Suitcase Sefton
and the
American Dream

Also by Jay Feldman

Hitting: An Official Major League Baseball Book

When the Mississippi Ran Backwards

Suitcase Sefton
and the
American Dream

◆

A NOVEL

To Jim,
goody buddy, kindred soul,

Jay Feldman

Jay Feldman

TRIUMPH
B O O K S
CHICAGO

Library of Congress Cataloging-in-Publication Data
Feldman, Jay, 1943–
Suitcase Sefton and the American dream : a novel / Jay Feldman
p. cm.
ISBN-13: 978-1-57243-812-5
ISBN-10: 1-57243-812-6
1. Japanese Americans—Evacuation and relocation, 1942–1945—Fiction.
2. Japanese American baseball players—Fiction.
3. Japanese American families—Fiction.
4. Pitchers (Baseball)—Fiction. 5. Baseball players—Fiction.
6. Baseball scouts—Fiction. 7. Arizona—Fiction. I. Title.
PS3606.E386S85 2005
813'.6—dc22
2005053881

This book is available in quantity at special discounts for your group or
organization. For further information, contact:

Triumph Books
542 South Dearborn St., Suite 750
Chicago, IL 60605
(312) 939-3330
Fax (312) 663-3557

Printed in U.S.A.

ISBN-13: 978-1-57243-812-5
ISBN-10: 1-57243-812-6

Design by Sue Knopf

To my father and
to the men and women
who were interned

"My baseball career
was a long, long initiation
into a single secret:
that at the heart of all things
is love."

—SADAHARU OH
A Zen Way of Baseball

ACKNOWLEDGMENTS

The inspiration for *Suitcase Sefton and the American Dream* came from a long magazine article I wrote more than fifteen years ago about baseball in the internment camps ("Baseball Behind Barbed Wire," *Whole Earth Review,* Winter 1990). In the course of researching that story, I traveled throughout California and spoke to many former internees, a number of whom have since passed away. At that time, more than four decades after World War II had ended, many of them were still coming to terms with the emotional scars of the internment experience, and their dignity and humanity impressed me deeply. In many cases, the stories and anecdotes they told me have found their way into the novel.

My good friends Isao Fujimoto and Kerry Yo Nakagawa provided many helpful details during the writing of this book. They showed not the slightest impatience with my endless questions and read the manuscript for accuracy and content.

Phil Asakawa, John Bowman, Larry Greer, Jim Kaplan, Ian Martin, James Rodewald, Lester Rodney, and my agent Alex Smithline also read the manuscript and made helpful suggestions.

Dusty Baker, a man among men, was kind enough to introduce me to Tom Bast, editorial director of Triumph Books, and Triumph honored me by choosing *Suitcase Sefton and the American Dream* as its first fiction release. Kelley White, my editor, was instrumental in helping me refine and tighten up the story.

As ever, my wife Marti, my first reader and biggest fan, was supportive throughout the writing process. I still have the card she left for me just after I'd finished the manuscript. "Dear Suitcase," it says. "What a story! Love, Annie."

J. F.

Part I
1942–1943

1

GREAT TRAILING CLOUDS OF DUST BILLOWED UP BEHIND the two-tone green Packard coupe as it barrelled along, hell-bent, through the middle of nowhere. Paying closer attention to the radio than to his driving, Sefton fiddled with the dial in an ongoing battle to defeat the static that kept intruding on the broadcast.

"Well, this is the old ballgame, riiiight here, friends," drawled the announcer with exaggerated import. Sefton listened intently, a bundle of nervous energy. "Bottom of the ninth, bases loaded, full-count on the batter, as the Bears try to slam the door on this Tucson rally and chalk up a win. You can just feeeel the tension."

"You can say that again," agreed Sefton, commenting out loud to himself in the manner of a man who spends too much time alone.

"Okay, Cartwright has the sign. He sets. The runners take their leads."

"They'll be runnin' on the pitch," said Sefton.

"With two out and the count full, they'll be off with the pitch," echoed the announcer.

"That's what I just said," Sefton informed the radio.

"Now Cartwright steps off the rubber."

"Cartwright, you bum," said Sefton with amused disgust. "That's why you're still pitchin' in the bush leagues—'cause you got no guts." The radio crackled and whined. "Get in there and throw the damn ball, for Pete's sake."

"Okay, he's back on the rubber. He sets, he winds, the runners go, here's the payoff pitch . . . *OWEEEOOOOWOWEEEEEE. . . .*"

"What the hell?" snapped Sefton, reaching for the dial. He muttered to himself as he twisted the knob this way and that in a desperate attempt to tune back in on the game. Suddenly, he became aware of something in his path—a jackrabbit had dashed out into the road some twenty-five yards ahead of the car. Braking as he swerved to avoid it, Sefton overcorrected and went into a skid. The back end fishtailed out, and the massive Packard went sliding down the dirt road sideways. Sefton wrestled with the wheel in a urgent struggle until he was finally able to get the automobile under control. He glanced back to see the jackrabbit zig-zagging crazily through the sagebrush. "Damn jackrabbit."

"I'll be loving you," crooned an oily voiced tenor. Sefton quickly grabbed the dial and tried for a few futile seconds to get the game again. He smacked the top of the dashboard in vexation and switched off the radio. "Damn radio."

He drove on in silence for a few seconds. Without the game to occupy him, he focused on his surroundings, realizing all at once that it had been an hour since he had given any thought to his location.

"Where in the Sam Hill am I?" Sefton asked himself.

Still driving at a good clip, he opened the glove compartment and took out a road map. Keeping one eye on the road ahead, he opened the map and consulted it. Finally, he reached a conclusion.

"Lost is where I am." He looked around at the saguaro cacti that dominated the landscape. "I am lost."

He continued on for a few minutes before he noticed the darts of steam escaping from under the hood of the car. In a panic his eyes flew to the temperature gauge: the needle was pinned over the red H on the right. "Shit."

Sefton glided the Packard to a stop and got out. He immediately felt wilted by the blistering heat. "Holy hell," he gasped, "must be a hunnerd and twenty." In the distance he saw a group of turkey vultures circling lazily in the afternoon sky. "I could fry out here. My bones'd be bleached by the sun by the time anybody found me."

He limped to the front of the car and stood for some moments watching the steam dance up from the narrow gap between the hood and the body. He took out his handkerchief and lifted the hood, releasing an angry ball of vapor. The radiator hissed and sputtered. In his impatience, he briefly considered prying off the cap, but his better sense prevailed. "Let it cool down a bit," he advised himself.

Sefton limped to the back of the car and spread out the map on the trunk. He took out his billfold and removed a scrap of paper: Eddie Pulaski—Buckeye, Arizona. He went back to the map. "Buckeye," he said, fingering the word. He moved his finger southeast to Casa Grande where, after lunch two hours earlier, he had made the reckless decision to abandon the main road and cut across the desert on an unpaved road in an ill-advised attempt to save time.

He studied the map. I shoulda stayed in Tennessee, he thought. This ain't my territory. I don't know my way around here. Jeez, I could end up dyin' chasin' some high school kid who probably can't even throw hard enough to break a pane of glass.

Sefton leaned against the car. He watched a lizard scoot across the sand. Those mountains on the horizon—were they twenty miles away or two hundred? Jesus, what kinda godforsaken land is this? Nothin' but cactus and sagebrush. He thought of the Western movies he had seen and half expected a bunch of Indians suddenly to appear out of nowhere and come swooping down on him. Instead, a prairie dog made a mad dash along the ground; when it reached its hole, it sat up on its hind legs and looked straight at Sefton for a few seconds before disappearing into the earth. The air was so hot it rippled.

For a brief moment, Sefton considered heading back to Tennessee, but as soon as the thought presented itself, he ushered it out of his mind. On the other hand, he thought, this kid could be the real McCoy. There's always that chance. . . .

He looked at the map again, trying to determine where he was. What made no sense was that judging by the sun, he was traveling east, and Buckeye was northwest of Casa Grande. Somehow, he had gotten turned around on these back roads and spent the afternoon chasing his tail. Now, here he was in one hell of a pickle.

In this heat, it could easily be an hour before the water in the radiator cooled down enough for him to get rolling again. Resigned to his misery, Sefton hobbled around to the shady side of the car, opened the door, and sat down on the running board.

The midday skies began to cloud up, and he could see a rainstorm in the distance. Soon it was as dark as it could be and still be daytime. Elaborately branched streaks of lightning momentarily lit up the scenery, followed by thunderclaps that grew increasingly ominous. Sefton decided he had better get moving.

He went to the front of the car and gingerly touched the radiator cap. It had cooled enough for him to remove it. He peered into the radiator, and there was a decent level of water still remaining. Still, best to keep the speed down, he figured. He replaced the cap, shut the hood, climbed into the car, and started it up.

He decided to keep driving east, that sooner or later he was bound to hit a paved road. After a few miles he came upon what appeared to be an irrigation canal that had a road alongside it.

He had been on the canal road for a couple of minutes when all at once the sky opened and a torrent of rain the likes of which Sefton had rarely seen began falling. Quickly, he rolled up the windows and turned on the windshield wipers, but they were wholly inadequate against the sheets of water that were teeming down.

After a hundred yards of driving blind, Sefton gave up and brought the Packard to a stop. He turned off the engine and sat listening to the rain pummel the cartop. In fifteen minutes, the storm began to taper off; five minutes more and it was done. The level of water in the canal had risen by a couple of feet.

Sefton rolled the front windows down, started up the engine, and drove. Ten minutes later, he was astonished to see that the surface of the road was bone dry. He scanned the desert—nowhere was there any evidence that rain had ever fallen. The air, however, was noticeably refreshed. It was still hot as hell, but it was no longer as stifling.

Sefton saw a roadside sign that made him honk the horn with joy: SACATON 5 MI. "Civil-eye-zation, here I come," he cried jubilantly, and a mile down the road he was still so elated at the prospect of getting back on track that he burst into song. "How ya gonna keep 'em down on the farm, after they've seen Paree?" Sefton sang with great gusto. "How ya gonna keep 'em away . . . from . . . Broadway?"

The song petered out as Sefton caught sight of something up ahead. "Now what have we got here?" As he approached, he was able to make out a fenced compound with a watchtower. When he got near enough, he saw that the fence was barbed wire and there was a uniformed guard in the tower. "Huh. Prison camp of some kind."

He looked at the map, but nothing of that sort was indicated. As he pulled alongside the camp, he saw through the fence that a baseball game was in progress. "Well, I'll be," said Sefton, tickled. "Now don't this just beat all? The American pastime. Nothing like a game of baseball to take a man's mind off his troubles."

He stopped the car, got out, stretched, and limped over to the fence. The ballfield was nothing but bare ground. The first- and third-base lines were filled with spectators sitting in folding chairs or standing.

Taking up a position between home plate and first base, Sefton watched the infielders fire the ball around the diamond as they do after chalking up an out. The third baseman, close to the mound, returned the ball to the pitcher and trotted back to his position. As the catcher squatted behind the plate, a new batter stepped in.

The pitcher, a lefty, looked in for the sign, nodded, then wound and delivered a blazing fastball that caused Sefton to blink with disbelief. The batter watched it go by. "*Steee-rike!*" bellowed the umpire.

"Do that again," muttered Sefton.

The pitcher peered in, nodded, and smoked another one by the hitter, who swung feebly and way too late. "*Twooo!*" the umpire roared.

Sefton's attention was riveted on the mound, his eyes as big as saucers. The pitcher went into his windup. "Curve, down and in," said Sefton to himself.

The pitcher threw. The batter cocked his bat and strode into the ball. At the last moment, the pitch altered its course and dove toward the right-handed batter's shoetops. He tried to check his swing, but it was too late, and he lunged weakly, waving his bat at thin air. The crowd erupted in cheers, and the players in the field came running in toward the first base bench to take their turn at bat. Sefton squinted to make out the name on their jerseys: FRESNO. Fresno, he thought, ain't that in California? What're they doin' out here in Arizona playing in some prison camp?

Sefton called to a group of fans ten yards inside the fence. "Hey, pal. Psssst."

A man turned. He was Asian and wearing a baseball cap. "Me?" he asked.

"Yeah, you. Ya know that pitcher?"

"Sure do."

"What's his name?"

"Jerry Yamada."

"Eye-talian boy."

"Huh?" said the man inside the fence.

"The pitcher," explained Sefton. "Eye-talian."

The man looked at Sefton for an uncomprehending moment, then turned his attention back to the field. From under the brim of his fedora, Sefton looked through the fence to the bench. His eyes found the pitcher, who was concentrating on the game as he toweled himself off.

Sefton suddenly became aware of the oppressive heat. He took out his handkerchief and mopped his face. He looked at his watch. Jeez, he thought, five thirty and it's still hot enough to boil spit.

The first batter of the inning drilled a sharp single to left, and the Fresno pitcher came to bat. Let's see if he can handle the bat, thought Sefton as the pitcher stepped in. He took the first pitch for a ball, then laid down a perfect sacrifice bunt that died halfway up the first base line. "Damn nice," said Sefton reflexively. "Damn nice."

He watched the pitcher trot back to the bench. He could not make out his features, but his body was small and tight. Sefton guessed he was maybe 5'7" or 5'8", 170 to 175 pounds. One of those tough little sneaky-fast southpaws. Like that Lombardi kid they got coming up in the Brooklyn organization. Or that little Polack, what's his name, Lopat, that the White Sox are bringing along. Maybe a little smaller than Lopat, but the same type. We should keep our eye on that Lopat. If he works out, we should grab him. He could win twenty for us pitching in the Stadium. I should talk to O'Neil about that.

Sefton took out his notebook and wrote himself a reminder. Then he turned to a new page, wrote "Fresno 8/4/42" at the top, and recorded what he'd already seen of this unexpected lefty.

For the rest of the game, Sefton watched him execute the many little things a pitcher needs to do to be a winner: he picked a couple of runners off base, he fielded his position deftly, he covered first on ground balls to the first baseman. Most of all, he had poise on the mound—when he gave up a single and double with one out in the eighth inning, he bore down and worked his way out of the jam without allowing a run. Sure, his mechanics could use a little work, but that was to be expected—he was a diamond in the rough and needed a little polishing.

When the game ended, Sefton called to the man inside the fence. "Hey, pal, could I talk to you for a second?" The man in the cap turned. "Do ya think ya could get him over here?"

"Who?" asked the man.

"The Fresno pitcher. I'd like to talk to him."

"I guess so."

"I'd sure appreciate it."

The man went to the knot of jubilant players around the first base bench. Sefton watched anxiously as the man talked briefly to the pitcher and pointed in Sefton's direction. The two of them began walking toward him. When they reached the milling spectators, the pitcher stopped to talk to a group of three people—a man and two women. What are women doin' here? Sefton wondered. He saw the pitcher point toward him and now all five came his way. Ten yards from the fence, the group of three—Sefton could now make out a young woman and an older couple—stopped and waited.

As the pitcher approached, Sefton was taken aback—he, too, was Asian. "Here's the guy that wanted to meet you," the man in the cap told the pitcher.

"Thanks, Tommy." The man nodded and walked away. "What can I do for you?" the pitcher asked Sefton.

Recovering from the surprise, Sefton stuck his hand through the fence. "Suitcase Sefton. My close friends call me Mac."

The pitcher shook hands. "Jerry Yamada. Pleased to meet you."

"That was a heckuva job you did out there today," said Sefton, turning on his best brand of sincerity.

"Thanks," said Yamada, matter-of-factly.

"I mean, I've seen some damn good pitchers, fella, and you're as good as any southpaw I've come across."

"Thank you."

"Have you ever thought about playing baseball for a living?"

"Not really."

"Well, here's your chance," said Sefton, pausing for effect, setting up his next line, the one that would make this kid's eyes pop. "I'm a scout for the New York Yankees."

If Yamada was impressed, he certainly did not show it. "I see," he said politely.

Ooh, this kid's a cool customer, thought Sefton. "I'd like to sign you to a contract," he said. Now that's gotta get him.

The pitcher thought for a brief moment. "I don't think that would work out," he said.

"You don't think it would work out? Maybe you don't understand what I'm saying. I'm offering you the chance of a lifetime, fella."

"I appreciate that, sir."

"So what's the problem?" Sefton asked with mild irritation. Yamada hesitated. "Look, if you're angling for more money already, you don't have to worry about that," Sefton offered. "I'll pay you what you're worth."

"It's not money," said Yamada.

"Then what, for Pete's sake?" Sefton asked, his voice rising.

"Do you know where you are?" asked Yamada. "Do you know what this place is?"

"Okay, you're a con," Sefton said reassuringly. "I understand. It ain't a problem. As long as you ain't an axe murderer, we can work out a deal with the authorities. We've done it before."

"This is not a regular prison camp," said Yamada. He turned and waved his hand toward the people inside the fence. "Look around. Do you notice anything about these folks?"

For the first time, Sefton looked closely at the players and fans. The first thing he noticed was that everyone who was not wearing a baseball uniform was in civilian clothes. This puzzled him, but before he had time to think it over, something else hit him. "Holy shit," he said involuntarily. "They're all Japs."

"Not Japs, Mr. Sefton," corrected Yamada. "Japanese Americans. This is an internment camp. Do you understand? The federal government sent us here. Even if I wanted to sign with you, it would be impossible."

Sefton was in an unfamiliar position—he could think of nothing to say.

"It was nice meeting you, Mr. Sefton," said Yamada. He turned to join the group of three who had been waiting for him. As they began walking away, Sefton came out of his daze and called after them.

"Yamada, wait!" The pitcher stopped but did not turn around. "Don't worry, I'll figure out a way to get you outta here."

Yamada shook his head in disbelief. Without turning, he lifted his glove in farewell. Sefton stood and watched the four continue on their way. After a few seconds, the young woman turned and looked at him. As preoccupied as he was with scheming to spring Yamada, Sefton could not help but notice how very, very black her eyes were.

2

"I'M TELLIN' YA, O'NEIL, THE KID THROWS BBS, AND HE'S got a curve that drops off the table." As always when he was excited, Sefton spoke loudly. "Not only that, he's got a pickoff move, and he can field. And to top it all off, he's a *lefty*!"

"Jesus, Sefton, keep your shirt on," said the voice on the other end. "You're gonna split my goddamn eardrum. You talk any louder, you won't need a telephone."

"Okay, okay," Sefton said, making a conscious effort to keep his volume down. "Listen, O'Neil, this kid is the genuine article."

"Where you calling from?" asked O'Neil.

"God's Ass, Arizona," replied Sefton. "Hot as a—"

"Arizona? What the hell are you doing out there?"

Sefton suddenly realized that in his fervor he had put his foot way down his gullet. Now how was he going to tell the boss he was fifteen hundred miles out of his territory, chasing a rainbow on a tip from some drunk in a bar? "I took a wrong turn," he said, stalling.

"A wrong turn?" said O'Neil.

"Never mind, it's a long story."

"Another one?" Sefton heard his boss take a deep breath and sigh on the other end. "Okay, what can you sign the kid for?"

"That's the catch," said Sefton.

"What's the problem?" asked O'Neil. "Parents?"

"Uh-uh."

"He wants too much?"

"No, that ain't it."

"What then?" said O'Neil with a trace of irritation. "C'mon, Sefton, I ain't got time to play Twenty Questions."

Sefton took a breath. "He's a Jap." He waited for a response, but none came. "O'Neil? You there?"

"Is this some kinda joke, Sefton?"

"You know me better than that, O'Neil."

"Jesus, Sefton," said O'Neil, exasperated. "You're a baseball scout, for the love of Mike, not the patron saint of lost causes. I don't care if the guy throws a hundred and fifty miles an hour. You know as well as I do we can't sign a Jap. In case you haven't heard, there's a war on, Sefton—with the Japs, as a matter of fact. They're gonna be draftin' our best guys into the army soon. Now get the hell back to Tennessee and find me some ballplayers I can use, will ya?"

Now there was a silence on Sefton's end.

"C'mon, Mac," said O'Neil, softening his tone. "Be reasonable."

Sefton pursed his lips. So that's that, he thought. "Yeah, you're right," he said, defeated.

"Atta boy," chortled O'Neil. "Now go back to Tennessee and beat those bushes for me."

"Right," Sefton agreed. "I hate it here, anyway."

"Call me next week, okay?"

"Okay."

"Take it easy."

"Bye."

Sefton hung up the phone. All at once, he was reminded of the heat. He took out his hankie and mopped his brow. "Shit," he said and spat on the sidewalk. He checked his watch. Almost eight. He surveyed the street, saw a diner down the block, and went limping toward it. When he got to the cafe, he saw through the window that the chairs were up on the tables. A woman was cleaning the counter. Just my damn luck, he thought, but tried the door anyway. It was open. He stepped in and a warm breeze hit his face. A large floor fan was on, not cooling the air but at least moving it around.

He turned on the big smile. "Any chance I could get a quick burger?" The woman gave him a weary look. He pressed his case. "I ain't eaten since breakfast. You wouldn't turn away a hungry wayfarer, would you?"

"You don't need to con me, hon," said the woman. "We'll feed ya."

"Bless your heart, sister," Sefton went on, continuing the sweet talk out of habit. "You are a true Christian." She handed him a menu, but he waved it aside. "Burger and fries, cup of coffee —black."

She wrote down the order, tore the sheet from her pad, and handed it through the kitchen window. In one seamless motion, she put a cup and saucer on the counter and poured Sefton's coffee. "Hot enough out there for ya?" she asked.

"How do you stand it?"

"You get used to it," said the waitress.

"No, thanks, not me," said Sefton, sipping his coffee. "Some storm this afternoon."

"Happens just about every day in the summer. Without that rain, we'd dry up and blow away."

"I guess so."

"Where ya from?"

"Tennessee."

"Wooo. Long way from home. You on vacation?"

"Yeah." Some vacation, thought Sefton.

"I'll give you a tip, hon," she said. "Come back in the winter. You'll love it. Nice and warm. Around here you can go in shirt-sleeves in January." She went back to her cleaning.

Sefton sipped his coffee. He could not get his mind off Yamada. That curveball . . . it could make grown men weep trying to hit that pitch. He reviewed the game in his mind, remembering all the little things the pitcher had done that impressed him.

Minutes later, Sefton's reverie was snapped by the cook: "Burger and fries," he called, putting Sefton's meal onto the window ledge.

The waitress came back, scooped up the plate, and put it on the counter. Sefton poured on a liberal helping of ketchup and dug in.

"Mmmmmmmm," he crooned. "Deee-licious."

"So, you doing some sightseeing?" asked the waitress as she went back to cleaning.

"What's to see?" asked Sefton in return.

"Right around here, not much. Just the Indian ruins and the Apache reservation."

"Mmmhh," said Sefton, chewing. "Apache reservation." He took another bite of his burger, his gaze on his plate.

"Yeah, about ten miles east of town. You take the old highway south, and you turn left at the second crossroads and just drive straight on out to Apache."

Sefton suddenly stopped chewing and lifted his head; his eyes lit up and a broad smile crept across his face. "Apache," he said through his mouthful. He sat that way for a few seconds, and then slowly, still smiling, resumed his chewing.

The grin remained on Sefton's face for the duration of the meal. When he finished, he leaned back in his seat. "Best hamburger I've ever had."

The waitress laughed. "I'll bet you say that to all the girls. Can I get you another cup of coffee?"

"No thanks, I'm fine," said Sefton as he stood up and fished in his pocket. "Where's the hotel?"

"Just around the corner," she answered, pointing the way.

Sefton took a dollar bill and put it on the counter. "Will that cover it?" he asked the waitress.

She glanced at the counter. "You're about sixty-five cents over, hon."

"That's for you."

"Why, thanks."

"My pleasure." He turned and started for the door.

"Don't forget to come back in the winter," she called after him.

"I'll do that," he said over his shoulder.

Out on the street, Sefton wondered when, if ever, it was going to cool down that night. He limped down the block to his car, opened the trunk, removed his suitcase, and continued around the corner to the hotel.

He had stayed in a million of these places. Before he even opened the door, he knew how the lobby would smell, what the front-desk clerk would be wearing, what his room would look like.

In the second-story room, Sefton fished his toiletries kit and pajamas out of the suitcase, then undressed. He took off his wooden leg, laid it on a chair, and gently massaged the stump that was his left knee. Five minutes later, he had showered and was in bed. He lay there thinking about Yamada, and about the plan he had hatched, and the Cheshire smile spread over his face again. Neither his excitement nor the heat nor the neon HOTEL sign flashing on and off right outside his window kept him from slipping quickly and easily into a deep and luxurious sleep.

3

A BEAD OF SWEAT ALREADY HAD FORMED ON SEFTON'S LIP when he pulled up to the front gate of the camp the next morning. On his way out of town, after breakfast at the diner, he'd noticed the thermometer on the bank—81 degrees at 8:30 AM— and stopped to ask directions to the nearest gas station, where he filled the Packard's radiator with water.

As Sefton rolled to a stop, the soldier on duty approached the car and bent down to peer in the window. "G'mawnin', suh," said the soldier, his thick New York accent absurdly out of place in the desert surroundings. "C'd I help ya?"

"Mornin', soldier," replied Sefton. "I'd like to see the director of the camp."

"D'ya have an appointment?"

"No, I do not." He had expected that there would be a certain amount of red tape here. The question was how to get around it.

"Could I see some I.D., suh?"

"Ya sure can, soldier." Sefton pulled out his billfold and removed one of his business cards, emblazoned with the aristocratic Yankees top hat. He handed it over.

The soldier read the card. "Ya woik for da Yankees?" he exclaimed. "Holy cow! Dat's my team!"

"Is that right?" asked Sefton, pleased at the prospect that this would make it easier for him to talk his way into the camp.

"Yeah, I'm from New Yawk. Da Bronx."

"Really? I never woulda guessed," said Sefton, laughing. The soldier laughed as well and extended his hand.

"Corporal Dominic Rizzolio. Pleased ta meetcha," he glanced at the card, "Mr. Sefton."

"Call me Suitcase, Corporal," said Sefton, shaking the soldier's hand but eager nevertheless to steer the conversation back to his own track. Before he could, though, Rizzolio put his foot on the running board.

"Hey, could I ask ya somethin'?"

He's my ticket in the gate, thought Sefton. "Shoot, Corporal."

Rizzolio leaned in and assumed a confidential tone. "I hoid dis here story about Babe Ruth . . ." He paused, trying to find a delicate way of continuing.

"It's probably true," said Sefton, sparing the soldier the embarrassment of having to lay out the details of the tale.

Rizzolio straightened up. "Git outta here!"

"Really, whatever you heard about the Babe, it most likely happened."

"Dis is a pretty wild story, if ya know what I mean," said Rizzolio, winking to make sure that there was no misunderstanding about so sacred an icon as Babe Ruth.

"In that case, it's definitely true," said Sefton.

"Sheeeez," responded Rizzolio, coming to terms with this new image of the Bambino.

Sefton saw his opportunity. "So, uh, how do I find the director?"

"Oh, yeah," said Rizzolio, returning. "He woiks right down dat street. 'Bout four blocks. Brown building on ya right. Lemme open da gate for ya."

Sefton smiled as he watched the soldier swing the steel gate open. "Hey," called Rizzolio, as Sefton drove through, "ya think DiMaggio'll get drafted at de enda duh season?"

"Who knows?" Sefton said, and waved as he went by. In the camp he drove by rows and rows of military-style barracks. On the dirt streets, occupants of the camp went about their business. Between two of the buildings, on a makeshift basketball court, a half-court pickup game was underway. In a jarring counterpoint to the apparent normalcy of life, soldiers with rifles patrolled the camp. The military presence was pervasive.

Finally Sefton saw the building that Rizzolio had mentioned. Alongside the walkway leading to the front door was a sign: Administration. Sefton became aware of a commotion on the other side of the entrance to the building. Several dozen people with picket signs were marching in a circle and chanting, as the two soldiers standing guard at the entrance kept a nervous, hostile eye on them. The GIs were spoiling for trouble. Sefton pulled up and parked.

Stepping out of the car, he stood and watched for a minute. The chant was now audible to him: "No more saltpeter—give us our flour and sugar! No more saltpeter—give us our flour and sugar!" What the hell are they talking about, he wondered.

Sefton limped down the walkway. Act as if you belong, he told himself. He had learned a long time ago that if you act with authority, most of the time you go unchallenged, whereas if you ask permission, too often the answer will be no. Besides, in this case, he could see that the soldiers were preoccupied with the demonstration. When he got to the building, he nodded to them and without breaking stride, muttered, "Mornin', boys," then opened the door and walked in.

Halfway down the corridor he opened a door that said Director. A stiff, prune-faced woman sat behind a desk, typing. A face only a mother could love, thought Sefton, and only on payday. When he entered the office, she glanced up but did not stop her work. He waited to be recognized. After a couple of minutes, she rolled the sheet out of the typewriter and put it in a pile. As she reached for another sheet, she addressed Sefton with mild annoyance. "Can I help you?"

"Yes, ma'am, you sure can," said Sefton, unfurling the charm. "I'd like to see the director if I could."

The secretary's frost did not thaw by even a degree. "And your name, sir?"

Sefton handed her his card. Without a word, she stood up, walked across the office, and knocked on a door at the other side of the room. From behind the door, Sefton heard, "Come in." She disappeared.

As he waited, Sefton looked around. There was the official photograph of Roosevelt on the wall, surrounded by documents with gold seals. Typical government agency, thought Sefton. Jesus H. Christ, I'd go nuts in one big hurry if I had to work in a joint like this.

The secretary returned. "Mr. Wayne will see you, sir."

"Thank you, ma'am." Sefton went into the director's office and walked straight to the desk holding out his hand. The director stood up and shook hands across the desk. The window was open, and Sefton heard the muffled chanting of the demonstrators in the street.

"I appreciate your takin' the time, Mr. Wayne," said Sefton. He sized the man up, taking in the starched, short-sleeved shirt and tie, and the precisely parted, tonicked hair.

"Close the door and sit down, Mr. Sefton," said the director, indicating a comfortable armchair. "It's not every day I get a visit from a major league scout."

"No, sir, I don't imagine it is."

"What can I do for you?"

Sefton was distracted by the chanting. "What's going on out there?"

Wayne smiled. "Oh, some of the camp residents are feeling their oats."

"Why are they saying, 'No more saltpeter?'"

Wayne laughed harshly. "Is that what they're saying? Well, you see, we have to keep the breeding down to a minimum here, or it could present all kinds of problems for us," he explained. "So we put saltpeter in the food to keep the hormones in check, if you know what I mean. Well, it seems the kitchen staff had been putting in a little too much, and it caused an outbreak of diarrhea. Unfortunate, but these things happen. We've cut back on the amount."

Sefton was still curious. "What are they saying about flour and sugar?"

Wayne snorted with disgust, no longer amused. "Good lord, somehow they've gotten the idea that the administration is siphoning off flour and sugar from the delivery shipments and selling them on the black market. I can't imagine where they'd get a notion like that." His eyes darted back and forth—as they tend to do when a man is not telling the truth. "Here we are taking care of them—housing them, feeding them—and do they appreciate it? No. They just look for trouble. That's the type of people they are."

From the street, someone shouted, "Hey, Wayne, c'mon out here and show your face!"

Wayne slowly got to his feet. "Not only that, but they're protected here." He continued talking as he moved to the window. "If they were out in society, there's no telling what might happen to them, what with the mood in the country the way it is toward the Japs right now." He closed the window and returned to his desk. "But surely you didn't come here to talk about this, Mr. Sefton."

"No, you're right, I didn't," said Sefton, hoping he had not set the wrong tone with the director.

"Well, then," said Wayne.

Sefton proceeded. "You have a fella here by the name of Yamada."

"More than one, I'd say." Wayne waited for Sefton's response, and when it wasn't forthcoming, he added, "Heh, heh, heh."

"Yeah, I bet," said Sefton, picking up the cue and chuckling at Wayne's feeble attempt at humor. "This particular fella's a pitcher. Lefthander."

"I see," said the director.

"Yes," continued Sefton. "Well, I saw this kid pitch yesterday, and I gotta tell ya, sir, he's got major league stuff."

"Is that right?" The director was visibly impressed. Just what Sefton had counted on.

"That's what I get paid for, Mr. Wayne."

"Yes, I suppose so. Go on."

Sefton took a breath. "Well, I'd like to sign this boy to a contract."

The director's demeanor turned serious again. "I'm afraid that's impossible, Mr. Sefton," he explained. "You see, he and the rest of his race have been sent here for the duration of the war. Our national security is at stake."

"Oh, yeah," said Sefton reassuringly. "I understand. Sure. But, see, there might be a way to get around that." He waited, but Wayne said nothing. Sefton decided to gamble. "I have an idea," he said confidentially.

"You do?" asked Wayne.

"Yup."

"And what would that be?"

Sefton leaned forward in his chair and whispered conspiratorially. "Pass him off as an Apache."

Wayne considered for a moment, then raised his eyebrows, impressed with the brazenness of the suggestion. "Interesting," he said. "Think it'd work?"

"Why, sure," said Sefton, sitting back, encouraged. "It's been done before."

"Really?"

"Hell, yes. John McGraw did it—had a colored boy by the name of Grant who he passed off as a Cherokee."

"You don't say."

"I sure do."

"I never heard of that," said Wayne, not wanting to show his excitement at being privy to an inside story, "and I'm quite a baseball fan. Tell me more."

"Well, back around the turn of the century, when McGraw was managing the Baltimore Orioles, he saw this real smooth infielder named Charlie Grant, who had light skin and what the colored folks call 'good hair.' McGraw was so impressed, he signed him up and gave him the name of Charlie Tokohama, full-blooded Cherokee Indian."

"I'll be. What happened to him?" asked Wayne.

"Unfortunately, Grant was very well known by the colored fans around Chicago, and Charlie Comiskey, the owner of the White Sox, got wind of the scheme and blew the whistle. But it almost worked."

"I don't guess you'd run the risk of this Yamada boy being too well known," said Wayne.

"Nope," agreed Sefton. He waited a few seconds. "So whaddya think?"

"It's an interesting idea," conceded Wayne. "It might work, but the problem still is, he's an internee, and that's not going to change until the federal government decrees otherwise."

"Right," said Sefton, keeping a close eye on Wayne's reactions, "but what if he were somehow able, I mean, what if we somehow found a way to get him out of camp?"

Wayne suddenly caught Sefton's drift and held up his hands. "Whoa, I don't know about that," he said, shaking his head. "You're asking me to take quite a risk."

"Oh, I understand that," Sefton assured him. "Of course, there'll be an incentive in it for you, don't worry about that." He rubbed his thumb and fingers together to indicate cash.

"Oh, I couldn't," said Wayne.

"Yeah, you could," countered Sefton.

Wayne thought for a moment. "Well, maybe I could."

Sefton smiled, pulled out his billfold, and removed a hundred dollar bill. He held it up for Wayne to see. The director shook his head, extended his hand with the palm up, and lifted it a couple of times to indicate that the ante needed raising. Sefton took out another hundred. Wayne lifted his hand again. Sefton held up a fifty. Wayne nodded and reached across his desk. Sefton handed him the money.

"So, Mr. Sefton, what else do you need from me?" asked Wayne, putting the cash in his pocket.

"I need to be able to get into the camp."

"Of course. By the way, how did you get in here today?"

"I sweet-talked the soldier at the front gate."

"Hmmmm. How much time do you figure you'll need?" asked Wayne.

"How much time can I have?" Sefton asked back.

"I can give you a seventy-two-hour pass."

"That should be enough."

"Fine," said the director, getting up from his chair and walking to the door. He opened it for Sefton and followed him into the outer office. "Miss Desmond, please give Mr. Sefton a seventy-two-hour pass," he instructed the secretary. She opened a desk drawer, took out a form, and gave it to Wayne to sign. Wayne scribbled his name and gave the paper back to her, then turned to Sefton and extended his hand. "Good luck, Mr. Sefton." They shook. "You'll be sure to let me know how this proceeds, yes?"

"I surely will, Mr. Wayne," said Sefton. "And thanks again for your help."

Wayne nodded and returned to his office, closing the door behind him. The secretary finished filling out the form and held it out for Sefton to take, dismissing him without a glance.

"Thank you, ma'am," he said, and tipped his hat. She raised her eyebrows.

Sefton limped down the hallway. When he got to the front door, he heard a commotion outside and remembered the demonstrators in the street.

"Lemme in," said someone angrily. "I wanna talk to Wayne."

"You can't go in there," came the emphatic reply.

Sefton opened the door. A few feet from him, two soldiers were scuffling with a man who was trying to get past them to enter the building. They blocked his path, holding their rifles in front of their chests as a barricade.

When the demonstrator saw the open door, he yelled down the corridor, "C'mon out here, Wayne, you coward." The crowd in the background echoed its support, demanding that the director appear.

"Look, buster, you better back off," said one of the soldiers, using his rifle to push the man backward.

Infuriated, the protestor pushed the soldier in the chest and shouted, "Don't tell me what to do."

The pushing escalated, and suddenly one of the soldiers swung his rifle and caught the man in the side of the head. The crowd jeered loudly and surged forward. The man took a step back, brought his hand up to his head, and sank down onto his knees. The soldiers moved in on him. One used his rifle to push the man down to the ground. The other took a pair of handcuffs off his belt, pulled the man's hands behind his back, and snapped the cuffs on.

The rest of the demonstrators closed in further, and the soldier who was holding the man down got up and moved menacingly toward the crowd. "Now get outta here, all of you," he growled, "or we'll take the rest of you in too."

The crowd slowly began to disperse. The other soldier lifted the protestor to his feet. The man's head was bleeding. "You're going to jail, buster," said the first soldier, pushing him toward the side of the building.

Sefton, who had been pretty much pinned in the doorway the whole time, was free to leave. He limped to the car and got in as the soldiers roughly escorted the demonstrator down the street. Sefton started the engine and pulled away, trying to make some sense of what he had seen and heard.

4

YAMADA SCRATCHED AT THE SANDY, BARREN GROUND with his hoe. This is pathetic, he thought, recalling the rich, fertile soil of the Central Valley. His mind drifted back to the farm, and he saw the lush fields, the house and the barns, the drying sheds, the silo, the flatbed truck, the chickens—all of it gone now.

He resisted the temptation to dwell on the memories, to indulge the feelings of sadness and anger. No point in that, he told himself. It can only lead to bitterness or self-pity, both of which his father had so often counseled against since the roundup and evacuation. Where would he be without the benefit of his father's wisdom?

Yamada glanced over to where his sister was working, then looked at his parents. It's hardest on them, he thought. Annie and me, we can start over when the war ends, but they're getting old. What do they have to look forward to?

Yamada took a deep breath, and as he bent over to resume his hoeing, he saw the white man in the fedora limping toward the garden. At first glance, Yamada did not recognize him, but when he raised his arm in greeting, the pitcher recalled Sefton's parting comment about finding a way to get him out of the camp. He was utterly surprised to see the scout, having given not a single thought to him since their conversation. In fact, he could not even remember the man's name.

"Hello, again," called Sefton, approaching the garden fence.

"Hello," Yamada said in return.

"It's gonna be pretty hot today, isn't it?" Sefton small-talked, as he opened the gate and came into the garden.

"It is," agreed Yamada politely.

There was an awkward pause. Then Sefton said, "Remember I said I'd find a way to spring you? Well, I've got it." He waited for a reaction, but there was none. "Yessiree, I've got a plan, and I'm betting it'll work."

More out of courtesy than interest, Yamada asked, "What's your plan, Mr., uh, Mr.? . . ."

"Sefton." Yamada nodded. Setting up his idea, Sefton waited a moment before playing his trump card. He rubbed his palms together and spoke slowly. "We're gonna pass you off," he paused for emphasis, "as an Apache Indian."

Yamada thought the scout was making a joke at first, but when he looked into Sefton's eyes, he saw that it was no such thing. He studied Sefton for a moment, then said simply, "You must be crazy."

"That's beside the point," said Sefton. "I told you I'd get you outta here to play professional baseball, and this is the way we're gonna do it."

"I'm sorry, but I'm not interested," said Yamada.

Sefton could not believe his ears. "What do you mean, you're not interested? How could *anybody* not be interested? This is a golden opportunity come knocking at your door, fella."

"I'm not an Apache, and I can't pretend I am," explained Yamada.

"Why the hell not? It's your ticket outta here."

"It's dishonest," said Yamada.

"Not necessarily," Sefton countered. "It all depends on how you look at it."

"Besides, I have my parents to think about," Yamada added, pointing in their direction.

Sefton saw a chance to beef up his argument. "Well, here's your best chance to give them a comfortable old age. You'll be earning some decent money, Yamada."

"That's not what I'm talking about."

"What, then?"

"I couldn't leave them here," Yamada said simply.

"Why not?" asked Sefton, making an effort to control his frustration. "They'll be taken care of here."

"I can't just break up our family like that."

"Dammit, Yamada, you're not making this easy on me."

"I'm sorry," said Yamada softly but firmly, and waited for Sefton to excuse himself and leave.

"Jerry," called a female voice behind the two men. Yamada turned, then Sefton. Fifteen yards away a young woman was crouched on the ground. By her eyes, Sefton recognized her as the younger of the two women who had been part of Yamada's group the day of the ballgame.

"Yes?" asked Yamada.

"Could you give me a hand pulling some of these weeds?"

"Sure thing. I'll be there in a minute." He turned back to Sefton. "And there's my older sister, Annie—I have to think of her too. You see, it's much more complicated than you ever imagined, Mr. Sefton. Look, I really appreciate your interest, but I'm afraid it's not gonna work. I don't mean to be rude, but I've got a lot of work to do before the sun gets too high."

"Okay, awright, I understand," Sefton admitted. "This is a big decision. You don't have to make up your mind right this minute. You think it over for a couple of days and we'll talk again later. How's that?"

Yamada hesitated. This type of aggressive insistence was foreign to him. It was not the way he had been taught to behave. Before he could say anything, Sefton jumped back in.

"That's all I'm asking. Just think it over, Yamada. That's not unreasonable, is it?"

"It's not unreasonable, but I'm not going to—"

"Just think about it," Sefton interrupted. "You got nothing to lose. Okay?"

Yamada looked at the ground. He felt trapped. "Okay."

"Great!" said Sefton with exaggerated enthusiasm. There was an awkward pause. Now that he had wheedled this concession out of the pitcher, he really had nothing more to say. "I'll let you get back to your work then."

"Thank you."

"See ya."

"Yeah."

Sefton started to limp away, but after a few steps turned back to Yamada, who had gone back to his hoeing. "When do you pitch again?"

Yamada did not look up. "Day after tomorrow."

"What time?"

"Six thirty."

"I'll be there," said the scout and continued on toward the garden gate. As he passed Yamada's sister, he raised his hat in greeting, smiled, and nodded to her. She gave him a shy smile in return, and in the quick moment before she lowered her eyes, he felt himself drawn into their dark warmth.

When Jerry was sure Sefton had left the garden, he looked up and watched him limp toward his car. Jerry shook his head in a combination of disbelief and grudging admiration. He leaned his hoe against the garden fence and went to help his sister.

"Wasn't that the man you were talking to after the game the other day?" Annie asked, as Jerry bent down to help her.

"Yes."

"Who is he?"

"He's a baseball scout. He wants me to sign a contract to play professional ball."

Annie looked over her shoulder. Sefton's car was driving away. "Doesn't he know the situation here?" she asked.

"He thinks he can pass me off as an Apache Indian."

She thought about it for a moment, then burst out laughing. Suddenly, Jerry too saw the absurdity of the situation, and the two of them enjoyed a good laugh. When it subsided, Annie went back to her weeding.

Jerry, however, was caught in a reverie. He saw himself in the old fields, working beside his parents. He remembered the sweet smell of the ripe prune plums wafting in on the breeze; the recalled fragrance brought with it the liquid glissando of the meadowlark and the abrasive squawk of the scrub jay. And now Annie was coming down from the house with lunch, and then the four of them were sitting under the huge live oak and eating with untroubled, leisurely pleasure.

All at once, the air was rent by the camp's lunch horn, and Jerry was wrenched out of the serenity of his daydream. "Lunchtime!" yelled someone. A second horn blast sounded. Jerry looked down at the bleak, desert soil. The pain caused by the memory of his earlier life and the contrast with his present situation wrapped itself around his heart, and a wave of sadness hit him.

This is what he was warning against, thought Jerry, remembering his father's admonitions against self-pity. Because a person could get stuck in it. He thought of those in the camp—and there were plenty—who were indeed fixated on the injustice of what had happened to them. Look at Yoshitake. He's consumed by rage. Hates all white people.

Still, it wouldn't be human not to feel some pain or anger. The important thing was not to dwell on those emotions. Let the feelings be there without resisting or encouraging them, he reminded himself. He drew a breath and looked up at the sky, where soft clouds were drifting by. He remembered what his father had told him so many times: feelings are like clouds—not one's true self. The true self is like the sky. The clouds always pass; only the sky remains.

He felt better. And it was a good thing because lunch at the mess hall awaited him, and if he allowed himself, the discrepancy between the memory of the peaceful lunch under the oak tree at home and the reality of the noisy, chaotic meal at the mess hall could cause yet more pain.

As Jerry rose from his crouch, he saw that Annie was already standing. She looked at him, concerned. "Are you okay?" she asked.

He nodded. "Yeah. I was just remembering how it used to be."

"I know," said Annie. "I think about it, too, sometimes."

"So, let's go get some lunch."

They started toward the gate, where their parents were already waiting. Annie put her hand on Jerry's arm. He stopped. She looked at him gravely. Now he was concerned. He knew by her expression that she had something important to say. She waited a moment more before speaking.

"An Apache Indian?" she asked incredulously, and the two of them laughed all over again.

5

SEFTON STOOD WITH HIS HANDS ON HIS HIPS IN CENTER field, waiting for the next batter to step in. The Yankees' pitcher was working on a no-hitter with one out in the eighth inning, and the stadium crowd was alive, a raucous beehive of sound that Sefton did his best to tune out. Shifting his weight, he extended his left leg in front of him, looked down at the ground, and caught sight of the pinstripes on the pant leg of his uniform. Pride welled up in his chest as it hit him once again—he, Mac Sefton, the farm boy from Oonoma, Oklahoma, population 217, was playing center field for the God Almighty world champion New York Yankees! He was living the honest-to-goodness American dream!

The batter entered the box and dug in his back foot. Sefton spread his legs, bent at the waist, and rested his hands on his knees in the classic outfielder's stance. As the pitcher went into his windup, Sefton tensed and rose up onto the balls of his feet. The pitcher threw, the hitter swung, and Sefton recognized the unmistakable crack of a well-hit ball.

Instantaneously, he took off to his left. He knew it was going to be very close, that it would take every bit of speed he had, and even then he might not get to the ball. He ran all out and, at the last moment, dove for the sinking line drive, his body parallel to the ground. He reached as far as he could, and the ball hit *smack!* in the palm of his glove. He rolled over several times and, lying flat on his back, thrust his glove into the air, the ball squarely in the pocket. The crowd went wild.

Suddenly, Sefton heard the noise of a loud motor. He lifted his head, panic-stricken, and saw the tractor bearing down on him. Just as it was about to run him over he opened his mouth to scream, but no sound came out.

Sefton sat straight up in bed, terror slamming at his heart as he awoke from the nightmare. He looked about the room in a frantic attempt to determine where he was. The neon HOTEL sign flashed on and off outside the window. As he surveyed the room, his gaze came to rest on the chair where his wooden leg lay. Slowly, a recognition of his surroundings surfaced, and a deep melancholy replaced the panic.

Sefton ran his hand over his head. His face and neck were damp with sweat. He swung his right leg over the side of the bed, dismounted, and hopped to the bathroom. He filled the glass on the sink with tap water and drank it down in one gulp.

Returning to the bedroom, Sefton fished around on the bureau-top for his wristwatch. He knew from long years of experience with this kind of dream that there would be no more sleep for him that night. He found the watch and squinted to read the illuminated dial. Twenty to four. Couple of hours till daylight, but even then, the diner doesn't open till seven.

These were the times he hated and feared, the times when the loneliness got way down inside him and carved out an empty place as deep and as wide as the Grand Canyon. The times when he stung so hard he thought he might just start screaming out loud. It was a much harder, much meaner pain than the one when he had lost his leg.

Sefton hopped over to the armchair. He picked up the artificial limb and tossed it onto the bed, then sat down in the chair. He looked out the window. A dog came loping along the middle of the otherwise deserted street, moving at a sideways angle the way dogs do when they are out on their own and enjoying the freedom. Suddenly the dog caught a scent on the pavement, turned sharply back from where he had come, made a wide, sweeping circle with his nose glued to the ground, and resumed his happy-go-lucky journey in the direction of his original destination.

Watching the dog's antics made Sefton feel a bit better. He started thinking about Yamada, and what he might offer him to change his mind. He couldn't figure this guy at all. Here he was in a prison camp, and Sefton was offering to spring him to play baseball, and the guy would rather stay put. Jesus, it takes all kinds. Still, there has to be something this guy wants, Sefton thought.

He also thought about what O'Neil was going to say when he learned that Sefton was still in Arizona. That one he could deal with, though. He and O'Neil went way back together, back to when they were teenage rookie prospects and roommates playing for Pine Bluff in the Cotton States League. Shit, those were some times. Sefton conjured up an image of the two of them, still wet behind the ears. What a pair. They had taken to each other right off the bat: O'Neil—red-headed, square-jawed, and jug-eared, the street savvy, smart-aleck, hot-tempered kid from the big city; and himself—lanky, blond, easygoing, good-looking hayseed with the sunny disposition and the winning smile.

By nature, Sefton was not given to introspection. But the memory of himself and O'Neil as youngsters caught him up, and the early morning hours coerced a measure of reflection from him. Easygoing? Sunny? Jesus, thought Sefton, could I ever have been that kid? As soon as the question formed itself, however, the answer rushed in behind it: when he lost his leg, everything changed.

It was perfectly understandable that he would have felt sorry for himself afterward—what else would you expect, at least at first, from a twenty-four-year-old whose bright future was suddenly thick fog. But he got kind of stuck there, and now, sitting in the dark of that hotel room he had to face it: in the past ten years he had grown into a pretty hard-driving, hard-boiled character. Spending so much time alone, his behavior was never reflected back to him, and without really meaning to or even knowing it was happening, he had acquired a bit of a cynical edge.

All the same, he realized, if I can still remember that kid, then some piece of him must undoubtedly have survived—something more, that is, than just the good looks and winning smile.

6

"HEY, SUITCASE, HOW YA DOIN'!" CALLED CORPORAL
Rizzolio when he saw Sefton's car pull up to the gate.

"Oh, I'm gettin' by, Corporal," Sefton replied through the window. "What about yourself?"

"Not dat bad."

Sefton took out his pass and showed it to Rizzolio. "Yeah, no problem," said the soldier and opened the gate. Sefton started to drive through, but Rizzolio held up his hand for Sefton to stop.

"I, uh," Rizzolio began hesitantly, but then trailed off.

"What's on your mind, Corporal?" asked Sefton.

"I wuz, uh, jus' wonderin', ummm," Sefton waited as Rizzolio shuffled his feet and tried to get his words together. After a few seconds, the soldier managed to blurt it out. "D'ya think ya could get me DiMaggio's autograph?"

"Gee, I don't know about that," said Sefton. "That could be kinda tough. Ya know, DiMaggio ain't real keen on givin' out his John Hancock. The players don't even like to ask him. He's just a guy that keeps people at a distance."

Rizzolio did his best not to show his disappointment. "Yeah, I unnastan'. I was jus' hopin'." He shrugged his shoulders.

"Sorry, Corporal," said Sefton. Rizzolio nodded, and Sefton guided the car on through the gate. He drove past block after block of barracks-type housing on his way to the ballfield. People were sitting and standing, strolling and chatting, as they might on any summer evening in any other neighborhood, the only difference here being the monotony of the housing, the barbed wire, the soldiers, and the guard tower.

When Sefton reached the field, the players were warming up. Some played pepper, others took infield practice, others shagged flies. Yamada was thowing on the sidelines. Another player stood near him, watching.

Taking up a position a respectful distance away, Sefton scrutinized Yamada's warm-up tosses with intense, professional concentration. When the pitcher noticed the scout, he tensed slightly and nodded hello. Sefton nodded in return. The player standing beside Yamada shot Sefton a hostile stare.

There was a sudden outbreak of excitement accompanied by animated gesturing among the older men who were sitting alongside the first-base foul line. They were all talking at once, and one man was writing furiously in a notebook. What's that all about? Sefton wondered.

When Yamada finished warming up, he, the catcher, and the third player walked toward the bench. Sefton could not help but notice the catcher's rock-solid build—built like a brick shithouse, he thought. Shoulda been a boxer. "Hey, your fastball's popping, Jerry," said the catcher. "You're gonna mow 'em down today."

Yamada took the compliment in stride. "Thanks, Isao."

As the three players passed Sefton, he spoke to Yamada. "I'll see you after the game, right?"

"Okay," said Yamada, noncommittal.

The trio walked on. When they were out of Sefton's hearing distance, the player who'd been watching the warmups spoke to Yamada. "Who's the white guy?" he asked with barely concealed disdain.

"It's not important," answered Yamada. "Don't worry about him."

"I don't trust him," said the other man.

"Yoshitake, you don't trust any white people."

"Damn right I don't. Why should I after what they did to us?"

Yamada knew there was no advantage in saying anything more, but even if he had wanted to, the umpire's cry of "Play ball!" made it a moot point. The Fresno team took the field.

Almond-shaped eyes followed Sefton as he made his way through the crowd to find a spot where he could observe Yamada. He saw the place where he wanted to be, but his path was blocked by a cluster of fans. He cleared his throat.

"Excuse me, please," Sefton said, causing several people in the group to turn around. When they saw him, they shied away, as they might from a leper. One woman did not back off, however, and when Sefton looked at her, he saw it was Yamada's sister. Those eyes.

"Oh, hello," said Sefton.

"Hello."

"I, uh . . . we met in the garden the other day."

"I remember." Annie could not tell why, but she was intrigued by this curious man.

"I didn't, uh, recognize you from the back."

"Mmm."

"I'm Mac Sefton."

"Annie Yamada."

Sefton considered offering his hand, then thought better of the idea. "Nice to see you again," he said instead.

"Yes, same here."

There was an awkward pause as they ran out of things to say. "Well, I'll, uh, let you watch the game," said Sefton.

"Thank you."

"See ya later."

"Okay."

When Sefton had worked his way over to an unobtrusive spot near the fence, he looked back in Annie's direction. To his surprise, she was looking at him and gave a smile that was at the same time shy and confident. He tipped his hat, smiled back, and turned his attention to the field.

Yamada finished his warm-up pitches and the first batter stepped in. The infielders started up their chatter. Yamada took the sign, wound, and fired a fastball; the batter let it go by.

"Stee-rike!"

Yamada came back with a curve that appeared to be out of the strike zone but dipped over the plate at the last second. The hitter was frozen.

"That's twoooo!"

Yamada looked in, shook off one sign, nodded at the second. He took a deep breath and delivered. The batter laced the ball to left field for a single.

The next man came to the plate. Yamada started him off with a curveball; the batter was taking all the way. "Stee-rike one!" wailed the ump. Yamada leaned in, got the sign, took a deep breath, and threw. The batter smacked a line drive to the gap in left-center field, but the left fielder got a good jump on the ball and held it to a double as a run came around to score.

The next batter advanced the runner to third with a sacrifice bunt, which made Sefton smile. Nobody out in the first inning, the pitcher a little shaky, the heart of the order coming up, and they're playing for one run. Strictly bush league. But he also realized it said something about the respect they had for Yamada— they obviously didn't expect to score too many runs off him.

The cleanup man stepped in and took a fastball for a strike. Sefton's eyes were fixed on Yamada, trying to pick up something in his delivery that might be off—or was it just possible that he could have been wrong about the kid? Yamada took that deep breath and delivered. The batter belted a long fly to right-center that looked like extra bases, but the center fielder ran it down and made a nice, over-the-shoulder catch. The runner on third tagged up and scored.

Now Sefton knew why Yamada was getting cuffed around, and it had nothing to do with his delivery. It was much simpler than that.

Before the next batter could step in, Yoshitake called time and went out to the mound to confer with Yamada. They were joined by the catcher. The three jawed for a minute and then the manager trotted back to the bench. Yamada struck out the next batter on three quick fastballs to end the inning. As he walked off the field he was shaking his head.

Sefton looked over in Annie's direction. A moment later she turned to look at him. Her furrowed brow formed a silent question. Sefton smiled and nodded.

Yamada struggled through the next four innings, giving up a bunch of hits and three more runs. After that he settled down, but by then the damage was done. At the end of the game, which Fresno lost by a score of 5–3, there was a flurry of activity among the older men along the first-base line as money changed hands. Now Sefton understood what the earlier excitement had been about—they were betting on the game. Yamada spent a few minutes commiserating with his teammates and then slowly walked over to see Sefton.

"Rough day, huh?" said the scout.

"Yup," said the pitcher. "Just didn't have my good stuff today."

"There was nothing wrong with your stuff." Out of the corner of his eye, Sefton could see Annie coming over to join them.

"Well, they sure knocked me around out there."

"They only hit one pitch."

Yamada seemed taken aback. "You could tell that?" he asked.

"Your change-up. Soon as you stopped throwing it they didn't touch you."

"That's true. Took me a while to figure out that's all they were hitting."

"Ya know why they were hitting your change-up?"

"I have no idea."

"You're tipping it off."

Yamada looked skeptical. "I am? How?"

Sefton reached over and took Yamada's glove and ball. He put the glove on his right hand, assumed the look of a pitcher about to go into his windup, and took a deep breath. "Get it?" he asked Yamada.

"I'm not sure I do," answered the pitcher.

"You're takin' a deep breath before you throw your change. You do it every time. It's the only pitch you do it on."

Yamada thought it over. "I wasn't aware of that."

"Course you weren't," said Sefton. "That's why it's a tip-off. They can't catch up to your fastball and your curve ties 'em in knots, so they wait for the change-up, and you're nice enough to telegraph when it's coming."

"So I better get rid of that breath."

"In general, I'd say yes," agreed Sefton, "but you can also use it as a setup."

"What do you mean, a setup?"

"Well, every once in a while, when there's nothing at stake—ya know, two out, you're up by five runs—telegraph it like ya been doing, and give 'em a free base hit. That way they'll keep look-ing for it. Then when you're in a tight spot—say, close game, two out, couple of runners on, two strikes on the batter—you take that breath, he's expecting a change-up, and you blow your best fastball by him. He'll be two feet behind it."

Yamada smiled, obviously impressed. "Not a bad idea. Thanks for the tip, Mr. Sefton."

"Don't mention it. And call me Mac, would ya?"

"All right."

"Yeah, there's a couple more things I could point out to you."

"Such as?"

"Hey, you can't expect me to give away everything all at once, can ya?"

"Why not?"

"Well, I gotta know what you're thinking first."

"About what?"

"About signing."

"What does that have to do with it? If you can help me, what's the harm?"

Sefton thought this over. It was a different way to deal than he was used to. What the hell, he'd play another card. "Okay. Here's something else. Your fastball's too straight. It doesn't move enough."

Yamada looked puzzled. "What's the difference if nobody can get around on it?"

"Here, no difference," said Sefton.

"So?"

"But when you go up against better hitters, I don't care how fast you're throwin'—if your ball doesn't move, the good hitters are gonna time it eventually, and they'll tee off on ya. Heck, I could hit your fastball usin' my wooden leg for a bat."

"What do you suggest?"

Sefton took the baseball and gripped it across the seams. He lifted the tip of his index finger. "If you throw your fastball off your middle finger, it'll move in that direction." He made a gesture indicating the direction of the ball. He put his index finger back down and lifted the tip of his middle finger. "If you throw it off your index finger, it'll move the other way." He gestured in the opposite direction. He handed Yamada back the ball and glove. Yamada tried the two grips.

"I'll have to work on that," he said. "I appreciate the help. You sure have a lot of baseball knowledge, Mac."

"Which is how I know you could be a big-leaguer, Yamada."

The pitcher stiffened. "I'm not going to pretend to be an Apache."

"Jesus, we're back at the starting line," said Sefton with no small degree of frustration. "Look, maybe you don't realize what this means to me."

"To you?" said Yamada. "I thought you had my interests in mind."

"I do, of course," Sefton said, realizing his mistake and quickly backpedaling. "Of course I'm thinking of you. But this is a big chance for me too. It ain't every day that I run into a southpaw of your caliber."

"Look, I'm sorry to disappoint you, Mac, but I've gotta be going. Thanks again for the tips." He turned to Annie, and the two of them began walking.

"Wait!" called Sefton desperately. "We gotta talk some more!"

Yamada stopped and turned. "Look, Mac, it's a lost cause. Nothing personal. I like you, but you're asking me to do something against my principles, and I can't do that. Just let it go, okay?"

Sefton and Yamada stood regarding each other for a few moments. Try as he might, Sefton could not come up with anything to say. He looked helplessly at Annie, hoping for her intercession, but she said nothing and looked away.

"Good luck, Mac," said Yamada. He and Annie turned again and continued to walk. After a few steps, Annie looked back at Sefton. In her eyes, he could see a desire to help coupled with the resigned awareness that she could not. After a few steps she turned away. Sefton sighed. He watched them for a few seconds, then sadly turned and walked toward his car. Once more Annie looked back, this time to see Sefton limping slowly and dejectedly away.

7

"WELL, THAT'S TOO BAD," SAID WAYNE SYMPATHETICALLY.

Sefton was agitated. "For Pete's sake," he continued, "here I am offering the guy a ticket outta here, and he turns it into a matter of principle."

"Inscrutable Orientals."

"You're telling me."

"So, where do you go from here?" asked Wayne, eager to change the subject lest the issue of repaying his two-hundred-and-fifty-dollar "bonus" arise.

"Back to Tennessee, I guess," answered Sefton, then immediately returned to his previous train of thought. "Jeez, it just kills me to lose a fish like that. One in a million."

"Well, at least you can console yourself with the knowledge that he won't be signing with anyone else," Wayne chuckled.

"Mr. Wayne, that is absolutely no consolation whatsoever to me."

"Yes, I see your point. But it's probably for the best, anyway."

"What makes you say that?"

Wayne's voice took on an ominous tone. "Shit, we don't know which of these people could turn out to be a spy for Japan. God knows they all look alike, and you can never tell what they're thinking. Yes, indeed, these people are different, Mr. Sefton. They are different. They are the yellow peril." The two men sat in silence for a short time, each one alone with his thoughts. Suddenly, Wayne sat up straight. "Now, if you'll excuse me," he said, indicating the six-inch-high stack of papers on his desk.

Sefton did not envy him. "Oh, yeah, sure. Well, thanks again, Mr. Wayne," he said, rising. He went to the director's desk and they shook hands.

"Not at all. It was my pleasure."

On his way through the outer office, Sefton tipped his hat to the crab apple then limped down the corridor to the front door of the building. When he opened the door he was hit by a blast of hot air that made him wince. That I'm not gonna miss, he said to himself.

Stepping out of the building, the blinding sunlight caused Sefton to look down for a moment. His eyes landed on a series of red spots on the pavement in front of him, and he suddenly recalled the beating he had witnessed a few nights back. The whole business did not make a lot of sense to him, but then, what did he know? If the federal government had put these people here for their own protection and for the security of the country, there must be good reasons for it, wouldn't you think?

Sefton drove to the front gate. "Ya gonna be aroun' much longer?" Rizzolio asked him.

"Leavin' today, Corporal. I'm takin' a powder."

"Aw, too bad. Ya gonna be back?"

"Not likely."

"Whut wuz ya doin' here in da foist place?"

"Wastin' my time. Chasin' a rainbow."

"Mmm. Sorry 'bout dat."

"Yeah, me too. Well, I better hit the road."

"Ya travel a lot, huh?"

"Comes with the territory. They don't call me 'Suitcase' Sefton for nothing. I put on about forty thousand miles last year."

Rizzolio whistled. "Forty tousand miles! Wow! Must get pretty lonesome out there. I'd go bananas. Don'tcha evah get tired of it? Don'tcha evah get an oige ta settle down?"

Sefton inhaled deeply and unconsciously dropped his guard. "Yep, sometimes I do," he admitted. "Sometimes I really do. Sometimes I think about what it would be like. . . ." There was a faraway look in his eye. "I sure do." He took another deep breath and came back. He looked at Rizzolio. "You better get outta the sun, Corporal."

"Yeah. Okay, I'll open da gate for ya." He made no move. "It sure has been nice knowin' ya, Suitcase. From now on, I'll think about you whenever I go down ta da Stadium after dis goddam war is over."

Sefton could not help liking this kid. "Hey, listen, next time you go to Yankee Stadium, you're my guest, okay?"

Rizzolio was unsure if his leg was being pulled. "No kiddin'?"

"You still got that card I gave you?"

"Sure do."

"You ask for Mr. Pat O'Neil, show him that card, and you'll get box seats courtesy of the New York Yankees."

"Heeeey!" sang Rizzolio and pumped Sefton's hand. "Wait till I tell da *paesani* on Gun Hill Road about dis! They're gonna piss in their pants! Box seats! *Mamma mia!*"

Sefton laughed. "You take care of yourself, Corporal."

"You take it easy yuhself, Suitcase. If ya ever get to da Bronx, I'll show ya 'round, okay?"

"You got a deal."

Rizzolio opened the gate. They waved to each other as Sefton drove through. Rizzolio was still waving when Sefton's car disappeared into the desert.

8

"THE RUNNERS LEAD. HERE'S THE PITCH. BERRY HITS a ground ball to short, should be an easy double play—*ohhh!*—Drummond kicks the ball, and the runners are safe all around." Sefton pursed his lips in disgust.

He had driven for a day and a night, stopping only for meals and the call of nature, before he had to quit and get some rest around the New Mexico–Texas border. After a few hours of sleep in the back seat, he drove another straight shot through the panhandle into Oklahoma. Toward the end of the day, he had found himself nodding off at the wheel, so around sundown he ate supper at the Consumers Cafe in El Reno and made for the hotel. It had been a miserable couple of days, and he was thoroughly exhausted and depressed. He had gotten no kicks on Route 66.

The next morning, however, he felt a bit better, the long sleep having somewhat restored his spirits. Now he was just west of Oklahoma City and thinking that with any luck at all he would be in Memphis by mid-morning tomorrow.

"Oh, fans, lemme tell ya, that was a tailor-made double-play ball if I've ever seen one. The Miners should have been out of this inning. Instead they have the bases loaded with one out, and the ever-dangerous Jack Sutton coming up to bat."

Sefton had seen Sutton play. Classic minor league hitter. Could powder a fastball. Had a cup of coffee in the National League—Sefton could not remember with which club—but he never stuck because he could not handle the big league curveball. After they figured that out it was all the poor guy saw. Steady diet of benders. And that, son, is the difference between Triple A ball and the majors: in the Big Show, not only can you be sure they'll find your weakness, but you better believe they've got the ability to exploit it.

"Now here comes McSorley out of the dugout, and he's making his way out to the mound. This might mean a pitching change for the Miners."

A hundred yards ahead Sefton could make out a figure walking along the side of the road. As he drew near he saw it was a G.I. toting a duffel bag on his shoulder. He pulled up and lowered the radio volume just enough so he could talk to the man. "Where ya goin', soldier?"

"Just about five miles up here."

"Throw your duffel bag in the back seat and hop in."

As they got rolling, Sefton turned the radio back up. "So Larson takes the long walk to the clubhouse. He'll be charged with five runs on seven hits, and the three runners on base are still his responsibility. Now, while Tuffarelo takes his warm-up tosses, let me ask you a question, fans. Do you have trouble getting a close enough shave?" Before the announcer could answer his own question, Sefton reached over and snapped off the radio.

"You like baseball?" asked the soldier.

"Yep. You?"

"Sure do."

"Ever play much?" Sefton inquired.

"Oh, 'bout the same as everybody else. High school, American Legion. You?"

"Oh, yeah. Played a lot."

"What position you play?"

"Outfield."

"Were you any good?" the soldier asked.

"I was a pretty fair ballplayer. Had to give it up, though."

"How come?"

"Had an accident."

"Oh, that's a darn shame."

"Yeah." They drove in silence for a short while. Sefton thought about turning the game back on but decided against it. It had been two days since he had any kind of decent conversation, and this was a good chance to get just enough of one to hold him for a bit. "You on leave?" he asked the soldier.

"Yessir. I got three days before I ship out."

"Where to?"

"They ain't told us yet."

"You on your way home right now?"

"Yessir. I'm gonna see my wife and folks. My wife is staying with them till I get back."

"Oh?"

"See, my dad owns a garage, and I work with him. Have since I been about fifteen. But he's gettin' up in years, and he's been tryin' to teach me the business end of it so's I can take it over when he retires." The soldier paused and shook his head. "Well, I'm a real good mechanic, but I don't have the head for business. My wife, now, she's a natural at that part, so Dad's teachin' her, and Mary and me, we're gonna run the shop together when the war ends."

"No kiddin'? You're already thinking about what you're gonna do when the war ends?"

"Sure am," answered the soldier. "The war ain't gonna last for-ever. I got dreams that I'm holding onto, and when the war's over, I'm goin' after my dreams. The way I see it, if you have dreams, you better go after 'em. You might not make it all the way, or it might not turn out exactly how you had in mind, but at least you're tryin' for somethin', and who knows, you might get another somethin' else along the way that's just as good—or maybe even better."

Sefton chewed on that for a while as he drove, neither man speaking. Oh, yeah, he had dreams once, but they had been crushed. And now? Now, it seemed more like he was just put-ting one foot in front of the other, living out the days without anything more in mind. Okay, so what would be a dream at this point? Shit, just left one behind. That Yamada—now, that was a dream. That boy was made for Yankee Stadium.

"That's it up ahead," said the soldier, yanking Sefton out of his musing. He pointed at a farmhouse just up the road. Sefton slowed down and pulled off the road, stopping alongside the picket fence that enclosed the front yard. A border collie came racing out from behind the house, barking for all it was worth. "That's Honey," said the soldier. "Sweetest dog in the world, but oh, does she like to bark."

The soldier got out, reached into the back, and pulled out his duffel bag. He shut the door and leaned into the front window. "I sure do thank you for the ride, mister."

"Don't mention it. And good luck with your dreams."

"Same to you." They shook hands.

The soldier turned and opened the gate to the yard. He knelt down, and the dog was all over him, licking his face and wagging her tail to beat the band. The screen door of the house flew open and a nice-looking young woman came running out. She ran to the soldier and threw her arms around his neck. They hugged and kissed as the dog ran circles around them.

After a moment, the screen door opened again and an older man and woman came out. They hurried over to the young couple and each embraced the soldier in turn. They were all talking at once. The soldier turned and pointed to Sefton's car. The whole group waved at him. Sefton waved good-bye as he eased the car back onto the road.

Before he got up to cruising speed, he reached over, popped the glove compartment open, and took out a map. He meant to look and see if there were any places where he should be stopping in Arkansas, any players he had been keeping an eye on that he should be checking out on the way through. Instead his eye fell on—or was instinctively drawn to—a town about seventy-five miles north-northwest of where he now was.

Sefton stared at the name: Oonoma. Jesus, he had not realized, at least not consciously, how close he was. It had been a good ten years since he had been around these parts. He was down near Natchez when he got the tip on Eddie Pulaski, and he had driven through Louisiana, the heart of Texas, and southern New Mexico on his way to Arizona. Never got close to Oklahoma. No, it had been a long time. And there was no telling when he might be by this way again. Why not? he thought. It'll only take me a few hours outta my way. He turned north at the next crossroads.

A few miles south of Oonoma, he turned right on a gravel road and followed it down about three miles until he hit the bridge over the little creek that had long ago run dry. The familiar sound of the bridge planks under the wheels of the car triggered a rush of feelings and associations. Every tree, every fencepost, every everything was familiar and held memories for Sefton.

He turned onto the dirt road that ran along the east side of the dry creekbed. Long-forgotten scenes rushed up to greet him. Under that cottonwood was where they had been fishing when Sonny Redbone had his eye put out by a fishhook. Oh, Jesus, he could see it right now, happening all over again. Sonny was never right in the head after that, God help him. And, oh yes, right here at the bend of the creek was where Charity Bennett had been charitable enough to surrender her maidenhood to him on that moonless night in July of what the hell year had it been? Thank you, Charity, wherever you are right now. And, of course, this pasture—well it ain't a pasture anymore—this was where little Morris Tomlinson had beat the living crap outta that fat bully, what's his name, Buddy something—Buddy Klein, that's it. Buddy had been terrorizing Morris for years, and the little guy finally snapped. He was like an animal. Took off his belt and whupped Buddy real bad till they realized he didn't mean to quit, so three of 'em jumped in and grabbed Morris and held him back or he was like to kill that boy.

Jesus, there's nobody left, thought Sefton as he drove past the abandoned homesteads. Used to be people living all along this creek. All gone now.

Just as he began to wonder if maybe he hadn't recognized the old place, or if maybe it wasn't even still standing, there it was. Dilapidated, but looking just as he remembered it. Clearly, the bank never kept it up after he had sold it. It was one of the few places that had not been lost to taxes after the land dried up and the Depression hit. Sefton had been one of the only people in the area who had been able to hang on to his house, well, his father's house, thanks to his earnings from baseball. But after the accident and his father's death, he just wanted to get away from there as fast as he could, so he sold the place to the bank for next to nothing. He thought it was worth more than what they wanted to pay, but what choice did he have?

Sefton got out of the car and limped over to the house, taking care not to let his gaze wander to the fields beyond—that was a memory he did not want to dredge up. The house was nothing fancy on a stick, just a wooden frame job like all the others around there. He tried the front door. It was locked. Jeez, when he lived here they never locked the door, but now that it's empty it's all shut up. Sefton shook his head at the irony. Just one more thing that didn't make any sense.

He walked around the place trying the windows until he found one that opened, and he climbed into the house. Immediately, he could feel the ghosts, and soon enough he saw them as well—his mother, father, and himself as a boy, moving through the small farmhouse. It had not been a very happy home. His father had been a difficult man, too difficult for even his mother to get along with for any stretch of time. And the drinking, of course, that made it all the more difficult. Sefton shivered at the memory. Lucky he had been such an easygoing, happy kid, or it coulda gotten to him a lot worse than it did.

Sefton walked from room to room, barely noticing the haphaz-
ard miscellany of relics—an old throw rug in the living room,
here and there a faded picture hanging off-kilter, a rusted sauce-
pan still sitting on the kitchen stove—the detritus of their lives
that had been left to molder.

He went into the small bedroom that had been his. He was the
only kid he knew who had his own room. Most of his friends had
ten or twelve brothers and sisters, but he was an only child. He
had never really thought much about it, but now he realized why.
His parents just hadn't liked each other very much.

Standing in the bedroom, Sefton recalled how the roosters would
get going two, three hours before dawn. First some early riser would
crow and wake up a few of the others, then one of those would give
a blast, then a third, and soon all over the plains there would be
cocks crowing as like to wake the dead. And it being so flat and
open, at night the sound traveled with wings, and you heard every
last one of 'em. Then they'd pipe down for twenty minutes or so,
till some go-getter remembered what being a rooster was all about,
and he'd set off another chorus. And so it went, till by about the
third or fourth round you couldn't sleep anymore anyway, so you
might as well get up and get going on your chores.

Sefton moved around the little room. For no reason at all, he
opened the closet door. It was dark in there, but he could make
out something in the corner on the floor. He bent down and
picked it up. As soon as he had it in his hand, he knew what it
was, even though he could not see it very well in the dark, and his
heart gave a little jump. Instinctively, he slipped his hand into it,
or rather stuffed his hand into it, because it was too small for him
now, and he brought it out into the light. His first glove. He went
to the window where he could get a better look at it. He turned
his hand over several times, examining the palm side and the
back, and he pounded his fist in the pocket. He smiled broadly,
remembering how he had first seen the glove in the window of
Pearl's Hardware on Main Street, with a drawing of a baseball

stamped in the leather and Spalding written inside the baseball, and on top of that the letters XR and the word "Champion." He went right in to talk to Mr. Pearl about it. He was thirteen and already had a bit of a reputation as a phenom—everybody for fifty miles around knew this kid could play. Mr. Pearl took it out of the window and let him try it on. "I'll tell you what, Mac. That glove costs two dollars. If you can bring me twenty-five cents, I'll put it away for you, and you can pay it off a little bit at a time until you've paid me the whole amount, and then you can take the glove home. Does that sound fair to you?" Sefton laughed at the memory. He had run out of the store and gone knocking on doors asking for any kind of work in order to earn enough to save up the quarter that would take the glove out of the window. He earned thirty cents the first week, and it took him about three months to scare up the rest. That glove was a dream come true.

Sefton looked around his old bedroom and down at the glove on his hand and knew he had found what he came for. There was nothing else he needed here. He climbed out the window, shutting it behind him. He limped to the car and got in, tossing the glove on the seat next to him. He started up and drove away without even a glance back at the house.

Driving south, Sefton thought about some of the plays he had made with the glove. In fact, he had used that glove until he broke into pro ball. By then he needed a bigger and better model, and besides that, this one was pretty well played out, so when he went with Pine Bluff he bought a new one, a pro job, with his first paycheck. Oh, yes, he had dreams then.

Dreams. He thought about the soldier he had given a lift to earlier. He thought about Yamada. He saw him on the mound, winding up and throwing, his tight, wiry delivery a picture of economy. And then, to his surprise, he thought of Annie and her dark, dreamy eyes.

When he got to Route 66, Sefton turned west and headed back to Arizona.

9

AS YAMADA AND HIS FRIEND MADE THEIR WAY TOWARD
the rec hall, the second man danced on his toes and threw phantom combinations of punches into the evening air. Puffing and
sweating, Nishimi looked like a wind-up toy gone haywire.
People turned to watch as the two men went by.

"Be careful, Isao," Yamada cautioned, "you don't want to wear
yourself out before the fight."

"I know what I'm doing, Jerry," grunted Nishimi.

Yamada smiled. The two of them had been best friends since
childhood, and Nishimi had been Yamada's catcher for ten years,
ever since the first team they had played on. Nishimi was a good
person and a great friend, but he was not a moderate man. In that
sense, the two complemented each other quite well; as reserved
and deliberate as Yamada was, so was Nishimi ardent and exu-
berant. Whatever he did, he threw himself into with zealous
abandon.

Boxing was his current infatuation. He was an accomplished
karate man, the holder of a second-degree black belt, and when
the camp sports committee organized another evening of prize-
fighting, Nishimi eagerly signed up, despite never having been in
a ring before.

These evenings were always well attended. Boxing was not as
popular as baseball, of course, but it had its loyal crowd of devo-
tees. The manly art of self-defense was especially popular among
those who loved to bet, and bet they did on each bout.

Nishimi was matched up with a more experienced boxer, a guy
named Ichikawa, from Merced, who had fought in the Golden
Gloves once. To make matters worse, Ichikawa was a lefty.

"Which is where you come in," Nishimi had said to Yamada when he informed him of the impending bout. "I need you to be my sparring partner."

"No, thank you," Yamada had responded. "I have no desire to get my nose broken. And I sure don't want to injure my pitching hand belting you in the kisser."

"No, it's not like that," Nishimi protested. "We're not really gonna fight."

"Then what are we gonna do, dance?"

"No, I just need to practice against someone left-handed."

"But what do I know about boxing?" Yamada protested.

"I'll teach you," countered Nishimi.

"What do *you* know about boxing?"

"What is there to know? I saw a film of a Joe Louis fight once. All you have to do is hit the other guy harder than he hits you."

"Have you told your old man about this?" Yamada asked.

"No."

"You think the backers are going to let you risk getting your face pushed in when we're in first place and you're leading the team in hitting? You're gonna catch hell from the backers."

Yamada had a point. The Fresno team's issei backers—older, first-generation immigrants, Nishimi's father among them—were not apt to take kindly to the possibility of their catcher and the team's leading hitter getting hurt in a prizefight. After all, they were the ones who had put up the funds for the gloves, the bats, the uniforms and spikes—not to mention the money they collected on bets every time the team won a game. No, this stunt was not likely to please the backers.

"I won't tell 'em," said Nishimi. "They won't find out till just before the fight, but when I win they'll be happy, and then the next time I fight they'll bet on me and clean up."

"What if you lose?"

"I won't lose," Nishimi insisted.

Finally, he wore Yamada down, and the two of them went into training in secret. Lacking gloves, they "fought" openhanded, slapping at each other, pulling their punches so as to avoid injuring one another or themselves.

As Nishimi became accustomed to the angles and direction of a left-hander's punches, his confidence grew until now, the evening of the fight, he was almost cocky. Yamada was not so sure. There had to be more to boxing than what they had been able to figure out on their own.

Men were arriving at the rec hall from all over camp. Inside, they sat in folding chairs and stood in groups, chatting quietly or animatedly arguing. Cigarette and cigar smoke shared the air with excitement and anticipation. In the center of the room, at floor level, there was a makeshift boxing ring, defined by one simple strand of rope. The wooden corner posts were precariously anchored in burlap bags filled with sand.

After a short time, the head of the sports committee ducked under the rope and into the ring. In Japanese, he called for attention. When the large room quieted down, he thanked everybody for coming and introduced the referee, who was greeted with polite cheering as he entered the ring. The referee and the head of the sports committee bowed to each other, and the latter ducked back out of the ring and took a seat.

The referee announced the boxers for the first match. At the mention of the names, a flurry of betting broke out among the issei, and the combatants entered the ring. The fighters and their seconds met in the center of the ring with the referee, who went over the rules. At the end of his talk, the fighters bowed to one another and went to their corners.

The match began. Excited voices called encouragement to both men. It quickly became obvious that neither had much in the way of experience, and the fight was a sloppy affair. It went the full three-round distance without either fighter landing a significant punch, but at the end they were both worn out from the energy wasted by lack of technique, and they had to hang on to each other just to remain upright. The referee declared the fight a draw, a decision greeted with disapproval by the fans.

The seconds helped the boxers out of their gloves and passed them along to the second pair of fighters, whose names were called out by the referee. The issei went into another betting frenzy.

A minute into the first round, one of the fighters tripped and went careening into the rope, which collapsed under his weight and took the two adjoining corner posts down. The referee called time, and the posts were reset, but the fighter who had taken the tumble had sprained his ankle in the fall and was unable to continue. The fans grew a bit more restive.

When the referee announced the names for the third bout, there was a gasp of shock from a group of fans seated near ringside. Nishimi's father shot up out of his chair in stunned disbelief, but the son and his second were already making their way into the ring. As Yamada laced on the gloves, Nishimi fixed his gaze on his hands so as to avoid looking toward his scowling father or any of the other Fresno backers in attendance.

The referee gave the fighters their instructions as the bets went down. The boxers bowed and returned to their corners.

"Good luck," said Yamada as the cowbell sounded.

Nishimi advanced to the center of the ring and kept going. His opponent circled and backpedaled, but Nishimi went directly for his man. That was the way he had seen Joe Louis do it, and it had worked.

Ichikawa suddenly lashed out with two right-handed jabs that snapped Nishimi's head back. The crowd, finally given something to react to, buzzed with enthusiasm. Nishimi shook his head and kept coming at his foe. Ichikawa threw a jab that Nishimi slipped and countered with a punch to Ichikawa's chest. Ichikawa circled and Nishimi pursued. The fans were electrified; finally, they had what they had come for.

The fighters tied up in a clinch near Ichikawa's corner. The referee called for a break and stepped in to separate them. Yamada looked away from the ring to the Fresno group; the backers were watching with glowering intensity. Yamada's attention swung back to the ring.

The fighters broke, and the referee backed away. Ichikawa took a couple of steps toward Nishimi, who suddenly squared away in a karate stance, with his elbows drawn back, fists facing up. There was a collective intake of breath from the crowd. Nishimi let out a ferocious, *"Hah!,"* and for a split second, Ichikawa's mental guard fell. In that instant, Nishimi sprang forward and unleashed a pair of lightning, karate-style punches, right–left, both of which caught Ichikawa on the chin. The Merced man buckled. The crowd rose as one, and a tremendous roar filled the hall.

Ichikawa was on his hands and knees. The referee directed Nishimi to a neutral corner. The man on the floor shook his head, trying to clear the cobwebs as the referee began his count. At four, Ichikawa tried to get up, but his arms slipped out and he went sprawling. At ten, the referee went to Nishimi and lifted his arm. The rec hall was in a state of bedlam.

The referee took a jar of smelling salts from his shirt pocket and waved it under Ichikawa's nose. Nishimi crossed the ring to where Yamada was standing.

"Not bad, eh?" shouted Nishimi over the din and held out his hands so Yamada could unlace the gloves.

"You had that planned all along, didn't you?" Yamada shouted back. Nishimi smiled and nodded.

Yamada got the gloves off and handed them to the referee. With his back to the Fresno group, he leaned in close to Nishimi and, wiping his friend's face with a towel, said, "Take a look at the backers."

"Oh, yeah, the backers—I almost forgot about them." He looked over Yamada's shoulder to where the Fresno group was sitting. Their expressions had softened, but they were not celebrating. "Uh oh," said Nishimi. "Time to face the music."

Nishimi's father beckoned to his son, who immediately ducked out of the ring and went over to the group of older men. Yamada followed. When they reached the group, Nishimi's father turned without a word and led them all out of the rec hall.

After the tumult of the crowd and the closeness of the air inside, stepping out into the night made for instant clarity. Nishimi and Yamada hung their heads, waiting for the chastisement that was surely coming their way. Nobody said anything for a minute or more. Finally, Nishimi's father spoke in Japanese.

"Why weren't we informed about this?"

Nishimi waited a moment before speaking. "Forgive me, I should have told you."

"You do as you wish now?" the father asked rhetorically, controlling his fury. "Since we came to this place, the sons think they can act as they please without asking the fathers' permission?" Nishimi said nothing. "Is that the way things now stand?"

"No, Papa-*san*."

"Then please explain yourself."

Nishimi cleared his throat. "I wanted to . . . I thought . . . I could . . . I'm not really sure anymore."

"Yes. Well, at least you won the fight," said Nishimi's father. "That is undeniably to your credit." Nishimi and Yamada breathed a sigh of relief. This acknowledgment of Nishimi's success meant that as inexcusable as his behavior had been, he was going to get off with a tongue lashing. "But what if you'd lost?" There was a flash of real anger in the father's voice now, and it rose in volume. "And what if you'd been hurt so you'd been unable to play baseball?"

Nishimi was thoroughly chastened. "Please forgive me," he said in as firm a voice as he could. "I was thoughtless and selfish."

"From now on," roared Nishimi's father, "no more boxing! From now on, you stick to baseball!" He turned and stormed back into the rec hall, the rest of the Fresno backers sucked along in his wake.

Nishimi and Yamada stood in the warm night air, absorbing the magnitude of their blunder. Finally they began to shuffle home, each absorbed in his own thoughts.

When they reached Nishimi's barrack, Yamada gave his battery mate a pat on the back and said, "Smart fight."

Nishimi laughed. "I'm retiring undefeated."

"Good idea."

"No kidding."

"Game tomorrow at six," Yamada reminded him.

"Yeah. Who do we play?"

"Merced."

"Oh, no," groaned Nishimi. "Man, are they gonna be riding me."

"You better watch yourself on any close plays at the plate."

"Well, at least Ichikawa isn't on the team."

"Oh, yeah, that's all we'd need."

"I better get a few hits, too, to get in good with the backers again."

"They're gonna be giving you the cold shoulder for a while, no matter how well you do," said Yamada. "Just to make sure you've learned your lesson."

"I know."

"Okay, see you tomorrow."

"Yeah. Thanks again, Jerry."

"'Night."

Yamada continued along to his building. He thought about what Nishimi's father had said. It was true, of course. The age-old relationships between the generations had begun to crumble here in camp, and many of the younger nisei did as they pleased. Normal family life was no longer possible in these circumstances, and without a strong family structure, who could tell what misfortune might befall the community? In fact, the whole community structure had been undermined when the government ordered the election of camp officers but forbade any noncitizens from holding office, which usurped the natural leadership role of the older generation. Yamada shook his head at the perversity of the situation.

When he entered his family's room, he bowed respectfully to his father and mother and acknowledged Annie with a polite nod of the head.

10

SEFTON DECIDED TO TAKE IT EASY GETTING BACK TO Casa Grande. He had busted his ass driving east, so why not slow down a little and enjoy some of the sights on the way back? No dawdling, of course, but no traveling at night, either.

Driving west on Route 66, Sefton could not help but remember the years when the "mother road," as that Steinbeck writer had called it, was the main escape route from the Dust Bowl. Sefton could see, in his mind's eye now, the river of migrants flowing west, all their worldly possessions piled onto their cars or trucks. "Okies" they were called with scorn, as if they were some lower form of life.

One memory in particular pushed its way into Sefton's mind. He was on his way home after the 1931 season; he knew it was 1931 because it was the year he tore up the American Association with Columbus and had been given a $50 bonus on the day the season ended. "You're on your way up, son, we all know it," the owner of the club had said as he handed him the envelope with the money. Sefton took it to mean that the following year he would be in the Big Show.

He had taken the bus to Oklahoma City and was hitchhiking the rest of the way—fifteen miles on 66 and then up to Oonoma. His first ride only took him a short bit outside the city, and he had been walking for a few miles on the mother road when he came across a family pulled over on the side—nothing unusual in that, lots of those old jalopies broke down on the trip to California.

The man was sitting on the ground, playing a guitar and sing-ing, but there was something so mournful about these folks, with the woman weeping and the kids, all boys, about five or six of them, leaning on the car so solemn like, that Sefton could not help but stop to see if there was anything he could do. As he reached the people, he heard the familiar melody and words of "We'll Understand It Better Bye and Bye." Sefton put his suitcase down and sat on it.

When the song ended, the fellow with the guitar did not acknowledge Sefton directly, but he nodded his head, indicating a little blanket roll on the ground in front of him and said simply, "That's our little baby girl in that there blanket. Died this morning. She was three weeks. Just cain't bear to say good-bye yet. Gonna hafta bury her right here 'fore we push on. Won't even be able to make her a proper box."

Sefton sat in silence for a few minutes, then asked, "Can I help you with the diggin'?"

The man waited a little before responding. "That'd be mighty neighborly of you." He nodded to the oldest boy, about eleven, who walked around to the back of the car, rummaged around in the trunk, and took out a shovel. The boy kept his gaze on the ground as he approached Sefton, but as he handed over the tool, he glanced up with the most uncomprehending look of sorrow in his eyes.

Sefton walked ten or fifteen yards back off the road. It took him about half an hour to dig the grave, during which time the father kept playing his guitar and singing hymns. When Sefton finished the digging, he turned his back to the group and reached into his pocket. Except for bus fare and a few meals, he had not spent anything of his bonus money. He removed a twenty-dollar bill, folded it up, and tucked it into his fist.

When Sefton returned to the family, it seemed that nobody had moved. The father was singing "Gathering Flowers for the Master's Bouquet." At the end of the song, Sefton handed the shovel back to the boy.

"Thank you, friend," said the father getting up off the ground.

"I guess I'll be goin' now," said Sefton, picking up his suitcase.

"God bless you."

Sefton held out his hand. As the man took it, he felt the folded paper being pressed into his palm and looked down at their clasped hands. He separated his hand from Sefton's just far enough to see the money, and his eyes came back up to meet Sefton's again. After the briefest moment, the guitar slid out of the man's other hand and fell to the ground as the dam broke and tears began rolling down his face. Sefton gave the man's hand another hard squeeze and withdrew his own, leaving the money behind as he turned and walked down the road.

Ten years later, driving by what could well have been the very spot, Sefton could not recall the man's face, could not, in fact, remember any details about the people save the look in the boy's eyes. That he remembered vividly. The eyes pleaded with him to explain the inexplicable. Little could Sefton have known at the time that he would soon have an unexplainable sorrow of his own to try to comprehend.

His thoughts were pulled back to the present when he suddenly saw a similarity in the plight of the Oklahoma refugees and the people in the internment camp in Arizona. "The federal government sent us here," Yamada had said, and Wayne told him they'd been shipped there "for the duration of the war." Jeez, Sefton realized, that must mean they were forced to leave their homes. Not that different, when you come right down to it. He resolved to find out more about this business when he got back to Arizona.

Thirty miles over the Texas border, the tree-dotted grasslands ended and the panhandle opened up into forever. Sefton instinctively pushed the gas pedal toward the floor. He needed to get himself back to Arizona and do everything in his power to convince that mule-headed Yamada to sign a contract to play baseball. He looked at the map. If he traveled only by day, he could make Amarillo tonight, Albuquerque tomorrow night, and with any luck be back at the camp the following day.

Aside from the occasional thousand-foot-high plateau that interrupted the desert landscape, the panhandle held no interest for
Sefton, but he made up a couple of games to help the miles pass.
The first was a simple tally: the number of armadillos, alive and
dead, that he saw. The second was more challenging: the towns
in the panhandle were ten to fifteen miles apart, and he noticed
that when he left one town behind, the next one's water tower
would loom up in the distance. After he had been through a few
of these burgs, it occurred to him that the size of the water tower
was in direct proportion to the number of people living there, so
he began guessing at the population of the oncoming town on the
basis of the size of its water tower.

By the time he got to the New Mexico border, Sefton had seen
seventeen live armadillos and eight dead ones, and could peg the
population of a panhandle town, give or take a few dozen.

He crossed the Sangre de Cristo Mountains and dropped
down into Albuquerque right on schedule. To his delight, the
Albuquerque club was playing El Paso that night, and after supper,
Sefton headed over to the ballyard to take in the game. He had
heard guys talk about how the ball carried in the dry desert air,
especially at night, and he saw it for himself when there were five
home runs hit in the game.

The next day Sefton was up and gone by nine, thinking he
might make it to Casa Grande that night. He took the high desert
of northern New Mexico at a good clip and bombed through
the Painted Desert. But as he headed into the mountains south
of Holbrook late in the afternoon, the Packard overheated, and
he had to stop to wait for it to cool back down. It was far enough
into evening when he hit Snowflake that, after briefly considering
continuing on, he decided he was too tired and it would be better
not to push it.

He slept late and had a leisurely breakfast the next morning,
figuring he had an easy day's drive ahead of him. In the early
afternoon, he was coming down out of the mountains and moving

right along, barreling down a long, curving grade when out of the clear blue nowhere there was a road sign: SPEED LIMIT 25. It came up so fast that Sefton had no chance to slow down, and he cruised through the sign at fifty-five. He heard the siren immediately and knew he had been caught in your basic speed trap. The motorcycle cop came roaring up behind him and pointed to the side of the road. Sefton pulled over and got out.

"Morning, officer," he said, as the cop dismounted his bike. He had talked his way out of many a ticket over the years, and he had found by experience it was better to be polite with these guys.

"Morning," nodded the officer as he sauntered over to the car. He wore jodhpur pants; a leather belt ran on a diagonal across his chest. "Speed limit's twenty-five here, and you were doin' about fifty-five, sixty."

"Fifty-five, actually, but you see that sign came up in an awful hurry. Didn't see it till I was right on top of it."

"Yessir. C'n I see your driver's license, please?"

The guy was all business; Sefton sensed the futility of his position. He took out his billfold and removed the license. He also handed the cop one of his business cards, which was usually enough to help him skip away with just a warning. He would tell a couple of funny stories about some of the crazy antics that went on with ballplayers and that would be it.

The cop read the business card and handed it back. "I hate baseball." He glanced at the driver's license, then put it in his breast pocket and said, "Follow me, please, Mr. Sefton." He walked back to his motorcycle, started it up, and got back on the highway heading east. When Sefton saw that the officer was backtracking, he groaned. He was as irritated about the delay in his travel schedule as about the fine he would likely have to pay.

The cop waited for Sefton to fall in behind him, then led him back up the road to Globe, traveling at about ten miles an hour. When they reached town, the officer parked in front of the hotel and indicated for Sefton to follow him in. A raggedy-looking bum was sweeping the floor of the lobby. Sefton wondered why he had been brought here. A second later he had his answer.

"Your honor, this man was speeding," said the cop.

Sefton looked around. There was nobody else besides himself, the cop, and the bum. The bum walked behind the counter, leaned his broom against the wall, and took off his apron. He opened a drawer and came up with a gavel, which he smacked on the counter. "Court's in session," he said.

Amazed as he was, Sefton said nothing. The officer laid Sefton's license on the counter. "Your Honor, this man was going fifty-five miles an hour where the posted speed limit is twenty-five."

The judge looked at Sefton's license. "Mr. Sefton, I'm afraid yer gonna have to stand trial." Sefton sighed. The cop took the pair of handcuffs that were hanging on his belt and went to snap them on Sefton's wrists.

"Hey, what gives?" said Sefton with alarm.

"Well, you'll have to stay in jail till yer trial, of course," said the judge.

"When's the trial?"

"Week from next Tuesday."

"What?"

"Unless you wanna post bail, that is."

"What if I'm not around for my trial?"

"In that case, you forfeit bail."

Sefton suddenly saw how it worked, and he knew he was cooked. "How much?"

"Thirty dollars."

"Thirty dollars?"

"One dollar for every mile over the speed limit."

Sefton was incensed at the kangaroo court. "I've seem some speed traps in my time, but this is one of the cutest I've ever come across."

"Watch yourself here, son, or you could find yerself in contempt of court."

Sefton knew it would be pushing his luck to go any further. He took out his billfold, and the cop put the handcuffs back on his belt. All Sefton wanted now was to be the hell out of this place. He put the money on the counter, and the judge gave him his driver's license back.

"I need a receipt," said Sefton, figuring he could get O'Neil to foot the bill on this one.

"Don't give no receipt," said the judge and rang up the money on the hotel cash register.

Sefton's jaw dropped. It was even worse than he'd thought. Before he could think it over, he blurted, "Well, how do I know this money goes to the state of Arizona?"

The judge brought his gavel down hard. "Contempt of court." The policeman took the handcuffs off his belt again.

Sefton knew when he was whipped. "How much?" he asked.

"Twenty-five," said the judge.

Sefton paid the money, turned on his heel, and limped out. He looked at his watch as he got into the car. It was almost three. The episode had cost him fifty-five dollars and more than two hours' traveling time. Now he would really have to step on it if he wanted to get to Wayne's office before closing.

11

CORPORAL RIZZOLIO WAS TRYING HIS BEST TO KEEP from falling asleep on his feet. The heat was bad enough, but the boredom was what really got to him. Most of the day's action took place in the morning—delivery trucks, camp workers from Casa Grande or Chandler, occasional government people. By two o'clock the traffic usually died down, and the rest of his shift was sheer tedium. And sweltering tedium to boot. The small wooden overhang offered some relief from the direct sun, but it was still over a hundred degrees in the shade.

Rizzolio looked at his watch: twenty to five. Another hour and twenty minutes and he would be off duty. He shook his head from side to side. He blinked hard several times and rolled his eyeballs in their sockets. Sing a song, he told himself. Any song. He tried to think of a funny one. Oh, yeah, dat's a good one. He looked around to see if anyone was within hearing distance and then started singing to the tune of the "Colonel Bogie March":

> Hitler, he only has one ball,
> Göring has two but dey are small,
> Himmler has somethin' simluh,
> An' Goebbels has no balls at all.

Rizzolio laughed out loud. Another one, he said to himself. Oh, yeah, I got it:

> Whistle while you woik,
> Hitler is a joik,
> Mussolini pulled his peenie,
> Now it doesn't woik.

He roared with laughter, as much at the song as at himself for carrying on like this. I been out in da sun too long, he thought. He looked around once more. Dis one I sure wouldn't want anyone to hear:

> My country 'tis of dee,
> Sweet land of Germany,
> My name is Fritz.
> My father was a spy,
> Caught by de FBI,
> Tomorrow he will die,
> My name is Fritz.

He was still chuckling when he saw the two-tone green Packard a hundred yards down the road. Couldn't be, he thought. What would he be doin' back here? Sure enough, though, as the car drew near, Rizzolio could make out the face. "Hey, Suitcase," he called. "Whaddya say? What a surprise!" The car rolled to a halt and Rizzolio bounded over to the window. "Hey, *compa, come stai?*"

Sefton had been around enough Italian-American ballplayers to know what Rizzolio was asking. "I'm fine, Corporal. How about yourself?"

"Terrific! 'Specially since da Yanks are runnin' away with da pennant again! So what's up? What brings ya back?"

"Oh, some unfinished business," said Sefton evasively.

"No kiddin'. I thought I'd never see ya again."

"No such luck, Corporal." Sefton didn't want to seem too eager, but he knew he had only a few minutes left to catch Wayne in his office. Trying to sound casual, he asked, "So, could you, uh, open the gate for me?"

"Sure, could I see ya pass?"

"I don't have one."

Rizzolio's face fell. "Then I can't let ya in, Suitcase."

"Why not? You let me in before."

"I know, but they're really cracking down now. I caught hell for lettin' ya in da foist time without no pass."

"Oh, for Pete's sake."

"I'm sorry, pal. I wish I could."

"I know, Corporal. It's not your fault. What about Mr. Wayne? Could I speak to him?"

"He's gone till Friday."

"Crap. That's a lousy deal." Sefton shut off the engine and thought. "All right, listen, could you do me a small favor?"

Rizzolio brightened up again. "Sure, Suitcase, just name it." He felt better at being able to do something for Sefton.

"Do you think you could find out when the Fresno team plays again?"

"Foist chance I get."

"Great. And when you find out, call me at the hotel in town and let me know, okay?"

"Sure thing."

"I appreciate it."

"Don't mention it. It's nuttin'. I'm happy to help ya out." Rizzolio was about to say something else but stopped.

"Something on your mind, Corporal?" asked Sefton.

"Yeah. Could I ask ya a question?"

"Sure."

Rizzolio looked around, then lowered his voice. "Ya lookin' at a ballplayer on da Fresno team?" Sefton hesitated. "So dat's it! Wow!"

"That's strictly confidential, Corporal. Top secret."

"Oh, yeah, sure. Don't worry. You can trust me. I won't say nuttin' to nobody."

Sefton could tell Rizzolio had another question that he was reluctant to ask out of politeness. "Now what?" he asked the soldier.

"Could ya, ya know, like, gimme a hint about who it is? Ya know, who ya got yer eye on?"

"I'm afraid I can't do that, Corporal."

"Yeah, I understan'. But, Suitcase, ain't ya gonna have a problem? Ya know what I mean? These guys, dey look like da enemy. An' when ya think about it, who knows, maybe some of 'em could actually be in cahoots wit' Japan. I suppose ya already thought about dat, huh?"

"Yeah, that's the tricky part, all right. I'm working on that. I've got a couple of ideas."

Rizzolio winked. "Yeah, I betcha do."

"So you'll call me, right?" Sefton asked.

"Soon as I know somethin'. Ya c'n count on me, Suitcase."

"I knew I could, Corporal." Sefton started up the engine, waved to Rizzolio, made a U-turn, and headed off to Casa Grande.

As Rizzolio watched him drive away, he could barely contain his excitement. Hey, I'm in on somethin' here, somethin' big, he told himself. I'm helpin' Suitcase with a ballplayer. *Marrone!* Hey, he suddenly realized, what if dis guy makes it all da way to da Yanks? An' I helped Suitcase land'm! He saw himself and his *paesani* in a field-level box in Yankee Stadium—he was introducing them to this guy from Fresno. Dis is da guy I helped Suitcase sign up back in Arizona. He saw them all shaking hands. Yeah, he told himself again, dis is somethin' big.

He had no trouble staying awake for the last hour of his shift.

12

"THIS IN ITSELF WAS WORTH COMIN' BACK FOR," SAID Sefton, taking another bite of his hamburger.

The waitress laughed. "You can sure lay it on, hon," she said affectionately.

"No, I mean it. You're talkin' to a guy that travels a lot, and I know one hamburger from the next. I'm tellin' the truth when I say y'all got one of the great ones here."

"Well, thank you, we appreciate it," said the waitress. Sefton nodded. "So you're really thinking of moving out here?"

"I'm thinking about it, yeah."

"Ain't much work around here, hon."

"Don't need a job. I work for a large company, see, and I'm on the road all the time, so I'm thinkin' about changin' my territory."

"You a salesman?"

"No, I'm a baseball scout."

"Is that right?" asked the waitress. Sefton nodded and took a sip of his coffee. She turned around and called into the kitchen. "Charlie, c'mon out here. This fella's a baseball scout."

A beefy face appeared in the kitchen window. "No foolin'?"

"No foolin'," said Sefton.

Charlie emerged from the kitchen wiping his hands on his apron. He extended his right paw to Sefton. "Charlie Moore, and this is my wife Josie."

"Suitcase Sefton."

"Nice to meetcha." They both shook hands with Sefton. "What team ya with?"

"The New York Yankees."

Charlie whistled. "Not bad. You ever sign anybody famous?"

Sefton nodded. "A couple of my guys are in the Big Show."

"Like?"

"Like Charlie Keller."

"You discovered King Kong Keller?"

"I did."

"Good ballplayer that Keller. I like him. Same name as me." Sefton smiled.

"Mr. Sefton's thinking of moving out here," said Josie.

"Is that right? Hey, listen, we got some pretty decent ballplayers in our neck of the woods," said Charlie. "Baseball is a year-round sport in this part of the world."

"That's good to hear," said Sefton. "That is definitely good to hear."

"Course, ya gotta know where to find 'em. Things are pretty spread out in the desert."

"Well, maybe you can help me with that."

Charlie was pleased. "I'd be glad to."

"It's a deal," said Sefton, and attacked his hamburger with renewed gusto.

"How's the burger, Mr. Sefton?" asked Charlie.

"The best, Charlie. The best. And call me Suitcase, will ya?"

The door of the coffee shop suddenly swung open. "Charlie, what the hell are you doin' outta yer cage?" said a raspy voice. Sefton slowly spun his stool ninety degrees to see who had come in. A duffer with a stubble beard and wide red galluses shuffled across the floor and took a seat a few stools down from Sefton.

"Evenin', Jess," said Charlie and Josie in unison.

"Never mind all that, just get the hell back in there and cook me up some supper," the old man said, then turned and winked at Sefton.

"Since ya ask me so nice, I guess I'll have to oblige," said Charlie. He turned back to Sefton, but before he could say anything more, his eye went to the street. "Whoops, here comes the rush," he said, and retreated toward the kitchen. "I'll see ya later, Suitcase."

"Right," said Sefton.

In the next fifteen minutes, the coffee shop filled up. Sefton took his time, watching the regulars interact with the sometimes-easy, sometimes-strained intimacy of people who had spent all their lives in the same locale. He had a second and a third cup of coffee, paid his bill, and went over to the hotel.

As Sefton approached the front desk, the clerk put his newspaper aside and nodded with only the vaguest sense of recognition. When Sefton realized no greeting would be forthcoming, he said, "I'd like the same room I had last week if it's available." The clerk peered closer, hoping the fog would lift. How quickly they forget, thought Sefton. "Mac Sefton. I was in the room next to the neon sign."

"Oh, yeah. Mr. Sefton. Right. I didn't recognize you for a minute there." He looked at the room chart. "That room is available." Suddenly something clicked. "Oh, right, Mr. Sefton. There's a message for you." Sefton was puzzled—who knew he was here? The clerk reached into one of the mail slots, pulled out several slips of paper, and took off the top one. Handing it across to Sefton, he said, "Just came in about fifteen minutes ago."

Sefton read the note. Mr. Sefton: Cpl. Rizzolio called at 6:15. Fresno plays tomorrow, 7 PM. Sefton smiled. Boy, this is a kid you can rely on. He must have run right over to find out about the game as soon as he was off duty.

"How long you be staying?" the clerk asked, writing Sefton's name in the register.

"Hard to say."

"I'll just leave that part blank." He handed Sefton the room key and returned to his newspaper.

Sefton made his painstaking way up the stairs. Funny, he thought as he opened the door to the room, how the little bit of familiarity from the few nights already spent in here makes it feel a heap more comfortable than one of the other rooms. Familiarity. Comfort. That must be what normal people feel in their homes. Sefton had to wonder, as he now and then was prone to do—though he never knew when it was apt to come over him—what it would be like to be a normal person, with all the circumstances that went along with such a condition.

Well, that was just speculation. He had a more important issue on his mind, namely, how he was going to handle the red-headed, short-fused O'Neil. He lay down on the bed and thought about his old friend. Pat O'Neil had been one helluva shortstop. Soft hands, great reflexes, arm like a rifle. Only problem was all field, no hit. Even before the beaning. Never could handle the bat worth a damn. A real punch-and-judy hitter. 'Course you could still play in the minors if you were as good a fielder as O'Neil was, even if you couldn't hit your weight.

Baseball was different in those days, thought Sefton, before Branch Rickey turned the minor leagues into a farm system for the Big Show. Back then, all the bush league teams were independent, and the way the club owners made money was to buy the talent, let him play, then sell him to a club at a higher level. By an amazing turn of luck, Sefton and O'Neil had their contracts sold to the same teams three times.

Sefton tried to teach O'Neil to hit, and he was actually coming along a little, but then he took that pitch in the noodle. It was early in the 1928 season, their fourth year in the pros. As Sefton thought about it, he once again heard the heart-stopping sound of the ball hitting O'Neil's head, like a melon being dropped on the pavement. It hit him square in the temple, and he crumpled like he had been shot. As it turned out, it was not that bad of an injury—O'Neil was only out for two weeks—but after that he was always afraid in the batter's box. He would be bailing out, stepping in the bucket all the time. Toughest little bird you would ever want to meet—5'8", 155 pounds, and no fear of any

man on earth—but that little white horsehide had him intimi-
dated real bad.

Sefton smiled at the recollection of the next part. O'Neil was
no dummy. He could see that his career as a player was finished.
So after the season, he went back to Hell's Kitchen, put on a shirt
and tie, took the subway up to Yankee Stadium, and marched into
Colonel Ruppert's office. He introduced himself to the owner and
proceeded to tell him how the Yankees had better get themselves
a farm system like Mr. Rickey was building up for the Cardinals
or they were going to be left behind, because the days when you
could just buy the talent were over and the future was in developing the talent. And yessir, he, Patrick G. O'Neil himself, was just
the man to put the thing together. Twenty-one years old and telling Jacob Ruppert about the business of baseball. You talk about
brass balls!

But the Colonel was impressed with O'Neil's cockiness. In
fact, the Yankees were just starting to acquire some minor league
teams, and while Ruppert was not about to let the kid run the
whole farm system, he did hire O'Neil to head up the scouting
department. He would have had to give one of the scouts a raise
in pay to take the position, and besides, none of them would have
wanted a desk job anyway. So the kid was perfect. One of the
first things the boy wonder did was see to the purchase of Sefton's
contract and have him assigned to a Yankee farm team.

Lying in the hotel bed, Sefton thought about the best way to
talk O'Neil into letting him stay on in Arizona. He tried out various schemes in his mind, but none of them seemed quite right.
Then he suddenly remembered something and took out his billfold. He found the scrap of paper that had started this whole thing:
Eddie Pulaski—Buckeye, Arizona. *That* O'Neil would go along
with—at least, Sefton hoped he would.

13

O'NEIL HAD BEEN VERY SUCCESSFUL IN HIS FRONT-OFFICE job. He was personable, aggressive, and bright. He knew baseball on the field, and he picked up the business side of the game quickly. In fact, he learned in a hurry that baseball was first and foremost a business—it was only to kids and fans that baseball was a game. Oh, sure, the players had fun at it, but to most of them it was a job—at least to the good ones it was, and the good ones were the only ones of interest to the New York Yankees organization.

O'Neil saw how, as in many other fields of investment, money and ruthlessness could combine to produce a cartel—in this case, one focused on winning baseball championships. In the eight seasons between 1921 and the year O'Neil joined the organization, 1928, the Yankees had won six pennants and three World Series thanks to the deep pockets and business savvy of brewery magnate Jacob Ruppert.

O'Neil learned how to bend the rules where possible and how to operate outside them when necessary. He found out how you could hide players in your minor league system to keep other clubs from developing an interest in them. He discovered the forbidden practice of secretly owning more than one club in the same league in order to get around rules on waivers and options so as to extend your minor league rosters beyond the prescribed limits. You did what you had to do in order to win, and if that included illegal or unethical activity, well, everybody else did the same, and let's face it, it was a dog-eat-dog business. As Colonel Ruppert himself had once said, "I found out a long time ago that there is no charity in baseball, and that every owner must make his own fight for existence."

After bringing Sefton into the Yankees fold, O'Neil had taken good care to make sure that his friend's path to Yankee Stadium was well oiled. Sefton delivered and was moved up a level each year. When he won the American Association batting and RBI titles in 1931, there was nowhere left for him to go but the Big Show. The timing was perfect. Ruth would be thirty-seven and Combs thirty-three in 1932. Sefton could break in easy, a year or two as a reserve before becoming the starting center fielder.

Then came that goddamn accident. O'Neil may not have been as devastated as Sefton, but he was a close second. With spring training just about to begin, however, he had to wait a couple of months before he could go and visit. As soon as camp broke, O'Neil took the train from Florida out to Oklahoma. When he arrived, Sefton was in a bad way. He was glad to see O'Neil, but his whole aspect had changed. In place of the sunny, happy-go-lucky athlete O'Neil had known, he found a dark, brooding amputee. O'Neil did the only thing he could for Sefton: he offered him a job. Sefton said he would think it over, and the next winter, O'Neil received his letter accepting the offer.

O'Neil was pleased. He figured a change of scenery would be best and assigned Sefton to the west Tennessee area, which included the neighboring portions of Alabama, Mississippi, Arkansas, Missouri, Illinois, and Kentucky. Sefton turned out to be a good scout. He had an eye for talent, and because he had no family, he did not mind being on the road much of the time. If he was a little unpredictable now and then, well, that was Sefton. In the long run, O'Neil knew he could count on him.

They were both proud to be part of a powerful, efficient organization, and they had both had a hand in developing the Yankees juggernaut that had won five out of six pennants and World Championships between 1936 and 1941, including four straight from 1936 to 1939. And with less than a month to go in the 1942 season, the Yankees were sewing up another American League flag.

O'Neil looked up at the framed photos on the wall over his desk: *To Pat, with all best wishes, Babe Ruth; To Pat, from your friend, Lou Gehrig; To Pat, Regards, Joe DiMaggio*. There were many more pictures around the rest of the room—other ballplayers, Yankees teams, and even a few show business celebrities. But these were the three that O'Neil cherished most—especially the one of DiMaggio, which Joe had given him at the end of last season, the season DiMag had hit in fifty-six straight games. Looking at the photo, O'Neil had a thought that had occurred to him more than a few times before: but for Sefton's accident, he, not DiMaggio, could now be patrolling center field for the Yankees.

The phone rang. "O'Neil speaking."

"Howdy, Pat. It's Mac."

"Mac, how are ya? I was just thinkin' about ya. Great to hear from ya. Ya back in Tennessee?"

Sefton cleared his throat. "Uh, well, actually, no. I'm, uh, I'm still in Arizona."

"What the hell? I thought we agreed that you were going back to Tennessee."

"I know, I know, but listen, I been thinking." Sefton took a big breath. "I've decided that I'd like to be transferred out here."

O'Neil hit the roof. "What! What the fuck are ya talkin' about? I thought you hated Arizona."

"I thought so too, but I dunno, it's growin' on me. I'm really startin' to like these wide-open spaces. Didja know they play baseball year 'round in Arizona?"

"Hey, c'mon, Mac, don't bullshit me. We've known each other too long. What is goin' on?" Suddenly O'Neil knew what it was. "It's that Jap pitcher, isn't it? I know you, Sefton. When you get ahold of something, you can't let go. You're still after that Jap pitcher, ain't ya?"

Sefton had anticipated this, and he had the answer ready. "No, uh-uh. There's this kid named Eddie Pulaski that I've heard about, and I'm gonna take a look at him. Right-handed pitcher. They say he throws real hard. He's the reason I came out here in the first place."

"Where'd ya hear about this kid?"

"A guy in Mississippi told me about him."

"You went halfway across the country on the word of some hillbilly?"

"It wasn't exactly like that. This guy was from Arizona, and he played against Pulaski."

"Oh, okay, now I get it," said O'Neil, his voice tinged with sarcasm. "Some scrub couldn't get a hit off this guy in high school, so he figures he must be big-league material."

"No, I been askin' around," Sefton fibbed, "and everybody I talk to says the same thing about him."

"In that case, may I ask why ya haven't seen this guy yet? Ya been out there two weeks already."

Sefton hadn't thought of that one. He was silent for a few seconds as his mind raced to come up with an excuse. "His team's on the road. American Legion tournament. Be back after this weekend."

"Mac, if you're shittin' me. . . ."

"I ain't shittin' ya, Pat."

O'Neil sighed. "You're a ballbreaker, Sefton, ya know that? Okay, go ahead and take a look at this kid. But I ain't promising nothing."

"Fair enough. I'll get back in touch with you as soon as I catch up with Pulaski."

"You damn well better."

"Thanks, O'Neil. Talk to ya later."

O'Neil hung up without saying good-bye. This is what comes of hiring your friends. Sefton knows he can get away with all kinds of shit. Anybody else woulda gotten his ass fired on the spot. Oh, well, it wasn't the first time Sefton had pulled a crazy stunt, and it surely wouldn't be the last. The whole thing would blow over in a week, and soon enough Sefton would be back in Tennessee where he belonged.

14

THE COFFEE SHOP HAD BEEN TOO BUSY AT LUNCHTIME, so Sefton went over again a little before five, figuring he could talk to Charlie and catch an early supper before heading out to see Yamada pitch. When he walked in, Josie looked up from cleaning the counter.

"Hi, hon. You're turnin' into our best customer."

"Why not?" said Sefton, playing along. "Y'all got the best food in town."

"How do you know that? Where else have you eaten? You had supper here last night, then breakfast, lunch, and supper today."

"I don't need to try the others. I know when I've found the best."

"Okay, hon," she laughed, "you convinced me." She put a cup and saucer in front of him and handed him a menu. "So what'll it be?"

"Actually, I need to talk to Charlie while it's still slow. I'll order after that."

Josie called into the kitchen. "Charlie, c'mon out. Suitcase is here, and he wants to talk to you."

Charlie peered out and saw Sefton. "Hey, Suitcase." He came out of the kitchen. "What's up? What can I do for you?"

Josie moved out from behind the counter, went and sat down at one of the tables, and lit up a cigarette.

"Charlie, you ever hear of a guy named Eddie Pulaski?"

"Are you kiddin'? Everybody's heard of Eddie Pulaski," said the cook. "From Buckeye. Hardest thrower we've ever seen around here. I mean, this kid throws aspirin tablets."

"So I've been told."

"He's only got one problem."

"And what would that be?"

"Gettin' the ball over the plate."

Sefton nodded. "I should've guessed. How old is he?"

"Twenty-one, twenty-two."

"Who's he playin' for now?"

Charlie shook his head. "He ain't playin' no more."

"Why not?"

"Nobody'll bat against him. You take your life in your hands when you face Eddie Pulaski."

Sefton was pleased. "That bad?"

Charlie nodded. "Oh yeah. Worse than you can imagine."

"That's good. Good. How long since he's pitched?"

"Oh, I dunno. Coupla years."

"Do you know where I can find him?"

"Now that you mention it, seems to me I haven't seen him around in a while."

Josie spoke up from her table. "Last I heard he was working at the lumber yard up in Prescott. I think maybe he lives somewhere around there too."

"Thanks, Josie," said Sefton.

"You gonna go see him?" asked Charlie.

"Yeah. I'll go up there and watch him throw."

"But he's not playing."

"There are five things I always have with me, Charlie: a bat, a ball, a right-handed glove, one for a lefty, and a catcher's mitt. I'll have him throw to me."

"Okay. But there's one thing you're missing."

"What's that?"

"A suit of armor."

Sefton laughed. "I've seen some wild throwers in my time, Charlie."

"You ain't seen Eddie Pulaski yet, buddy."

"Don't worry, Charlie. I'll be okay."

"Yeah, I guess ya will."

"There's something else I'd like ya to do for me," said Sefton. "If it ain't too much trouble, that is."

"Just name it."

"Yesterday you told me there were some other pretty good ball-players around here."

"There are—quite a few."

"You don't suppose you could make a list for me, do you? Names and hometowns?"

"I'd be glad to, Suitcase."

"Thank you, Charlie," said Sefton sincerely. "You're a gentle-man."

"Don't mention it." Charlie paused. "Now I got a coupla questions."

"Shoot."

"Why did ya say it's good that Pulaski's so wild?"

"Well, the wildness in itself is not a good thing," explained Sefton. "What's good is that he throws real hard and that he intimidates people. Ya see, the heart of baseball, Charlie, is the duel between the pitcher and the hitter, and each one is always looking for any little edge he can find, like a touch of wildness, which keeps batters from gettin' too comfortable at the plate. If the hitter has it in his head that this guy is always capable of uncorking one, he ain't gonna be too likely to dig in against him."

"But if he can't throw the ball for strikes, what good is it?"

"You're right, of course. But if we can teach him to find the plate, we can make a pitcher out of him."

Charlie looked doubtful. "I guess ya know what yer talkin' about, but nobody's been able to tame him yet, and God knows, a few coaches have tried."

"What, high school, American Legion coaches? I don't mean to sound rude, but most guys at that level don't have the knowledge to turn someone like Pulaski around. See, there's any number of reasons why a guy is wild. It could be a mechanical problem—

something in his windup or delivery that ain't right. Or it could be something as simple as he's holding the ball wrong. Or releasing it wrong. Or it could be fear—he's worried about hitting a batter and hurting him bad, so instead of locking in on the catcher, he's watching the batter out of the corner of his eye."

Charlie was impressed. "I guess I'm gonna learn a little something about the game from you, Suitcase."

"My pleasure," said Sefton.

"Who's the toughest pitcher you ever saw, Suitcase?"

"Ya mean, including everybody?"

"Yeah, including everybody."

Sefton thought for a moment. "That'd hafta be Satchel Paige."

Charlie's eyes opened wide. "Ya mean the colored guy?" he asked, astonished at Sefton's unexpected answer.

"That's who I mean," Sefton nodded.

"Tougher than Feller? Tougher than Dizzy Dean?"

"Charlie, this guy can make a baseball sit up and whistle 'Dixie.' He fires BBs and he comes at ya from so many different angles ya can't ever get set. You don't dig in against Satchel Paige."

"I never woulda guessed," said Charlie.

Sefton laughed. "You'd be amazed at some of the ballplayers in the Negro Leagues. Josh Gibson—a right-handed Babe Ruth, and behind the plate, as good as Dickey. Oscar Charleston—best all-around player I ever saw. Cool Papa Bell—fastest man on earth. Double Duty Radcliffe—hard to say if he's a better catcher or pitcher. Judy Johnson, Ray Dandridge, Buck Leonard, Quincy Trouppe, Martin Dihigo, Hilton Smith—to name just a few."

"Where did you see all these guys play?"

"I never miss a chance to watch the colored teams if they got a game near where I'm workin'. Some of the best ball you'll ever see."

Charlie was about to ask another question when Josie spoke. "I hate to break this up, but we better get ready for the dinner rush, don't you think, Charlie?"

The cook nodded. "Yeah, I better get back to my cage, as Jess calls it." He turned and moved back toward the kitchen, then stopped. "Oh, yeah, one other thing I was gonna ask ya."

"I'm all ears."

"When I make up this list for ya, and ya start going around to take a look at these ballplayers, do you think I could, ya know, like on a Sunday when the shop ain't open, maybe tag along with ya sometimes?"

"I don't see why not. Sounds like fun."

"I'll make up some sandwiches for us to take along."

"Nothing with mayonnaise, I hope."

Charlie laughed. "Hey, you stick to baseball, I'll take care of the food."

"Sounds great, Charlie."

"I'll be lookin' forward to it," said the cook and ducked back into the kitchen.

Sefton picked up his menu and swung his seat around to face Josie. "Now, about supper. I'll have the grilled rattlesnake."

15

ANNIE YAMADA WAS A PERSON WHO SAW THE POSITIVE
side of things. It was not an attitude she had to try to cultivate or
maintain; rather, it was her nature. She had been blessed with an
accepting and patient temperament.

The roundup and evacuation of her family and their friends
and neighbors had strained that outlook, however. When they
had been forced to abandon their farms and businesses and were
taken to the assembly center and housed in horse stables, she found
it difficult to sustain her optimistic approach to life. There had
been a period of about two months when she had sunk into a
depression.

The turning point came with the move to Arizona. True, the
living conditions here were far from ideal, but they were so much
better than what they had been at the assembly center that her
affirmative nature reasserted itself. Instead of focusing on the miserable fate that had befallen them, she was now grateful that they
had a clean place of their own, however basic it was. By concentrating on the details of daily life, she was able to be her normal,
positive self once more.

She also participated in some of the activities the cultural committee had set up to help maintain a semblance of normalcy
in the camp. She took origami classes. She volunteered in the
library. With her mother, Annie attended theater and music
performances.

One of the things she enjoyed was baseball. Before the internment, she had been aware that her younger brother played the
sport, but it was not something she was concerned with, and certainly not to the point of attending a game. It was not that she

disapproved or found it distasteful in any way. It simply did not interest her. For one thing, it moved too slowly, and she was a doer not a watcher. For another, she really did not understand baseball very well.

In the months since coming to Arizona, however, she had more time on her hands, and so she had taken an interest in the Fresno team's ballgames. Little by little, she had come to understand the fundamental aspects of the game and had even begun to appreciate a certain beauty in it. If the fine points escaped her, she could always ask her brother to explain anything she did not understand.

Her brother's success in baseball pleased her. As his older sister, she had always felt protective toward him, and seeing him do well was important to her. Now, watching him pitch against Merced, she could see his mastery over the other team. By his own admission, he had learned a few things from that professional baseball scout who had been around last week, and he was now putting those lessons into practice, as the Merced batters appeared overmatched against Jerry's repertoire of pitches.

The game was into the sixth inning when Annie thought she heard someone call her name. She looked around and saw several people she knew, but none of them were trying to catch her attention. She turned back to the game.

"Annie."

It was louder this time. She looked around and again saw nobody who might be calling her, but as she turned back to the field, her eye caught someone waving outside the fence. She looked closer. My goodness, it's that baseball scout. He was smiling at her. She waved and smiled back, though she was puzzled at his being there. He made a gesture with his hand, indicating that her brother was pitching very well today. She nodded. He tipped his hat to her. She smiled again and went back to watching the game. That is one determined man, she said to herself in amazement.

As the teams changed sides at the end of the inning, Annie looked back to see if Sefton was still there. He smiled once again, and this time she noticed something more in this smile than she had seen before. She would have liked to make her way through the crowd to go talk to him, but decorum advised against it.

Annie was surprised at herself. What was it about this man, this stranger—this *hakujin* for goodness sake!—that interested her so much? She couldn't answer that question. She only knew that she felt drawn to him. She didn't know why. Oh well, it's nothing of importance. Don't turn around again, she told herself. She focused her attention back on the ballfield.

The game proceeded at a fast pace. It was a pitcher's duel, with Yamada nursing a 1–0 lead for the Fresnos. Both hurlers were sharp and working quickly, and the fielders held them up with crisp, clean defense.

In the bottom of the ninth inning, Yamada walked the leadoff batter. The following hitter laid down a nice sacrifice bunt and moved the man over to second. Annie could not be sure, but she thought her brother looked tired. The next man up grounded to the second baseman, who threw the man out at first, with the runner advancing to third. Yamada walked the next batter, which brought Yoshitake off the bench. The catcher joined them for the brief mound conference. Annie could see her brother shake his head, yes, I'm all right, and the manager trotted off the field.

Yamada went to work on the batter. The first pitch was a called strike. On the second pitch, the runner on first base broke for second, but the Fresno catcher had shrewdly called for a pitchout, and the runner looked dead. In taking the ball out of his mitt, however, the catcher was overanxious, and the ball squirted out of his hand and fell harmlessly at his feet.

With the tying and winning runs in scoring position, Yamada bore down. He broke off a wicked curve that the batter fouled off for strike two. His next pitch was just high. Two balls, two strikes. Bent over at the waist, Yamada mopped his brow, peered in for the sign and nodded. He came to a set, checked both runners, looked back in, and took a deep breath.

Annie suddenly remembered the advice that Sefton had given her brother about tipping off his change-up. She smiled to herself—it was the perfect time to put it into practice. Yamada rocked and threw. It was a searing fastball, and the *thud!* of the ball in the catcher's mitt recorded the final out of the game as the hitter's bat was still moving through the strike zone.

The crowd erupted. Yamada's teammates ran to him and mobbed him as fans poured onto the field. Annie turned around and waved to Sefton, then crossed the field to her brother. She waited while the players finished their celebration. Finally, she was able to get his attention.

"Guess who's here," she said.

"Who?"

"That baseball scout."

"Sefton?"

"Yes."

Annie pointed in Sefton's direction. Shocked, Yamada looked toward the fence. There was the scout, all right, grinning at him. Sefton looked Yamada in the eye and took a very deliberate, exaggerated deep breath. Yamada responded with a polite bow of his head. When he looked up, he saw Yoshitake glaring at him; there was disgust written on the manager's face.

"C'mon, Annie, let's go," said Jerry, and began walking. When they were clear of the ballfield, Jerry spoke again, with some agitation. "What is he doing here again? I thought I made it quite clear that I wasn't interested in his offer. Why can't he just leave me alone?"

Neither spoke for a few seconds, then Annie said, "I like him. He seems like a nice man."

"He may be," said Jerry, "but I don't think he has any idea of what we've been through, or what our lives are like. Especially now."

They walked back to their barracks in silence, each one deeply absorbed in thought.

16

THE NEXT MORNING, SEFTON WAS UP EARLY. HE SHOWERED, shaved, dressed, and was waiting outside the coffee shop along with Jess when Josie opened the door at seven o'clock sharp.

"Well, aren't you the early bird this morning?" she teased.

"Gotta make a phone call at eight," he said, and walked by her to take his seat at the counter as she propped open the door. "Mornin', Charlie," called Sefton toward the kitchen. Jess sat two stools down from Sefton.

Charlie looked out. "Howdy, Suitcase. I'm workin' on that list for ya."

"Thank you. Maybe weekend after next we'll do some huntin', whaddya say?"

"Sounds good to me."

Jess looked up. "You boys goin' huntin'?"

"Ya might say so, Jess," said Sefton, and winked at Charlie.

After breakfast, Sefton took a stroll around town to kill time. At five minutes after eight, he phoned Wayne's office.

"Wayne here," said the camp director.

"Mr. Wayne, hello. This is Suitcase Sefton."

There was a momentary blank pause, then, "Mr. Sefton, what a surprise. Where are you calling from?"

"Right here in Casa Grande."

"Really? I thought you'd gone back to, uh, where is it, Kentucky?"

"No, Tennessee."

"Tennessee, that's it. I thought you'd gone back there."

"Actually, the organization's transfered me to Arizona."

"What a coincidence. Actually, it's also fortunate that you happened to call me right at this moment. I just now got back into the office after being gone for a week."

"You don't say! That is a coincidence," agreed Sefton.

"So what can I do for you?" Wayne asked.

"Well, I've been thinkin'. Since I'm gonna be around here anyway now, I figure I might as well keep an eye on that Yamada." Sefton paused a moment to allow for Wayne's reaction, but the director was silent. Sefton resumed his spiel. "So, I was hopin' that you and I could reach some type of agreement whereby I could come into the camp every so often in order to maintain my contact with him." He waited again. Still nothing from Wayne. "Am I making myself clear?"

"I take it you're referring to an arrangement similar to the one we made last time. Am I understanding you correctly, Mr. Sefton?"

"You're understanding me perfectly, Mr. Wayne. That is exactly the type of agreement I had in mind."

"Well, I imagine we can probably work something out. Would you care to come to my office and discuss the details?"

"I'd be delighted."

"How would Monday work out for you?"

"Ya know what? On Monday I have to go up to Prescott to take a look at a pitcher."

"So you're already looking at prospects," said Wayne. "I'm very impressed. May I ask who this pitcher is?"

"Name's Eddie Pulaski. Supposed to be a real fireballer. Ya know him?"

"Only by reputation. I've only been out here for about nine months. We didn't start getting the camp ready until just after Pearl Harbor. But, yes, I've heard of Pulaski. He's a bit of a legend around here. They say he can't hit the broad side of a barn." Wayne chuckled at the cliché.

"Yeah, that's what I've heard too." Sefton paused and then changed the subject back. "Listen, how about if I came over in an hour or so?"

"Hmmm. I've got a lot to catch up on right now."

"This won't take us very long, Mr. Wayne. I'll be out of your hair in fifteen minutes."

"Sure, why not. What about nine thirty?"

"I'll be there."

"I'll tell Miss Desmond to expect you, and I'll notify the front gate."

"Perfect. Thank you."

When Sefton drove up to the gate, Rizzolio greeted him, as always, heartily. "Hey, Suitcase! How's tricks?"

"Great, Corporal. What about you?"

"Not bad. Could be worse."

"Say, Corporal, I wanna thank you for getting back to me so fast on that Fresno game."

"Didja catch it?"

"I did."

"Me, too."

"Really?"

"Yep. An' I think I figured out who ya prospect is."

"Ya did, eh?"

"Yeah, it was easy. There was one guy on dat field who was head and shoulders above."

"True."

Rizzolio raised his left hand and waggled his index and middle fingers in the universal gesture for throwing. A smile broke out across his face. "Am I right?" he asked Sefton rhetorically.

"You're right," conceded Sefton.

"I knew it."

"Confidential, Corporal."

Rizzolio turned serious. "My lips is sealed. So, how's it goin' with signin' him up?"

"It's gonna take time. It's delicate, if you know what I mean."

"I think I do, Suitcase." Sefton shifted his weight in the driver's seat, and Rizzolio realized he was ready to get going. "I guess ya got a meetin' with Mr. Wayne, eh?" he offered.

"I do," said Sefton, eager to get on with it.

"I'll get da gate for ya."

"Thank you, Corporal. And don't forget, not a word to anybody."

17

THE MEETING WITH WAYNE WENT ABOUT AS SMOOTHLY as Sefton had hoped. He gave the director five hundred dollars, in exchange for which he received a gate pass, which allowed him access to the camp provided he didn't "abuse the privilege," meaning he had to be out of the camp by midnight. Wayne also made it clear that should the pass be discovered by any higher authority than himself, he would deny having issued it or having any knowledge of its existence, and Sefton would be hung out to dry.

After the meeting, Sefton drove over to the garden. He parked his car and let himself in the gate. There were several people working amongst the rows, but no Yamada. Sefton was about to turn and leave when he spied Annie. She was kneeling, working in a patch of some green vegetable that was not familiar to Sefton. He limped over to her.

"Hello again."

She looked up at him, then down at the ground, then up again, and said simply, "Mr. Sefton." She was glad to see him but dared not show it.

Did anyone ever tell you that you have the most incredible eyes? thought Sefton. "Nice to see you again," he said instead.

"Thank you. It's nice to see you, too. I suppose you're looking for my brother."

"Well, yes, I was, but I can talk to him later. Actually, I was kinda lookin' for you too."

Annie looked skeptical—*what does he want?* "You were?"

"Yes. Would you like to take a little walk?"

I'd love to, she thought, but said, "I have to do my work in the garden." *This is very complicated,* she thought to herself.

"You can take a few minutes off, can't you?"

She thought for a few moments. "I guess so. Sure, let's walk."

Annie stood up and leaned her hoe against the fence. They went out the gate. Neither of them spoke for a couple of minutes, and in the silence Sefton became aware that people were staring at them.

"I guess we must look pretty strange," he said.

"People are not used to seeing a white man and a nisei woman together. Especially not here."

"Nee-say?"

"Second generation. My parents are issei—first generation, born in Japan, but the first ones in America. Jerry and I are nisei—born here."

"Oh. Why don't we walk down to the ballfield. There won't be anyone there to stare at us this time of day."

"Okay."

Sefton needed to understand more about what he'd stumbled into here. How could it be that he had never even heard about this camp? Never even known that the Japanese had been sent here by the government?

"How did you get here? I mean, how did all this happen?" he asked, and then added quickly, "If you don't mind my asking."

"I don't mind," said Annie. "Let's see, it started right after Pearl Harbor. FBI agents came and took away some of the issei men—nobody knew where to. White people we'd known all our lives were suddenly looking at us as if we'd committed some kind of unspeakable act. Oh, not all of them, of course. Some of our friends were very helpful and sympathetic. But most white people acted as if we were the ones who actually dropped the bombs on Pearl Harbor.

"There were all kinds of rumors flying around about what was going to happen to us. First there was an eight o'clock curfew, then we had to get a permit to travel more than five miles, and then one day we were told that the government had ordered all people of Japanese descent to be evacuated from our area. We were given a week to get ready and told to report to the fairgrounds. They kept us there for a couple of months, and then they transferred us out here."

"Just like that?" asked Sefton.

"Just like that. All of us. Even the ones who are American citizens, like me and Jerry. Actually, about two-thirds of the people here are American citizens."

Sefton's eyes narrowed as he absorbed the significance of what she was saying. They walked without speaking until they reached the baseball field. Sefton was right—aside from some kids who were playing ball, the only other people around were over on the other side of the field.

"Can I ask you a couple more questions?" Sefton inquired tentatively. "I would really like to understand this better."

"Go ahead."

"Has it been very hard?"

Annie looked curiously at Sefton, wondering if he had led such a privileged life that he could not extend himself into imagining how hard it had been, but when she saw the earnestness in his face she realized it was just his way of asking her to supply more details.

"Yes, it has," she told him. "When we got to the fairgrounds and saw the barbed wire and the soldiers, it hit us real hard that we were prisoners. At the fairgounds we lived in converted horse barns with seven or eight of us in a twelve-by-twenty-four-foot room. The stench was awful. We had to wash in horse troughs. The latrines were disgusting.

"Then when it came time for us to leave there, they sent some of us here and some to Arkansas. Friends, relatives, people that had grown up together, known each other all their lives were suddenly separated. Our whole community was torn apart.

"It's better here than it was at the fairgrounds, but still, we're not free. You see the soldiers everywhere. There have been more than a few incidents of people being roughed up for no real reason.

"And there's no privacy. My brother and I, we're young. We're more adaptable. But for my parents, for them it's been horrible. Losing our farm, everything they've worked for—their whole way of life has been disrupted and uprooted. And for no other reason than being who they are."

"You lost your farm?" asked Sefton.

"If you don't make your mortgage payments, the bank takes over your property. Most people lost everything they owned. Homes, cars, businesses, land—everything. They hardly had time to fill a few suitcases. Remember, we only had a week to get ready. A lot of people sold what they owned at very low prices just to get a little money together. I've even heard some people here say that's why we were sent away—so the white people could get their hands on our property, but I don't know if that's true or not. The thing I do know is that when the war ends, we'll have to start over again with nothing."

After a while, Sefton said, "I had no idea about any of this."

"That's because you don't live on the West Coast."

"You said some people were sent to Arkansas. So this isn't the only camp?"

"Oh, no, there are more; I don't know how many all together. I know of three others. But all Japanese-Americans in California, Oregon, and Washington were sent away, so there have to be even more than three. The rumor is that there are about ten in all."

Sefton remembered what Wayne had told him. "Maybe the government brought you here for your own protection. Ya know, there's a lot of hatred out there right now toward the Japanese."

Annie pointed to the top of the perimeter fence. "If that were the case, why would the barbed wire at the top of the fence be angled in toward us? Wouldn't you think it'd be the other way around? If we're here for our own protection, why do the soldiers patrol the inside of the camp instead of the outside? No. We're prisoners, Mac."

Sefton was quiet again, watching the kids on the ballfield as he mulled over what she had told him. The sounds of the game grabbed Annie's attention as well. "Your brother's a good baseball player, you know," said Sefton.

"Yes, he's pretty good."

"No, Annie, he's more than that. He's very good. He's good enough to get paid for playing—and paid well. Well enough to buy another farm."

She smiled. "He told me what you had in mind."

"Yes, well, obviously that's not gonna work. Why's he so dead set against it?"

"It's a matter of integrity. One of the things that's most important in our culture is personal integrity. We always strive to tell the truth. It's very basic to us." She looked at Sefton. "Do you understand?"

He nodded. "I suppose I do. My mother was a lot like that. She had a lot of dignity. She was about as honest as a person could be."

"Was?"

"She died of tuberculosis when I was fifteen."

"I'm sorry. And your father?"

"He was a hard man. Hard worker, hard drinker, hard brawler. Drank himself to death. I can't imagine two more different people. I don't know what drew them together."

"I guess opposites attract," said Annie.

She suddenly realized what she'd said and felt a flush of heat rise in her neck and face. She looked at Sefton to see if he'd picked up on it. "I guess that's true, isn't it," he said to let her know he had indeed. They smiled in shared recognition of their mutual attraction being out in the open, enjoying the sweet embarrassment of the moment. Neither knew where to go from there.

Before one of them could find something to say, their attention was diverted to a commotion coming from the ballgame. Some of the kids had gathered at the perimeter fence and were pointing at something on the other side of it. Sefton followed the line of their arms and his eye fell on their ball, which was lying some twenty or thirty yards outside the fence. The boys conferred amongst themselves, and suddenly a couple of them were lifting the bottom strand of barbed wire as one boy crawled underneath.

"No, don't!" shouted Annie with alarm. "Stop!"

But he was already under the fence, scrambling to his feet and going for the ball. Just before he reached it, a shot rang out from the watchtower, and inches from the boy's feet, the dirt kicked up in a cloud. He froze in panic.

Annie and Sefton reacted instantaneously to the shot, she running down to the group of boys at the fence, he hobbling crazily in the other direction, toward the tower, shouting as he went. "Don't shoot!" he yelled with furious urgency. "What's wrong with you? Are you out of your mind? That's a little kid out there! He's going after a baseball! You could have killed him! Don't you have any sense, soldier?"

The G.I. in the tower lowered his rifle. Sefton turned and hurried back the other way. He found Annie kneeling, trying to coax the terror-stricken boy back inside the fence. "It's okay, he won't shoot again," she told him. The boy made no move. "Just pick up the ball and crawl back under the fence." The boy looked at Annie. She nodded to him. "It's okay. Do as I say." The boy slowly came out of his fear-imposed paralysis; in a dream-like state, he picked up the ball and, staring straight ahead, walked back to the fence.

Annie looked up into Sefton's face. Now do you understand? she asked him with her eyes. Does this answer all your questions?

18

ANNIE PAUSED IN HER SEWING AND LOOKED AROUND the small room that she and her family had tried so hard to give a feeling of home. Her father was doing calligraphy and her mother folding origami; both were absorbed in their work. Annie recalled how, when they had first arrived, the wooden barracks was barely finished, nothing more than a roof, floor, and siding slapped on a frame.

The Yamadas were lucky though. They were assigned to an end room, with its considerable advantages of three windows and only one adjoining room. As a family of four, their room was the mid-sized, twenty feet by twenty feet. Smaller families had to make do in sixteen by twenties. Annie's childhood friend Michiko had been assigned to one of those. Michiko's father had died in 1938, and she, her sister, and their mother, as a family of three, had been shoehorned into the smaller space. The twenty-four by twenties went to those with four or more children or with children and elderly parents.

At first, the buildings had no interior walls. Each living area was defined by a wood stove, a droplight, and metal Army cots with stiff, straw mattresses. The government provided wallboard, and the men divided the barracks into the predetermined dimensions. Given the shortage of tools, the work took longer than it should have, but after a week or two of living with only a curtain to divide them from the neighboring room, the Yamadas had their own living space, inadequate and cramped though it was.

Dust and sand crept into the room through the gaps between the wallboards and again between the floorboards, leaving a thin film that needed to be dusted and swept constantly. After about a month, the government wrapped the outside of the barracks with tar paper, which cut down on what blew in through the walls but made it even hotter inside and did nothing to prevent the desert from continuing to steal in through the slits in the floor.

Annie smiled as she thought about how her father had improved that situation. There was an issei in the community who had been a matmaker in Japan, and one night when the moon was dark, the Yamada men secreted a bale of hay out of the garden and delivered it to the old man's room. A week later the Yamadas had tatami mats on the floor of their abode. The sand still worked its way in, of course, but at least it didn't come up through the mats. Once a day the mats were lifted and the sand was swept out the front door.

With scrap lumber, Jerry and his father built a small table, low to the ground in the Japanese style, at which the parents now were engaged in their meditative activities, sitting on the *zabuton* pillows that Annie and her mother had sewn from rags and scrap fabric. The two men also built chairs, shelves, and a few screens that could be moved around to afford the members of the family a minimal level of privacy. The women hung the few paintings and photos—family heirlooms—that they had been able to bring along with them. And with these few refinements, the Yamada family had mitigated the bleakness of their cell and made it marginally comfortable.

Annie turned her attention back to the hole in her brother's uniform pants. When the order to evacuate had come, Jerry went around collecting equipment and uniforms from his teammates and left what he had gathered in the care of a neighbor, a white farmer the family had known for many years. A few weeks after arriving at the assembly center, Jerry wrote to the man and asked him to ship the gear. Instead, the farmer loaded everything onto his flatbed and drove it down to the fairgrounds, a small and unexpected act of decency that lifted the Fresno team's spirits.

Having their uniforms was a tremendous psychological advantage. While the other clubs were playing in scrounged or improvised outfits or even street clothes, Fresno was the only team out there that did not look rag-tag. Still, Annie thought as she glanced at all the previously patched tears and holes in her brother's pants, these have to be four or five years old. As she finished up the mending, she began to think about how it might be possible to fabricate a new set of uniforms, and soon she was working out the details of a plan in her mind.

"Your uniform is wearing out," Annie said to Jerry as she handed him the pants when he got in from working in the garden.

He looked at her handiwork. "Thank you," he nodded. "You're right. These pants have been living on borrowed time for the past season."

Annie smiled but kept her idea to herself. Instead, she said, "Mr. Sefton was looking for you today."

Jerry tensed. "What for?"

Annie shrugged. "I guess he wants to talk to you."

Jerry shook his head. "He's a stubborn man."

"I think he wants to apologize," Annie offered.

"To me?" asked Jerry, suspicious.

"He's concerned that he may have offended you. He respects you."

Jerry snorted. "He respects my fastball."

"Yes," Annie agreed, "but it's more than that."

"Well, this ought to be interesting. I've certainly never had a white man offer me an apology before."

Annie chose her words carefully. "He's different. I can tell. There's something about him." Catching something in her tone, Jerry looked up, but before their eyes could meet, Annie looked away, once again feeling that heat in her face. "Anyway," she continued, hoping to steer the conversation in a slightly different direction, "I invited him to tea."

Jerry was incredulous. "Here?" he half exclaimed.

Both Mr. and Mrs. Yamada looked up from the low table. They understood very little English, but the change in their son's voice was immediately perceptible to them. He raised his hand slightly and gave a small bow of the head to indicate that everything was under control, and they went back to their work.

Jerry took a moment to compose himself. "You invited Sefton here?" he asked in a more tempered tone.

"I thought he'd understand more if he saw how we're living," she explained.

"I don't care if he understands or not," countered Jerry.

Annie paused to let the air clear before she dropped her next bombshell. "Listen, Jerry," she began tentatively, "I don't want you to take this the wrong way, but I've been doing some thinking. Maybe you should go ahead and do it."

"Do what?" asked Jerry, not following her drift.

"Sign up to play baseball."

Jerry winced and waited several moments before responding. "I can hardly believe what I'm hearing," he said, in as measured a manner as he could manage.

"I understand," said Annie. "But, listen, if you could save up enough money to buy us another farm, wouldn't it be worth it?" said Annie eagerly.

Now Jerry understood what was happening. "Sefton's gotten to you."

"We talked," she acknowledged. "But that's not why I'm saying this. I've thought it through carefully, and it seems like a good chance for us—maybe our only chance."

Before he could reply, the dinner horn sounded. Taking the interruption as a chance to end a conversation that had gotten away from him, Jerry folded his uniform pants and went to lay them on the shelf across the room. Mr. and Mrs. Yamada put their materials away, and the family was ready.

Jerry opened the door and stood aside. Annie waited for her parents to leave and then followed. As she passed her brother, he asked, "So when is he coming?"

Annie smiled sweetly. "Next Sunday evening."

Jerry rolled his eyes. They stepped through the door and joined the stream of humanity coursing toward the mess hall. As they walked, Annie glanced sideways at her brother. She could not be sure, but she believed she saw him chewing his lip in that distracted way he had when he was seriously considering a new idea.

19

SEFTON SWUNG INTO THE GATE OF THE LUMBERYARD
and parked alongside the office. He sat in the car for a minute,
enjoying the air. It had started to feel different about an hour back
as the Packard climbed into the mountains, and it just kept getting more agreeable all the way to Prescott. This is more like it,
thought Sefton.

He got out of the car and limped over to where a couple of
millworkers were sitting on the ground, leaning against the side
of the office as they ate their lunch. The men were covered with
sawdust: it was on their clothes, in their hair, in their eyebrows.
Sefton was reminded of how the dirt got into your pores after a
day of plowing.

"Howdy, fellas." They nodded in return. "Either of you know
where I could find a guy named Eddie Pulaski?"

The taller of the two men hastily swallowed his mouthful and
said, "I'm Eddie Pulaski."

Eddie Pulaski, thought Sefton as he extended his hand—the
only reason I'm here at all. "Eddie, my name is Suitcase Sefton."
Pulaski wiped his hand on his overalls, and they shook. "I'm a
scout with the New York Yankees, and I hear you've got one
helluva fastball."

"You hear right, mister," said the other millhand. Sefton looked
at the smaller man and nodded. "Isaac Martinez," said the man,
holding out his hand.

"Whaddya say, Eddie," coaxed Sefton, as he shook hands with
Martinez. "C'n ya show me your stuff?"

Pulaski lowered his head, uncomfortable. "No, sir, I really don'
think I could," he said. "Ya see, I ain't pitched in a couple years."

"I know, I've heard that too," said Sefton reassuringly. "But maybe you could just oblige me here by throwing to me a little bit."

"I dunno about that, sir. I'm purty wild. I woon' wanna hurt nobody."

"Eddie throws as hard as anyone you've ever seen, mister," said Martinez.

"Well, let's take a look."

Pulaski thought for a few seconds. "We can't do it aroun' here."

"Well, where can we do it?" asked Sefton.

Martinez looked at his watch. "There's another twenty-five minutes o' lunch hour left." He pointed at their food and then nodded toward the Packard. "Let's finish up and get in the car."

Sefton and Pulaski sat in the front. Martinez directed Sefton to the outskirts of town, where they stopped at an empty field and piled out.

Sefton went around and opened the trunk. "You throw right-handed, Eddie?" he asked, handing him a glove.

"Yessir."

Sefton took a burlap bag from the trunk, walked about ten feet to the rear of the car, folded the bag in half, and dropped it on the ground. "Awright, c'mon over here, Eddie." Pulaski walked to where Sefton was standing, looking at the ground the whole time. "Come with me," said Sefton and paced off sixty feet, where he drew a line in the ground with the heel of his shoe.

"Awright, now, I want you to just relax, Eddie. We'll play a little easy catch at first, and then when you're ready, you can turn it loose. Does that sound okay?"

Pulaski stared at the ground. "Yessir."

Sefton limped back to the car and took out the catcher's mitt and a ball. "Do you have a catcher's mask?" Martinez asked him.

"I'll be okay," said Sefton.

"Be better if you had a mask," Martinez advised.

Sefton laughed. He went over to the burlap bag and lobbed the ball to Pulaski, setting the pace for the beginning. Pulaski lobbed the ball back. After a few tosses, Sefton gradually increased the speed of his throws until he and the pitcher had a nice, smooth catch going, though Sefton had to reach for most of Pulaski's throws. Even at this three-quarter speed, Sefton could feel the power in Pulaski's arm. Kid throws a heavy ball, he said to himself, as the sting of the baseball came through the padded catcher's mitt.

"Lemme know when you're warm, Eddie."

"I'm warm, sir."

Sefton crouched down behind the burlap bag. "Awright, I just want you to relax and throw to the mitt. That's all, okay?"

"Yessir."

"Nothing fancy."

"No, sir."

Sefton raised the mitt and gave a target. Out of the corner of his eye, he saw Martinez edge behind the car. As Pulaski went into his windup, Sefton could not help but notice the hurler's awkward mechanics. The right-hander uncorked a pitch that sailed five feet over Sefton's head—the ball was by him before he could even think about getting out of his crouch and jumping for it. Jeez, he thought, even without a wooden leg I'da had trouble flagging that one down.

Martinez stepped out from behind the car. "I'll get it." He chased the ball down and ran it back to Sefton. "I told ya," he said as he handed the ball over. Sefton nodded. Martinez ducked back behind the car.

"Try and relax, Eddie," called Sefton and lobbed the ball back to Pulaski. "You don't have to try and impress me here. I just want to get an idea of how you throw."

"Yessir."

The next pitch bounced in the dirt, skidding under Sefton's mitt and cracking him in the shin. The scout howled in pain and rolled around on the ground. When he opened his eyes, Pulaski and Martinez were standing over him; Pulaski had a look of frightful anxiety on his face.

"I'm . . . I'm . . . I'm awful sorry, Mr. Sefton," he stammered.

Sefton rolled up his pant leg to assess the damage. The shin was already starting to swell and turn blue. In the middle of the developing egg he could see an impression of the baseball's stitches.

"Jeez, you got my good leg, Eddie. At least you coulda hit the wooden one. Here, help me up."

Pulaski extended his hand and lifted Sefton to his feet. Sefton hopped around gingerly for a few seconds, then put the mitt back on. "Awright, let's try it again. Just settle down, okay, Eddie?"

"Yessir."

Martinez picked the ball up from the ground and flipped it to his friend. As Pulaski walked back out to the line in the dirt, he held a little clubhouse meeting with himself in an attempt to get things under control. Once more he wound and threw. This time, before Sefton had a chance to react, there was a sound of glass shattering, and the passenger-side window of Sefton's car was in sudden need of replacing.

Sefton slowly got up out of his crouch and took off his mitt. His leg was throbbing. He hobbled over to assess the damage. The ball had hit the window squarely, leaving shards of glass everywhere. The ball lay on the back seat.

Sefton turned and waved Pulaski in. The pitcher slowly trudged over, his gaze fixed on the ground. "I shore am sorry, Mr. Sefton," he said when he reached the car.

"I know you are."

"I tol' ya I was outta practice."

"Can you throw any other pitches besides a fastball, Eddie?" Sefton asked.

"No, sir."

Sefton thought, the kid throws way too hard to pass up, but is he ever gonna take a lot of work. "I'll tell you what, Eddie. I believe we can make a relief pitcher out of you." Pulaski stared at the ground. He moved the dirt around with his foot but said nothing. "We've got some work to do on your mechanics, but with that fastball of yours, you could be successful coming out of the bullpen. Whaddya say? Wanna give it a shot?"

Pulaski was still silent.

"Eddie, he's offering to sign you up," said Martinez.

"What if it din' work out?"

"Nothing ventured, nothing gained," offered Sefton. "You're of legal age, aren't you, Eddie?"

"Yessir."

"Well, then, you can sign for yourself. I'll give you a hundred dollars to put your signature on the dotted line," said Sefton.

"Then what happens?" asked Pulaski.

"In February we pay your bus fare to come down to Florida for spring training. If you stick with the organization, we give you a one-year contract and assign you to a team."

"What if I don' make it?"

"Well, in that case, you're free to try out for another organization."

"No, I mean, would you pay my way back here?"

"Well, we don't usually do that," said Sefton, but when he saw Pulaski's reaction, he added, "but I suppose we could work something out. But let's take a positive outlook here. Let's not be startin' out thinkin' you won't make good."

"Go ahead and sign, Eddie," his friend encouraged. "Whaddya got to lose?"

Pulaski wavered. Sefton went to the trunk and opened his briefcase. He leafed through some papers, found the pile he was looking for, and extracted two sheets. He went into a different compartment and took out a piece of carbon paper. He filled out the blanks in the contract, signed his name to the bottom, and passed the papers and pen to Pulaski. The pitcher took what Sefton handed him, but made no move to sign. He hung his head.

"What's the matter, Eddie?" asked Sefton.

Pulaski looked up, making eye contact with Sefton for the first time since they had introduced themselves. "I can't read, sir," said Pulaski.

This was only a mild surprise to Sefton. In his territory, it happened enough that he knew how to handle it without further embarrassing the prospect. "I understand. Can you sign your name?"

"Yessir."

"Well, fine then. All this paper says is that I'm paying you one hundred dollars to try out for the New York Yankees organization next spring, and that we have sole rights to you as a ballplayer until the last day of April of 1943. Why don't you have Isaac look it over if you have any doubts at all?"

Pulaski shook his head. "No, that's okay. I trust you, sir. Show me where I sign."

When he had autographed the contract, Sefton gave him the carbon copy and put the original and the carbon paper back in his briefcase. He took out his billfold, removed a hundred-dollar bill, and handed it to Pulaski, who took the money and shoved it in the pocket of his overalls. They shook hands.

"Congratulations, Eddie," said Sefton. "Now, I'd best get you guys back to work. Whaddya say we clean some of this glass outta the car?"

"I'm awful sorry, Mr. Sefton," said Pulaski again.

"I know you are, Eddie. Forget about it. I'll go over to Phoenix and get it replaced."

Martinez retrieved the burlap bag and did a fairly decent job of cleaning up the back seat. Sefton drove the two men back to work, shook hands with them one more time, and hit the road.

Earlier in the day, passing through Phoenix on his way to Prescott, Sefton had been astonished at how sprawling the town was. Now, as he drove around in search of the Packard dealer, he saw just how spread out things were. He was also reminded that in just a few short hours in the mountains, he had managed to forget how oppressive the heat was down in the desert.

It was past midafternoon when Sefton located the car shop. They told him that it would take until noon the next day for the window to be replaced. He silently cursed his rotten luck, but when he consulted the Yankees' schedule, he discovered that the team was playing at home tonight, so even though it was early evening in New York, there was a good chance that O'Neil would be at the Stadium.

Sefton went into his charming mode. "Pardon me," he said to the car dealer, who was filling out the papers for Sefton's repair work. The man looked up from his writing. "Do you think I might be able to use your telephone to place a collect call?"

"Sure thing," said the dealer and pushed the phone across the desk.

Sefton rang the operator, who put the call through.

"O'Neil speaking."

"It's me." Pause. "I saw Pulaski throw." Pause. "He's unbelievable."

"Tell me more," said O'Neil, suspicious.

"He throws as hard as Feller."

O'Neil's attitude changed in a split second. "No shit?"

"No shit. Of course, he's all over the map."

"Figures."

"Doesn't have the faintest idea of where the plate is."

"Intimidating, huh?"

"Intimidating, nothing," said Sefton. "He's fuckin' terrifyin'."

O'Neil laughed. "You think we can use him?"

"Maybe in relief. He's so wild, if we put a pair of thick glasses on him, he'll scare the shit out of any sane man." O'Neil laughed harder, and Sefton knew this was good news for his chances of staying in Arizona. "But I gotta tell you, he's gonna be a major reclamation project. We might have to call in the Tennessee Valley Authority to tame this guy."

"Quit it, Mac," roared O'Neil. "You're killin' me. I'm dyin' here."

Sefton waited for O'Neil's laughter to subside. "Seriously, Pat, the kid is fast."

"What'd he cost us?"

"A C-note."

"Not bad."

"And," added Sefton, deftly tiptoeing into the next item on his agenda, "I've got a list of all the prospects within a hundred-mile radius of here."

"Good work," said O'Neil. He knew where Sefton was headed. "I guess you better start checkin' 'em out."

"Okay." Don't sound too eager here, Sefton told himself. "Does that mean I'm transferred?"

"It means you got six months to look around. We'll see what you show up with at spring training."

Sound grateful, Sefton advised himself. Humble, too. "Thanks, Pat. You won't regret it."

"That remains to be seen," said O'Neil, not wanting Sefton to feel too comfortable just yet.

"I owe you a favor," added Sefton for good measure.

"Are you fuckin' kiddin' me? Go tell it to your Aunt Tilly," said O'Neil with mock indignation. "You couldn't count as high as all the favors you owe me. And just in case you think you're slippin' something by me here, don't think I ain't on to what you're up to. I know this is all about that Jap pitcher. Fine and dandy. Just don't forget, Mac, baseball is a business. As long as you find me the ballplayers, I don't give a shit if you wanna chase some god-damn pipe dream."

"I gotcha," said Sefton, sobered.

"Mac, have I ever told you that you're a royal pain in the ass?"

Sefton was reassured. "Many times," he laughed, "but not recently."

"Well, it's still true."

"Thanks, again, Pat. I'll talk to ya later."

O'Neil hung up without saying good-bye, but Sefton didn't mind a bit. His future had brightened considerably. For the moment, his only real concerns were figuring out whether he wanted to go to a movie or a ballgame after supper, and how to kill the morning hours until his car was scheduled to be ready.

20

FROM THE POSITION OF THE MOON IN THE SKY, YAMADA guessed it was about three o'clock. He had been lying awake on his cot, staring out the window for more than two hours, his sleeplessness a combined result of the moon's radiance and his agitated state of mind.

When Sefton had made the suggestion, it was one thing; coming from Annie, it was quite another. In the days since she had first brought it up, Yamada had been haunted. If she truly believed that it would be best for him to play baseball as a way of helping the family, he could not just slough off the idea as he had when the scout had made the proposal. And he knew his sister well enough to know that she would not have offered such an idea lightly. No, Annie was very well aware of how he felt, and if she was now suggesting that signing with Sefton might be a good path to consider, she would most certainly have thought it out quite carefully.

Yamada was suffering: Sefton had thrown his life into turmoil. As bad as things had been after the evacuation, at least here in camp a semblance of stability had begun to emerge. True, like everyone else, he was making the best of a grim situation, but at least the circumstances were known, and he had reconciled himself to them. But Sefton's offer had unsettled the calm surface to reveal the turbulence deep down below. After all, it was not as if Yamada had not thought many times about what lay in store for him and his family. It was not as if he had not wondered how they were going to manage, starting over again with nothing.

Now, in the still of the early morning, Yamada mulled the options over and over to no resolution. He kept heading down the same blind alleys, running into the same brick walls. There was simply no good choice. He was firmly pinned on the horns of a dilemma.

Finally, after four o'clock, he fell back to sleep. He dreamt of being alone in camp, running in frantic desperation from one barracks building to the next, but finding no other people. Then he was on the old farm, and still he could find no one. Yamada was filled with a profound sense of isolation.

Nishimi appeared wearing boxing trunks and practicing shadowboxing. He danced wildly about, throwing punches without end. "Hey, Isao," Yamada reminded him, "your old man said no more boxing, remember?" Nishimi did not respond, but kept up his manic routine. "Stop," Yamada begged him, "I've gotta talk to you."

"Can't stop, Jerry," said Nishimi, punching. "Just turned professional. Gotta train."

"You turned professional? But why?"

"Good money, Jerry. Can't pass that up. See ya later." And he was gone.

Then Yamada was pitching to Sefton, who was using his wooden leg for a bat. Perfect time to use that change-up decoy, Yamada thought. He took an exaggerated deep breath and then threw a fastball; when it left his hand, he knew it was by far the hardest pitch he had ever thrown. But Sefton connected and blasted a monstrous drive. As Yamada turned to watch the ball disappear over the horizon, he remembered too late that it had been Sefton who taught him that setup move.

Sefton hopped to first base on his one good leg. "Too straight, Yamada. I told ya, your fastball's too straight. Doesn't move. Ya thought ya could sneak it by me, but I've got it timed."

And so it went, until Yamada was awakened by his sister just after six. "Time to get up and get going, Jerry," she said, as sweet as ever.

When he was dressed, the family moved toward the door. "Wait," Jerry said to the others in Japanese. "I need to talk to Papa-*san*. We'll join you at the mess hall."

Mrs. Yamada looked at her husband, who nodded. The women left.

Mr. Yamada was well regarded in Fresno's Japanese-American community. He was respected for his even keel and his common sense, and many people sought his advice. His son was no exception. Throughout his life, whenever his path was unclear, Jerry had consulted his father, grateful to benefit from the older man's experience and wisdom. He was well aware of how deeply his worldview had been shaped by the spontaneous talks his father now and then delivered to family and friends on life and how to live it.

Now Jerry paced the room while his father stood in silence for a couple of minutes. Perceiving his son's agitation and the difficulty he was having in expressing it, the older man finally said, "You seem troubled."

"I am indeed. I need your advice."

"Ahhh," said Mr. Yamada, and gestured for them to sit on the *zabutons*. When a comfortable amount of time had passed, the father said, "Now then," and waited.

Jerry searched for the words. "I seem . . . to be . . . confronted with a dilemma, and there doesn't seem to be a good solution."

"There never is—that's the nature of a dilemma," said Mr. Yamada.

"I suppose so. Then how do you decide the best course of action when you're facing an important choice, but neither of the options is satisfactory?"

"Can you be more specific?"

Jerry looked at his hands. "Forgive me, but I can't. Not yet."

"I see," said his father. He thought for a few moments and then spoke. "All right. I would say, first of all, that you should try to step back a bit to get some perspective. Keep in mind the impermanent nature of existence. Everything changes. This will too." Jerry nodded. Mr. Yamada paused, then asked, "I take it you've weighed the possible consequences of each choice?"

"Yes, I have. Many times over. And I'm still in a quandary."

"I understand. I would advise you then to consider the effects of each possibility on the other people concerned because it's always a good idea to choose a course of action that's beneficial to others." He paused. "Without knowing more, that's all I can tell you."

Knowing his father, Jerry was not surprised by his advice, but it was not especially what he wanted to hear. He sat for a few moments, then gave a slight bow of the head, acknowledging the end of their conversation. They rose and moved to the door.

Most of the time, Jerry experienced a liberating feeling when he left the confines of the small room for the outdoors, but not now. Now, he felt trapped.

21

"SO WHERE WE GOIN', CHARLIE OL' BOY?" ASKED SEFTON
when they had loaded the lunches into the trunk, bid Josie good-
bye, and were rolling out of town.

"We're headin' up to Globe," said the cook. "Little less than a
hunnerd miles northeast. Higher up. Be a bit cooler up there."

"That's fine by me," said Sefton as he reached over, opened the
glove compartment, and took out the Arizona road map, which
was folded open to the Casa Grande area. Sefton began unfolding
the map and scanning for Globe.

"Here, why don't I do that?" said Charlie, taking the map out
of Sefton's hand. "You watch the road. I'll read the map—maybe
just save us from gettin' killed."

Sefton laughed. "I don't usually have the luxury of a navigator,
so I've learned to read a map at sixty miles an hour."

"And lived to tell the tale," said Charlie, shaking his head.
"Takes all kinds."

When they were clear of town and the miles had started to glide
by, Charlie said to Sefton, "Tell me about scouting."

"Whaddya wanna know?"

"How it works."

Sefton thought a moment. "Scouting is the ground floor of professional baseball. Scouts can make or break an organization, but
most fans hardly know we exist. We're the unsung heroes of the
game." He looked over to see if Charlie was with him. Charlie
nodded. "We beat the bushes. We comb the sandlots of America
looking for prospects. That's why they call us 'ivory hunters.' The
most important thing in scouting is to beat the other guys to the
talent and sign it up. It's one helluva lonely grind, Charlie."

"I can imagine."

"Not that I'm feeling sorry for myself, you understand."

"I understand." Charlie thought for a moment, then asked, "Are most scouts pretty much like you?"

"Well, we've all been players, if that's what you mean, but I'd have to say the similarity ends there. You'd be surprised at some of the guys we got—guys that read Shakespeare and go to art museums and like to watch the opera and the ballet. And then there are plenty of other guys that are just about as ignorant as a plow mule and proud of it. They don't know shit from Shinola about anything but baseball. Me, I'm somewhere in between."

"Opera and ballet? Hunh." Charlie shook his head in disbelief.

"I wouldn't kid ya."

"Nah, I'm sure you wouldn't."

"What else ya wanna know?" asked Sefton, ready to talk.

Charlie considered. "Do ya'll use pretty much the same yardstick to judge a ballplayer?"

"No, sirree. Not by a long shot. Everybody has his own idea of what's what. There's an old-timer, a guy by the name of Larry Sutton, who was actually the first full-time scout. Now, ol' Larry is firmly and absolutely convinced that light-haired players hold up better in the heat of summer. Sounds ridiculous, but there you are. I know more than one guy who won't sign a player who throws left and bats right. Why? There's a superstition that such a player has to be uncoordinated—don't matter if he hits a ton and fields like a dream, these scouts won't touch him. Throws right, bats left, fine. Throws left, bats right, nope. Go figure, huh? Or you'll hear some scouts talk about 'the good face' or 'the good voice'—now what in the Sam Hill is that supposed to mean?" He snorted. "*The good face!* You ever see a picture of Ernie Lombardi, for Pete's sake? You ever see the mug on Carl Hubbell? Or Frankie Frisch? And believe me, I've seen plenty of ballplayers who look like movie stars but can't hit worth a damn."

"I take it you don't believe in any of that stuff," said Charlie.

"Nah, that's all a pile o' horseshit," Sefton said definitively. "It's malarkey, baloney. All that matters is if the kid can play. Hey, here's one for you: Cy Slapnicka for Cleveland—one of the best, he discovered Bobby Feller, now he's the general manager. He once had a chance to buy Lefty Gomez from the San Francisco Seals. He saw Gomez pitch two games against the Oakland Oaks, and he was ready to get him. So after the second game, he goes into the locker room to talk to Gomez, and Gomez is just coming out of the shower. Slapnicka takes a look at his pecker, which is a foot long, and that's it. Deal's off. Passes him up because he's sure a guy with a thing that big won't be able to keep his mind on baseball." They laughed. "Now, I don't have to tell you what Gomez has done for us in the past ten years."

"He's won quite a few games," Charlie put in.

Sefton nodded. "Very near two hunnerd."

"When you say that guy—what's his name?—was the first full-time scout, how'd they do it before that?"

"Before about 1920, there were only the 'bird dogs'—guys working on commission. They'd get a finder's fee for every player they found who got signed. But then, after Branch Rickey started the Cardinals' farm system and all the other teams followed suit, the big league organizations started putting guys on the payroll. Oh, sure, you still have the bird dogs today—mostly high school and American Legion coaches—but all the professional scouts are working for one of the big-league teams."

They had reached Florence, and Sefton left off his account to take in the burg and to pay attention to the street traffic. On the other side of town, he resumed. "Ya know, come to think of it, there *is* one way that we're all alike. Every scout I know dreams about finding a great one. One really great player. You know, you walk up to some ballgame in the sticks, and holy smokes, there's some kid with all the tools who nobody else has ever seen, and you sign him right there on the spot, just like that, and he goes on to become one of the all-time greats. That's what keeps every single one of us going."

Sensing that Sefton was off in his own little world, Charlie said nothing. The sage and saguaro flew by. Finally, Sefton came out of his daydream. "So exactly who're we goin' to look at today?" he asked.

"Well, there's actually two players," Charlie said. "Sam Montoya, the Globe shortstop, and Sidney Winchell, the centerfielder for Mesa."

"Sidney Winchell?" scoffed Sefton. "*Sidney Winchell?* Jeez, with a name like that, the kid'll be lucky to make it past Single A ball."

"What's his name got to do with it?"

"Sidney Winchell ain't a baseball name, Charlie."

"Didn't you just get through telling me the only thing that matters is if the kid can play ball?"

"I did," conceded Sefton, "but this is different."

"How is it different?"

Sefton thought. "Okay, I guess you got a point there. But still, have you ever heard of a big-leaguer with a name like Sidney Winchell?" Charlie laughed. "Well, have ya?"

"I guess not."

"My point, exactly."

"Why don't you wait and see him play?"

"Okay, I'll keep an open mind," said Sefton amiably.

Just east of Superior, off to the side of the road, they happened on a ballgame. Sefton glanced at his watch. They had plenty of time to stop and take in a couple of innings. "Shall we?" he asked Charlie, who nodded in agreement.

Sefton pulled the car over on the shoulder and they got out. "Now this is what you call a real cow pasture," said Sefton, taking in the uneven, scrubby playing field.

The players were in their teens. It was just a pickup game, with most of the kids in street clothes. No backstop, no benches, no coaches, just kids having themselves a good time. Choose-up ball. Sefton and Charlie leaned against the car and watched the action.

"So, Suitcase, what do you look for in a player?" asked the cook.

"What do *you* look for, Charlie?"

He thought. "I dunno. I guess good hands, a good swing, speed, good arm."

"Just about the same things I look for," said Sefton.

"C'mon now, there's more to it than that."

"Sure there is, but you got the basics. Look, it's a simple game—there are five tools: run, hit, hit with power, throw, and field. You need three of 'em to have a shot. If you can run, hit, and field, but you don't have a real strong arm, you might still have a chance at second base. Big, slow guy who can catch the ball and hit a mile, put him at first. Some guys have even made it to the Show with just three tools.

"Of course, to stick in the bigs, you gotta be able to field. To give you an example of a guy who couldn't, there's an outfielder named Smead Jolley in the Pacific Coast League—terrific hitter."

"Sure, I remember him—he had a few years in the majors."

"Played about three or four seasons with the Cubs and the Red Sox and hit three-hunnerd just about every year. Problem was, he couldn't play the outfield worth a shit. They tell a story about how ol' Smead once made three errors on one batted ball.

"Now, Branch Rickey, he always puts speed first on the list. A guy that can fly, Rickey'll sign him every time because that's the one tool you need on the bases *and* in the field. A fast man scores more runs, *and* he gets to more balls. Speed cannot be taught—you either got it or you don't. And speed never goes into a slump.

"So, if you got three tools, with one of 'em being fielding, you're a maybe. With four tools, you got a career. All five, and you're a star."

They turned their attention to the game. After a couple of innings, Suitcase asked Charlie, "You see anyone out there worth a second look?"

"Nope."

"Me neither. Let's go."

When they got to Globe, they found the ballpark and set up their lunch on a picnic table in the park across the street. Charlie had fixed a spread of fried chicken, corn on the cob, and sliced tomatoes, with apple pie and a thermos of coffee for dessert. The two dug in.

They took their time with lunch, enjoying the cool air. "Best meal I've had since this morning," said Sefton, as he loosened his belt to make room for a second slice of pie.

When the players began arriving for the game, Charlie and Sefton packed up what was left of the lunch, put it in the trunk, and crossed over to the ballfield.

Charlie started to ease into the second row of the wooden stands behind home plate, but Sefton caught his arm and pointed to the top row. With some effort, Sefton climbed the steps alongside the benches, Charlie behind him. When they reached the top, Sefton indicated the end of the bench on the first-base side of the plate, and they plunked themselves down.

"Any reason right here?" Charlie asked.

"Well, being up this high gives us the best view of the whole field, and since most batters are right-handed, I get a better look at their swing from this side."

Charlie nodded. Suitcase took out his notebook from his shirt pocket and leafed through until he came to a blank page. At the top he wrote, "Mesa at Globe 9/14/42." He turned to Charlie. "Now, tell me those names again."

"Globe shortstop, Sam Montoya," Sefton wrote. "Mesa center-fielder, Sidney Winchell." Sefton grimaced at the name and then looked over at Charlie to make sure he got the laugh he was playing for. During warmups, Sefton watched the two players. Montoya was a scrappy little guy, Winchell a big strong-looking kid.

During the early innings of the game, several ground balls were hit Montoya's way. He gobbled everything up and made accurate throws to first base. He also singled up the middle in his first at-bat.

In the third inning, the shortstop went deep in the hole to his right and made a good stop of a hard-hit grounder; he came up throwing, but missed the runner by a step. "Whaddya think?" asked Charlie.

"His arm ain't strong enough to play short in the pros," said Sefton. "He's got a great glove, but a real shortstop woulda had that guy at first."

"What about playing him at second, like you said?"

"He'll never have the size, Charlie. Look at the kid. He's 5'3", maybe 5'4", 115 pounds soaking wet with his galoshes on. I'd guess he's seventeen, maybe eighteen years old. So what can you expect him to fill out to—135, 140 at the most? You think that body is gonna stand up to the pounding you take over a hunnerd and fifty-four games a year? Not a chance. This Rizzuto kid we got at short now, he's 5'6", 150, and he's one of the smallest guys you'll ever see on a big-league diamond. It remains to be proven whether he's got enough strength. Most guys that size just don't last."

In the Globe half of the third, Sidney Winchell overthrew the cutoff man as he tried to get a runner going from first to third on a single, which allowed the batter to take second. Sefton clucked his tongue and made some notes in his book. When the next hitter singled home both runs, Sefton shook his head sadly.

After walking in his first at-bat, Winchell came up again with two out and nobody on in the fourth. He slugged a long, high drive to right field that looked like it would be caught until the Globe right-fielder lost the ball in the sun. Winchell coasted into second.

"Now, what do think of that, Charlie?" Sefton quizzed.

"My honest opinion?"

"I wouldn't care for anything but."

"He should be standing on third base right now."

"Exactly what I was thinking. He was loafin'." When Winchell was thrown out a moment later trying to steal third, Sefton said, "Nothing between the ears. I mean, ya don't hafta be Einstein to play this game, but there's such a thing as baseball sense. When I said all that matters is if you can play, that's not exactly true. There are certain intangibles like baseball sense, like attitude, like desire, potential—how a fella carries himself on the field. Now, have you noticed how this Globe catcher throws to second base after the pitcher's warmups?"

"I can't say I have," Charlie confessed.

"Kid's got a howitzer on him. If Winchell had been paying attention like he shoulda been, he'da seen that you don't run on this guy—especially you don't take a chance of gettin' thrown out stealin' third to end the inning. I told you, Charlie, Sidney Winchell is not a baseball name."

The cook laughed.

"Be right back," said Sefton, and he scooted down the bench a couple of yards until he was behind a man seated in the row below. He leaned over and spoke to the man; when the man responded, Sefton wrote something in his notebook.

The next time the Globe catcher came to bat, Sefton took out his stopwatch. The catcher grounded a slow bouncer to the left side of the infield; the shortstop charged the ball and made a good throw to get the runner. Sefton looked at his stopwatch, gave a satisfied nod, and wrote in his book.

Late in the game, the Globe third baseman booted an easy ground ball, and the hometown crowd got on him. "Yer a bum, Santos," called someone from the seats.

"He's not a bum," said Sefton to Charlie. "He's a stiff."

"What's the difference?" asked Charlie.

"A stiff doesn't have the tools to begin with, so ya can't get on him. You don't ride a stiff 'cause he's doin' the best he can. A bum is a guy who's got some talent but doesn't make the most of it. That third baseman is a stiff. Sidney Winchell is a bum."

"So, for you, I guess the day's a bust," said Charlie apologetically.

"No, not necessarily."

"How so?"

"That Globe catcher," said Sefton, pointing in the boy's direction. He consulted his notebook. "Name's Joe Branscomb. Not only can he throw, but he's also quick behind the plate. Not one pitch has gotten behind him all day, and there've been plenty in the dirt. I like the way he handles his pitcher and the way he takes charge out there. Have you seen how he's always moving the fielders around? He's also got pretty good foot speed for a backstop. Okay, he's just average with the stick, but a catcher who can hit is a bonus anyway. The main thing you look for is strong defense. Even if he never learns to be a real good hitter, he can play Double A, Triple A. Hell, there's plenty o' big-league catchers that have had decent careers hittin' two-fifty and less."

Charlie nodded.

When the game ended, Sefton said, "I need to talk to Branscomb for a coupla minutes. You don't mind, do you, Charlie?"

"'Course not. You take your time."

They made their way down to the field, and Sefton sought out Branscomb. The catcher then pointed to the seats; a man waved back to him. Sefton followed the kid over and shook hands with the father. He gave the man his card, and they talked for a few minutes. Sefton wrote in his book, then they all shook hands again, and Sefton limped back to where Charlie was waiting.

"Okay, let's hit the road," said the scout.

They crossed the street and climbed into the Packard. They were five miles out of Globe before either one spoke.

"Joe Branscomb," said Sefton, turning to Charlie with a sly wink. "*Joe Branscomb*," he repeated for effect. "Now *there* is a baseball name."

22

"THAT'S HIM," SAID ANNIE IN RESPONSE TO THE HESITANT knock. She took off her apron and crossed the room. She noticed that her heart was beating a bit harder than usual and stopped to smooth her dress and take a couple of breaths before opening the door.

"Mac, please come in."

"Thank you," said Sefton tentatively. He held a small bouquet of flowers. He had been uncertain about the wisdom of a visit when Annie had proposed it after the shooting incident at the fence, but she had assured him that it would be fine.

"How will I know how to act?" he had asked.

"When in Rome," she had said, and given him such a warm smile that it had been impossible for him to refuse the invitation.

Now, Annie moved aside, and Sefton climbed the two steps into the room, taking off his hat as he went. Stepping through the doorway, he saw Yamada and said, "Evenin'."

Yamada had not been in favor of this either. For one thing, he had to explain to his parents who this white man was that would be coming to tea—although in his account, he omitted the particular detail of Sefton's interest in signing him to play professional ball. More than that, he was reluctant to show the scout that he had any interest in taking him up on his proposal.

"Hello, Mac," said Yamada politely, albeit noncommittally. He gestured toward his parents, who stood stiffly by. "This is my father." Before Sefton could extend his hand, Mr. Yamada bowed to him. Remembering Annie's instruction, he returned the bow.

"And my mother." Mrs. Yamada and Sefton exchanged bows.

There was an awkward silence. Now what? thought Sefton. He remembered the flowers. "I thought you'd like these," he said, holding the bouquet out to Annie.

"Yes, they're beautiful. Let me put them in water." Annie took the flowers and Sefton's hat. She hung the hat on a nail by the door and grabbed a drinking glass. "I'll be right back," she said, and stepped outside.

Sefton was shocked. "You don't have running water?" he asked Jerry.

"Not inside."

"Nobody?"

"I've heard that the administration buildings have running water."

"But, I mean . . ." said Sefton, gesturing to include all the barracks.

"Us?" asked Jerry rhetorically. "No. Nobody."

Sefton took out his handkerchief and mopped his brow. "Whew, brother, I thought it was hot outside. Is it always like this in here?"

"Pretty much. It cools down some late at night."

Sefton shook his head. "Brutal."

Annie returned, carrying the flowers in water. "It's so long since we had such beautiful flowers," she said, placing them on the low table. "Well, shall we have some tea?" she asked no one in particular, and busied herself with bringing the teapot, teacups, and plate of sweets to the table. Her good friend Michiko, who worked in the kitchen, had made a pot of tea and a few simple treats for the occasion. Annie had been circumspect, telling her only that the family was having a visitor. Anything more would lead to many questions, and she really was not ready for it to get around the camp that a baseball scout was trying to sign her brother and that he was paying social calls to the Yamadas.

Watching Annie set everything down and arrange the zabu-tons, Sefton was seized with anxiety. Jeez, are we gonna sit on the floor? he wondered in a panic as everybody else moved to the table. Mr. and Mrs. Yamada and Annie took their places, sitting cross-legged. Because there were only four pillows, Jerry sat on his heels, samurai-style. Sefton stood rooted to his spot. Jerry gestured for Sefton to sit beside him. Feeling acutely out of place, Sefton inched over to the table and lowered himself gingerly to the floor.

Annie poured the tea. Sefton waited to see what would happen next. The older people raised their cups and sipped. Annie and Jerry did the same. Monkey see, monkey do, thought Sefton, lifting his teacup to his lips. The aroma of the tea caught him by surprise; the fragrance was so appealing he had no hesitation about tasting it. Again, to his amazement, though nothing like any tea he had ever had, it was thoroughly agreeable, a combination of husky, solid earth and sweet, delicate flower.

"Hey, this is good," he said involuntarily.

Jerry could not help laughing. "What did you expect, some kind of witch's brew?"

Sefton had to laugh at himself as well. "To tell you the truth, I didn't know what to expect."

"It would taste much better if we'd just made it," said Annie, "but we brought it back from the mess hall about half an hour ago. Try one of these too," she said, and offered the plate of sweets.

Mr. and Mrs. Yamada relaxed. Without understanding the conversation, the friendliness of the laughter and conversation signalled to them that the mood was lightening. Their smiles, in turn, caused Sefton to feel less constrained. He took another sip of the enchanted tea and looked around the room, all at once becoming aware of how small it was. He turned a quizzical face to Annie.

"Yes, all four of us live in this one room," she said, reading his mind.

A baby began crying in the next dwelling unit; its wails pierced the walls. "Not much privacy," observed Sefton.

"Actually we're fortunate," Annie said. "We're on the end of the building, so we only have one room next to us. If you're not on the end, you have other families on both sides."

Sefton tried to imagine it. He, after all, was a man who lived a pleasantly solitary life, seldom having his privacy intruded upon. "That could get a little, uh, tight."

"It does," said Jerry drily.

They sipped and nibbled. The silence was broken by Mr. Yamada, who spoke in Japanese. "My father says you're the first person he's ever met whose job was baseball," Jerry translated.

Sefton was suddenly on comfortable turf. He turned to Mr. Yamada. "Do you like baseball?" he asked. Jerry translated for his father.

The older man spoke briefly. "He says he loves baseball," said Jerry.

"Then you must be very proud of your son," said Sefton.

Jerry shook his head. "I can't say that to my father."

"Why not?"

"It would be immodest of me."

"Okay, then ask him if he likes to watch you pitch."

Jerry spoke in Japanese, and his father answered. "He says that before we came here he never saw me play."

"Why was that?"

After the question and response in Japanese, Jerry said, "Because he always had work to do on the farm when I had a game. Now, he says, he has a lot of time on his hands—there's not much to do here. So, even though he can see me play now, he would prefer if he had to work. He says he doesn't like to be idle."

Sefton looked at Mr. Yamada, pointed to himself, nodded, and said, "I understand. I don't much care for sitting around either."

The gesture and tone conveyed the meaning. Mr. Yamada nodded and smiled. *"Hai."*

Annie poured a second cup of tea, during which there was more small talk. When they had finished the second cup, Sefton knew it was time to go, but didn't want to seem impolite.

Annie came to his aid. "More tea, Mac?" she asked.

"No, thank you, Annie. I'm fine. Actually, I should be going."

Knowing he would have to face the issue of Sefton's offer sooner or later, Jerry said, "I'll walk you to your car."

"Sounds good."

They all got to their feet. "Thank you for coming, Mac, and thanks for the flowers," said Annie.

"You're welcome. Thanks for inviting me. This has been real nice." He turned to Mr. and Mrs. Yamada and bowed. "Thank you very much."

The parents returned the bow, and much to Sefton's surprise, Mrs. Yamada spoke in halting, heavily accented English. "Honor for family."

Annie moved to the door and took Sefton's hat off the nail. She held it out to him. "Don't forget your hat, Mac." He reached for it, and as she passed the hat to him, she gave his hand a fleeting little squeeze. Their eyes met in the briefest silent acknowledgment of this intimate gesture. "Please come again," she said, as much to cover any embarrassment over their secret moment as to prepare the way for a return visit.

"Thank you, I'd like to," said Sefton, understanding, as two people do when they are tuned into their own private frequency, all the implications behind, between, over, under, and around their words. The air between Annie and Sefton thickened with meaning and feeling.

Sefton turned to Yamada. "I'm ready when you are."

23

WHEN THE DOOR WAS CLOSED BEHIND THEM, THEY stood for a couple of seconds adjusting to the dark. In the time that had passed since Sefton's arrival, evening had passed into night. Yamada raised his eyebrows and pointed in the direction opposite from where he knew Sefton's car would have to be parked. Sefton thought for the briefest of moments before he caught Yamada's drift and nodded his approval. They began walking.

"You did well," said Yamada to break the silence.

"Thank you. I was nervous as a schoolboy."

"Hardly showed."

"You're just sayin' that to make me feel okay."

"You're right," said Yamada, and they laughed.

Intuitively, they both knew it would be best to save the real subject of their impending conversation until they reached their destination, and they continued their stroll without further small talk. When they arrived, they stood and looked out over it.

"It's very peaceful down here at night," said Yamada.

"A baseball field by moonlight is a thing of beauty," Sefton concurred. "Even this one."

"It's beautiful, all right."

Sefton looked at the ground and shuffled his feet. "Ya know I, uh, I never meant to insult you," he began.

"I realize that."

"Try not to hold it against me."

"Don't worry about it," said Yamada graciously.

"Good, 'cause I been thinking," he said, pausing to make sure he had Yamada's attention. "There's another way to handle this."

"What do you mean?"

Sefton had his new gambit pretty well thought out. "What I mean is, baseball's gonna be changing soon. There's been a lotta talk behind the scenes about bringing colored players into the game. See, there's just too much talent in the Negro Leagues, and that means there's a bundle of money waitin' to be made. Some smart owner is gonna find the right colored player and bring him along, and don't you think that every colored baseball fan in this country is gonna pay to see that man play in the major leagues? Darn right they will."

Yamada's face lit up. "Oh, I get it. You're gonna pass me off as a Negro."

Sefton looked at him blankly. What's this guy talkin' about? Yamada burst out laughing, and Sefton realized his leg had been pulled really hard. He had to laugh at himself. "That's a good one, Yamada. You had me there." He shook his head at being taken in, then resumed his train of thought. "No, what I'm sayin' is that once the color line is down, the game is gonna open up. So what I'm thinkin' is, we wait till the war is over, and then we make our move. You're gonna be the first Japanese player in American baseball."

Yamada stiffened. "Look, let me say this again: I am not Japanese. I'm a Japanese American. I was born here. I'm a United States citizen by birth."

"Of course, of course," Sefton tried to reassure him. "I understand that."

"I'm not sure you do."

"Yes, I do. It's just that most people are not gonna make that distinction. Okay, let's say you'll be the first American ballplayer of Japanese ancestry—you get the idea of what I'm saying."

"Yes, and I have to tell you that you're wrong there too."

"What?"

"Kenso Nushida."

"And what exactly is that?"

"Not what," said Yamada. "Who. Kenso Nushida was a pitcher who lived in Stockton and played for the Sacramento Solons in the Pacific Coast League about ten years ago."

"No kiddin'?"

"He was way past his prime, but he could still get the ball over the plate with some zip. I think it was probably more or less a publicity stunt to get the Japanese Americans out to the ballpark. And it sure worked. Man, he was our hero. I was about thirteen and just starting to really play, and when I saw him, I decided I'd be a pitcher. So you see, I wouldn't even be the first."

"All right, so I'm wrong about that part. But that's not the most important thing."

"You're right, it's not. The most important thing is that I'm not interested in being a professional baseball player."

Sefton felt himself growing agitated. "Not just a professional baseball player, Yamada. You have the potential to be a major leaguer!"

"Okay, a major leaguer," Yamada shot back. "I do not want to be a major league baseball player!"

Sefton was dumbfounded. This was a new one on him. In all his years, he had never encountered anybody with the slightest lick of baseball skill who did not harbor the dream of playing big-league ball. "What are you talkin' about? How can you not wanna be a major league ballplayer?" he asked, as much to get Yamada's answer as to try to figure out for himself how it could be possible. "Everybody wants to be a major league ballplayer. Every kid in this country dreams of playin' in the big leagues."

"Not me," said Yamada, setting the record straight.

"Why the hell not?" demanded Sefton, his frustration growing.

"Because I'm a farmer," answered Yamada.

"For Pete's sake, you can still be a farmer! You can buy one helluva farm with the money you'll make!" Sefton realized he was shouting and turned away for a moment in an effort to bring himself under control. "Forgive me, I tend to get a little excited."

Yamada nodded. Sefton continued in a more controlled tone. "It's just that I'm talkin' about the American dream here."

"Look, Mac, you don't have to tell me about the American dream. I know all about the American dream. I was living it one day, and the next day I woke up to a nightmare."

"Well, here's your way out! Listen, maybe you don't understand what you're turning down. Bein' a New York Yankee means goin' first class. The best hotels, the finest eating places, the most exciting cities in the country—Boston, St. Louis, Chicago. That's what it is to be a big leaguer!"

Yamada spoke softly. "That's not what I want out of life. I'm not interested in being on the road all the time. I've got my parents to think of. I have to take care of them. Besides, I don't like cities. I love farming, Mac. I love working the earth. I love plowing and tilling the soil. I love planting. I love the harvest. Sure, I like baseball, but it's just recreation for me. Something for enjoyment, to relax with on Sunday afternoons. If baseball was my job, it wouldn't be fun for me anymore, and I'd always be longing for the farm, just like I do now. I dream of those fields."

There was a long pause. Neither man said anything for several minutes. Finally, Sefton spoke. "Farming is for the birds."

Yamada looked at him. "How would you know?"

Sefton's gaze drifted out over the ballfield. "How I would know is, I grew up on a farm. I thought it was just fine too, till the land dried up and turned into a dust bowl. My father never got over it. He'd put everythin' he had into that land, and when it went bad, he pretty much lost his mind."

"Where was that?" asked Yamada, suddenly much more interested in Sefton.

"Oklahoma. Forty acres of cotton and soybeans. Rich, beautiful black loam—till the drought hit. Then the wind just blew the topsoil right off. I couldn't get the ol' man to quit, though. I offered to help him move—it was the Depression, and I was making decent money in Triple A ball—but he just kept trying to farm that worthless piece of sand. I could see what was happenin' to him. I tried to reason with him, but it wasn't no use."

"You played in Triple A?"

"I was on my way to the Big Show—everybody knew it. I had a year in 1931 that most guys can only dream about. Yep." He smiled at the memory. "So I went home after the season, and he was worse than ever. He was drinkin' real heavy, and his mind was just about gone. He thought it was springtime, and he kept talkin' about how we had to get to plantin'—wouldn't listen to anything anyone told him. So, I went out to work with him every day to make sure he didn't do himself some harm by accident." Sefton took a deep breath and continued. "Well, one day we were plowin', and the tiller blades snagged onto somethin'—I don't know if it was an old tree stump or what—and he put the tractor in idle and I climbed off to see what was goin' on."

Sefton stopped, closed his eyes, and rubbed his brow. It had been a long, long time since he had gone back over the details of this. He surely had not intended to dredge it up now. But here he was, for some reason telling the story to this kid he hardly knew. Sefton opened his eyes and looked at Yamada, whose gaze was fixed on him, somehow understanding that Sefton had unwittingly drifted into territory that was ordinarily fenced and posted with No Trespassing signs, signs intended to keep even himself away from the area. Sefton saw the recognition in Yamada's eyes and momentarily considered going no further with his story. Ah, what's the difference, he said to himself, and resumed his tale.

"I went around in back and kneeled down and started scrapin' around in the sand, and God only knows how, but the tractor slipped into reverse. He had enough sense left to see what was happenin', but by the time he could reach over and shut off the engine, the blades chewed up my left foot. They had to amputate just below the knee. My ol' man blamed himself, and that was the final straw for him. He went into a shell and died a few months later." He paused. "So I know all about farming, and as far as I'm concerned, you can have it."

Sefton was surprised at how little emotion there was left in his memory of the accident. Speaking about it now, more than ten years later, it felt to him more like a bad dream than something that had ruined his life.

"So you became a scout," said Yamada, yanking Sefton back from his thoughts.

"A good friend of mine from my playing days had gone to work for the Yankees in their scouting department, and he offered me a job. After my father died, I took him up on it. It ain't the greatest, but it's a decent living. And at least I'm still part of the game. See, I dream about a field too—center field. Which is where I'd be today if it wasn't for my leg. And there's always that hope of findin' gold. That's what keeps you goin'. You beat the bushes week after week, month after month, lookin' for that one ballplayer that'll make you into a legend. Like Paul Krichell—he works for the Yankees too. He once told me that when he first saw Lou Gehrig play, he knew right then and there he'd never have another moment like that the rest of his life. Now, I'm not saying you're Lou Gehrig, but when I saw you pitch, I knew I'd struck gold. A southpaw like you in Yankee Stadium with that huge left-center field is twenty-four-karat gold. And ain't it just my rotten luck to find the ore but have no way to mine the claim."

"As you said earlier, try not to hold it against me."

"I just hate to see a talent like yours go to waste. Look, let me ask you something. Don't you ever get mad about what's happened to you and your family?"

"Sure I do," Yamada conceded. "I wouldn't be human if I didn't. But I try not to dwell on that because what good would it do me? It's like your leg—there's nothing you can do about it. You just have to pick up the pieces and move on."

"And what, exactly, are *you* gonna move on to? You have nothing. You're so damn pig-headed. Have you thought things through at all? What are you gonna do after the war? What chance do you have? You talk about taking care of your parents, but exactly what are you gonna be able to do for them? I'm offering you a real way to get what you want. Signing to play ball is the best thing you could ever do for your parents."

Yamada knew it was true, and after what Sefton had revealed, he felt he owed it to the scout, and to himself, to be equally forthright. "Okay, I'll be honest with you. It's not that I haven't thought of what you're saying. Even Annie thinks I should sign to play. You seem to have understood why I can't pretend to be an Apache Indian, and I appreciate that." He took a deep breath. "So, here's what I've been thinking about. I'm still not eager to leave my family, and I still don't really want to be a professional ballplayer, but I see this idea as a compromise I'd be willing to make." He paused to gauge his companion's expression and found it acceptably open; for once, Sefton actually seemed to be receptive. "A number of guys have been allowed to leave camp to attend colleges back east. I guess the government figures if they can get us away from the West Coast, it's safe to let us out on the streets." He made a scoffing noise. "Anyway, it's a program sponsored by the Quakers. They collect signatures vouching for a person, and the person is released in their custody. I don't know how many signatures are needed, but the whole thing takes a few months to complete."

Sefton seemed puzzled. "I'm not sure I'm followin' ya here. How is your goin' to college gonna help us?"

"Well, they play baseball there, don't they?"

Sefton's eyes opened wide. "Ohhhh, I getcha. Hey, that's not a bad idea." As the implications began to sink in, his mind started racing. "Oh, yeah, that's it. I know a few college coaches that would just love to have you on their pitching staff. And they could really give you some help. These guys've played pro ball, and they know the game inside out. Yessirree, that is one heckuvan idea."

He was suddenly struck by a brainstorm. "Now here is somethin' I bet you haven't thought of."

Yamada was a bit uncomfortable with Sefton's untempered enthusiasm and with how quickly he had managed to adapt his thinking. Still, the pitcher was curious. "And what would that be?" he asked.

"You can study agriculture!"

Now it was Yamada's turn to be enthusiastic. "Wow! You're right. I hadn't thought of that. That is one heckuvan idea, to quote a friend of mine. Mac, you've made the whole thing start to look good."

Sefton was cooking. "What we can do, see, is find a college somewhere in my territory. That way, I can keep an eye on ya. Then, as soon as the war ends—well, assuming the talk about bringing in colored players is true—when the war ends, we sign you up."

"That's a big assumption."

"Yes, it is. But like I said, there's been quite a bit of talk on the inside, and you know how these things go. First people talk about somethin' for a while and then, by golly, the next thing you know, it happens. You watch and see if I'm not right."

"Okay."

Sefton thrust out his hand. "Put 'er there, Yamada." Yamada hesitated. "Whatsa matter?"

"How come I call you Mac, but you call me Yamada?"

"I don't know. I never thought about it."

"Call me Jerry."

"Okay, Jerry."

They shook and started walking back. When they reached the barracks, Sefton started to slow down, but Yamada indicated for them to keep on. "I said I'd walk you to your car, didn't I?" As they approached the Packard, Yamada asked, "Doesn't it get to ya, Mac, all the traveling?"

"'Course it does. Jeez, here I am thirty-five years old, no roots, no family, no place to hang my hat. Sometimes I ask myself, what would it be like to be a normal guy with a wife and kids? It sounds good, but then I think, how would I make a living?"

Yamada smiled. "There's always farming."

"Yeah, well. . . ." He reached for the door handle and began to turn it, but stopped in the middle. "Ya know, your sister invited me back to visit your family again."

"I know, I heard," said Yamada, and he laughed.

"What's funny?"

"You and Annie like each other, don't you?"

Sefton was taken aback. "Is it that obvious?"

"I know my sister very well."

Okay, thought Sefton, it's out in the open. "Actually, we like each other a lot. Whaddya think your parents are gonna say?"

"Well, that remains to be seen. My parents are more broad-minded than a lot of people in their generation, and my father's a pretty wise man in many ways, but it's still not gonna be easy for you. You're gonna have to win them over. They'll be interested in your character. In fact, they'll be pleased to learn that you know farming—that's definitely in your favor. Yeah, come to think of it, you should visit us some more and get to know my father. You could learn a few things from him."

"Okay. What about next Sunday?"

"Sure, why not?"

"I'll be there." Sefton opened the car door and started to get in, then thought of something. "Say, you got any ballgames this week?"

"Wednesday."

"I'll see ya then."

"Okay, Mac."

"Good night, Jerry."

After Sefton drove off, Yamada took a short walk rather than return directly to the room. It was still early enough that there were a few people yet about. In half an hour, however, anybody out of the barracks would inevitably call attention to himself—not something a person wanted to do here.

Yamada had a lot to think about. He was about to take a big step and, he had to admit to himself, a step that—now that Sefton had come up with the idea of his studying farming—he could actually look forward to. This was something he could truly feel good about, something that could turn out to be of real benefit to his family.

He also did not want to talk to Annie just yet. He knew she would want to hear about his conversation with Sefton, but he was equally concerned about her. How serious was her interest in Sefton? How serious, for that matter, was Sefton's interest in her? Yes, he needed to talk to her, but not now. He was not quite ready. First he needed to let the noisy chatter that filled his head settle down.

24

AS ANNIE WALKED TO THE MESS HALL, SHE WAS PREOCCUPIED with the same pair of issues that had absorbed her attention since her brother had talked to her about his idea. For the past two days, she had turned these matters over and over again in her mind.

Jerry's leaving the family would be very difficult. When she had suggested to him that he sign to play ball, she was only thinking of the potential gain for the family; she had not really thought through the day-to-day implications of having him gone. Now, though, the real possibility of his being away made her consider rather more specifically what it might mean to her and her parents. The adjustment would be enormous. The consolation that made the sacrifice bearable, of course, was the promising outcome. Most important, Jerry's idea of attending college was a plan that her parents would surely approve of.

Then there was the subject of Mac. It was not as if she had not thought of the questions Jerry brought up about him and about their blossoming interest in one another. She certainly had been aware of those concerns, but she had managed to push them to the back of her mind. Her conversation with her brother, however, had forced her to face the issues squarely. Did she really want to let her relationship with Mac develop? When she was in his presence, there were no qualms in her mind, but now, apart, the doubts crept in. Of course, it was still very early in their friendship and who could tell how it might work out? It might just be a passing fancy. But then again, it might not—and that's where things could get sticky. Back and forth she went.

As Annie approached the mess hall, her engrossment in her thoughts was temporarily sidetracked. She went around to the kitchen door and entered. The oppressive heat and ear-piercing din was only partially tempered by the savory smells as the cooks carried out their frenzied preparations for lunch.

"Michiko," she called, catching sight of her friend. The other woman looked around, and Annie waved to get her attention. Michiko smiled and came over, wiping her hands on her apron.

"Hi, Annie," she half-shouted in order to be heard above the clatter.

"It's always so loud in here," Annie shouted back. "And hot."

"This is nothing. You should come over in the afternoon when we're preparing supper—then it's really hot."

"I can imagine."

"How was the tea?" asked Michiko.

"It was really delicious. Do you think I could ask you to do it again for me this Sunday?"

"Sure, why not?"

"Thanks."

"And just who is this mysterious guest?"

Annie smiled. "Oh, just somebody."

"Does my old friend have a beau?" asked Michiko.

Annie blushed. "No, nothing like that. Just a friend of Jerry's." Michiko grinned coyly to let Annie know that she was not completely convinced. Annie waved her off and changed the subject. "What about the rice bags? Do you have any more?"

"Yes, as a matter of fact," said Michiko.

"I was hoping you did."

"I'll get them," said Michiko, and disappeared into the pantry.

Annie looked around the kitchen; it appeared to her an intense, frenetic beehive. She could feel the tension and the pressure of the work and said a silent prayer of gratitude for having a garden job.

Michiko returned with the bags. "I've got twelve this time," she shouted.

Annie did some quick arithmetic in her head. "Oh, that's great. I'll only need eight more."

"I should probably have those for you by the beginning of next week."

"You're so kind."

"Come by with the teapot on Sunday and I'll fix you up."

Annie took a roundabout way home so she could stop at a few places to distribute the bags. The rice bags provided Annie a distraction, a chance to focus on something besides her brother and Sefton. In thinking through the specifics of her plan, she had estimated that if the brand name was turned to the inside instead of cut away, it would take four bags for each uniform. Now, as she walked, she rubbed one of the cotton bags between her fingers. Not the best material for the use, but the only thing available. And certainly better than the threadbare suits they were wearing now. Since Michiko had been furnishing her the bags, Annie had quietly been handing them out to the wives or mothers or girlfriends of each of the other twelve players on the team, with the explicit instructions that the entire project was to remain a secret until all the uniforms were finished, at which time they would all be presented together. For letters and numbers they used old sheets or pillow cases that they dyed blue at the arts and crafts shop.

After the three stops to drop off the bags, her thoughts turned quickly back to Sefton. She knew that getting involved with him would put her on shaky ground in terms of community reaction. She had only ever heard of two niseis who had taken up with white people—and both of those were men. As far as she knew, no woman had ever married a *hakujin*. If such a situation was not explicitly forbidden that was only because it was simply unimaginable. But why should it be any different for a man than for a woman, she asked herself with mild indignation.

She gave a sudden intake of breath as she realized that here she was thinking in terms of marriage! Heavens, she hardly knew the man. Still, she did know this—she liked him very much and was fairly certain she could love him. After all, she was not completely green when it came to men; she had had boyfriends before, and she knew what she wanted in a man. And Mac was the first man she had known who really captivated her. There was something about the way he looked into her eyes that was at once both disarming and vulnerable. When she was around him she felt good; her body felt more alive.

But there was something else that concerned her deeply. More troubling than the unspoken taboo on marrying a *hakujin* was Mac's work. He was on the road for such long stretches at a time, and she knew she could not be married to a man whose job kept him away from home so much. That was the real key to whether or not it could work out between them. She could defy the traditional mores of the community for a man like Mac—but only if he were willing to settle down and leave the road life behind.

25

"HOW YA DOIN', SUITCASE?" ASKED CORPORAL RIZZOLIO, with a nonchalant wave.

So listless was Rizzolio's greeting that Sefton was immediately worried that something serious might have happened. "Jeez, Corporal, is everything okay?"

"Not really, Suitcase. I can't believe da Yanks lost da Series. I'm down in da dumps."

Sefton smiled. "Oh, is that all? I thought someone in your family died."

Rizzolio shook his head sadly, "Four games to one?"

"St. Louis is a good club, Corporal. They got some good ball-players—Slaughter, Marion, that rookie Musial. Ya gotta give 'em credit. They just outplayed us."

"I suppose." He shrugged, still trying to come to terms with the state of affairs. "I'll let ya in."

"Thanks."

"Ya gonna catch da Fresno game today?" asked Rizzolio over his shoulder as he opened the gate.

"I am, yeah."

"How's it comin' with dat southpaw? Ya makin' any progress?"

"Maybe a little, but it's still top secret, Corporal."

"Hey, Suitcase, ya got my woid. You ain't gotta worry about me."

"I know that. And cheer up, okay? As they say in Brooklyn, 'Wait till next year.'"

"Okay."

Sefton waved as he went through the gate. I guess that's the price of success, he thought, as he drove over to the ballfield. You win most of the time, they expect you to win all the time. What do they call us over there in Brooklyn? Oh, yeah—"U.S. Steel." Well, that's the way it goes when you're the best there is.

As Sefton limped from his car to the field, he could see that the game had already started. When he reached the fringe of the crowd, he looked first for Annie; when he spotted her and she immediately waved to him, he realized that she had been looking for him as well. He joined her.

"What's the score?" he asked.

"Five to one," she said.

"Ours?"

She nodded.

Sefton noticed something missing. "Where are your parents?"

"Working in the garden. Lifelong habit."

"I understand."

They turned their attention to the game. Little by little, they inched together in order to close the gap between their bodies until they came to rest against one another, her shoulder joining his upper arm. If Annie had any lingering doubts over how she felt about him, they were dissipated by the excitement she felt as they stood side by side, their arms touching.

Sefton wanted to put his arm around her waist, but he knew the impropriety of such a gesture and instead simply stroked the back of her hand with his finger. After a few seconds, she responded by hooking her index finger in his. He gave her finger a light squeeze. Soon they were secretly holding hands, communicating with the subtlest of touches.

The game was a rout, and Yamada coasted to an easy victory. After the final out and the congratulations, he approached Sefton and Annie. He was accompanied by Nishimi, who still wore his chest protector and shin guards and carried his catcher's mitt and mask in his hands.

"Hello, Mac," Yamada said, extending his hand.

"Jerry," said Sefton, taking Yamada's paw.

"Mac, I'd like you to meet my good friend Isao Nishimi. Isao, Mac Sefton."

Sefton offered his hand. Nishimi quickly tucked his catcher's mask under his left arm and shook hands. He acted shy and seemed nervous.

"Pleased to meet you, Isao."

"Same here, Mr. Sefton."

"Please, call me Mac."

"Oh, okay."

"Isao wanted to ask you a baseball question, Mac."

"Shoot," said Sefton amiably.

"Well, I was, um, wondering if, ya know, um, you could, ya know, give me a couple of pointers."

"On what?"

"Ya know, hitting."

Sefton whistled. "It looks to me like you've got that pretty well figured out."

"Isao's our best hitter," said Yamada. "He's leading the team in just about everything."

"You've got a sweet swing, Isao," Sefton told him. "I wouldn't change anything."

"Oh, okay." Nishimi seemed disappointed.

"Well, I could give you a tip on situation hitting," offered Sefton, not wanting to let Nishimi down.

The catcher perked up. "Yeah?" he said enthusiastically.

"Sure. Let's say you're up at bat early in the game with two out and nobody on base. The count goes to two-and-two or three-and-two. Now the pitcher comes in with a good pitch that's in your favorite part of the strike zone, and you just know you can hit it a country mile. But instead of powderin' it, you purposely swing through it for strike three. Now why do ya suppose you'd wanna go and do a fool thing like that?"

Nishimi thought. "Gee, I don't know."

"I'll tell ya why. Because you're settin' him up. Now, when you come to the plate in the late innings with runners on base and the game on the line, that pitcher is gonna feed you that same fat pitch thinkin' you're gonna whiff on it again. Only this time, you knock the cover off the ball."

"Wow," exclaimed Nishimi.

"Now this only applies if your team ain't too far behind in the early innings," cautioned Sefton. "If you're losin' by three, four runs, your job is to get on base. But if the game is close, give up the early at-bat and gamble that you'll get your pitch later on in the game."

"That's terrific, Mr. Sefton," said Nishimi.

"Mac," Sefton corrected him.

"Mac," repeated Nishimi. "Wow, that's really some idea. I can't wait to try that."

Sefton suddenly became aware of a pair of eyes on the back of his neck and turned to see a Fresno player, perhaps twenty-five feet away, glaring at him. There was no mistaking the look—pure hatred.

"Hey, what's with him?" Sefton asked Yamada.

"That's our manager, Tom Yoshitake. He doesn't like white people."

"Well, if his look is any indication, I'd say that's puttin' it mildly."

"That's the kind of prejudice we've faced since Pearl Harbor," said Yamada. "Wherever we went. It's probably good for you to get a taste of that."

"Listen, Jerry," Sefton said sternly, but without animosity, "let me tell ya somethin'. I come from Oklahoma. You ever hear the term 'Okie'?"

"I have."

"Know what it means?"

"It means someone from Oklahoma."

"Not exactly. It means poor white trash from Oklahoma. You get the difference? After the Depression hit and the land dried up, a whole lotta people lost ever'thin'—just like you folks here—and all of a sudden they was poor." Without Sefton's being aware of it, talking about Oklahoma stirred up long-dormant feelings in him, and he lapsed into old speech patterns, patterns he'd consciously worked at smoothing over in an effort to remove the stigma of being an Okie when he played up north. "They was poor and they was white. But they warn't trash. They was decent, hard-workin' folks who just got dealt a real bad hand. So a lot of 'em took off for California 'cause they was desperate and they been told a pack o' lies about how much money they's gonna make, but when they got out there, they found it warn't nothing like they heard about, and now they was fifteen hunnerd miles from home without a pot to piss in. 'Scuse my language, Annie. And ever'body looked at 'em with fear and hate in their eyes and called 'em Okies like they was some sorta animal."

Sefton's voice wavered ever so slightly, and he took a deep breath to collect himself. Annie, Yamada, and Nishimi were focused on him, waiting attentively. "That year I played in Newark, I had a teammate by the name of Jack Templeton. He was a cocky kid from California, and he didn't seem to like me, but I never could tell why. One day, we were in the clubhouse, and someone said somethin' to me that I didn't catch, and I asked him would he repeat it. Well, Templeton pipes up and says, 'Don't bother, he won't understand it anyway. He's an ignorant blankin' Okie.' Now, it was bad enough him callin' me an Okie, but ignorant was a real slap in the face, as if the two went together. I happen to have graduated from high school. When my mother was dyin' she made me promise I would finish school before I went in the pros. So I walked over to Templeton, and I said, 'Come again?' And he said, 'You heard me, ya dumb Okie.' So I coldcocked him. Knocked him flat with one punch. Only time in my adult life I ever hit a man. He never said one other word to me the whole rest of the season."

Sefton stopped again and pointed toward Yoshitake. "So don't tell me I need that, Jerry. I don't need that any more than I needed

Jack Templeton, any more than you needed the way white people looked at you after Pearl Harbor."

Nobody said anything for a time, until Yamada spoke softly. "I understand," he said, chastened. "I'm sorry if I offended you."

"It's okay," replied Sefton by way of conciliation. "I know you didn't mean to."

"Well, if you truly can forgive me, I've got a favor to ask of you."

"Your wish is my command," said Sefton, taking off his hat and making a grand, sweeping gesture with it as he bowed low. Annie laughed. It was a display designed to show Yamada and the others that everything was okay between them and him, and it had its intended effect.

"The guys have been asking me if you would come to a practice and help out," said Yamada.

"How did they know who I am?"

"Well, they've noticed you at the games, and I kind of confided our plan to Isao here, and well, ya know, things just kinda got around."

"What do they want me to do?"

"Oh, ya know, just give us some tips on the fine points of the game. Most of us have never really had any formal instruction."

Sefton nodded his head in Yoshitake's direction. "What about old sourpuss over there? I wouldn't want to tangle with him."

"It's not his team," said Yamada. "He's just the manager. I'm sure the backers would be very happy to know that a major league scout was helping us."

Sefton thought a moment. "Well, sure. Why not? Actually, I'm flattered."

"Wow, thanks, Mr. Sefton," said Nishimi.

"Mac."

"Mac. Thanks, Mac."

Sefton glanced at Annie. The mixed look of discovery and joy in her eyes told him that their bond was growing stronger.

26

SEFTON STOOD AT HOME PLATE, BAT AND BALL IN HIS HANDS. "Awright, here's the play," he called, loud enough for all the out-fielders to hear. "Runner on first, ball's hit to the gap in left-center. Shortstop goes out to shallow left to take the relay. Shortstop, make sure you're on a line with the outfielder and home plate, and throw up your hands so he can see you. First baseman, you come across the diamond and line up with them. If the runner's gonna score, the catcher'll tell you to cut off the throw and make a play on the batter at second or third. Otherwise you let the ball come through for a play at the plate. Okay, here we go."

He threw the ball up, and the left fielder and center fielder broke for the gap. Sefton caught the ball. "No cheatin' now. Wait till I hit the ball." The outfielders stopped and returned to their positions.

Sefton fungoed a line drive to left-center field, and the shortstop headed out to shallow left field. The center fielder ran the ball down and made his relay throw to the shortstop. The throw was off-line to the shortstop's right, so he took a couple of steps and reached across his body to backhand the ball, then whirled and threw a strike to the plate. Nishimi took the throw and put a tag on the phantom runner. Everybody on the field cheered. Off to the side, Yoshitake, the Fresno manager, glowered.

Sefton dropped the bat and, moving faster than usual, went hobbling out to where the shortstop stood, waving his hands and calling as he went. "Okay, everybody listen up!" All the players turned to look at him. When he reached the shortstop, he asked, "What's your name, son?"

"Raymond Kurima."

"Awright, Ray. That was one heckuva throw you made to the plate. But watch this now." He took Kurima's glove and put it on his hand. He spoke loud enough for everyone to hear. "When you get out here to take the relay, if you see that the throw is gonna be off to your right, you need to get yourself over there to make sure you catch the ball on your left, because if you hafta reach across your body to backhand the ball, then you've gotta pivot in order to make your throw to the plate." As he talked, he animatedly illustrated his points. "Now, that's gonna take an extra second, which could allow the run to score—no matter how good of a peg you make. But if you make sure the ball's on your left, you can turn sideways, catch the ball, and throw home all in one motion. See what I'm sayin'?"

"I sure do," said Kurima.

"Okay, let's try it again." He started back to the plate, then turned and called to the center fielder. "What's your name out there in center?"

"Kenso Matsumoto, sir."

"Ken, ya suppose ya could make that same throw again, off to his right? And keep those throws down now—none of these rainbows."

As Sefton limped back to the plate, he caught Yoshitake in his peripheral vision, seething on the sidelines. Sefton hit a similar shot to left-center, and Kurima executed the play perfectly. "Now, that's more like it," shouted Sefton enthusiastically. "Okay, let's take some infield. Outfielders, take a breather."

He started with some easy bouncers around the infield and then turned up the intensity, banging harder ground balls, forcing the fielders to move left and right. Everything went smoothly until he rapped a sizzler to the second baseman that took a bad hop at the last second and bounced up to hit the fielder, Nishimoto, square in the nose. The fielder dropped his glove and threw his hands up to his face as everybody rushed to his aid. When Sefton reached the scene, there was blood everywhere; he pulled out his handkerchief and handed it to someone to use to stanch the blood. They laid the man down with his glove for a pillow, and Kagawa, the big first baseman, attended to him. All eyes were focused on the prone figure.

"Make sure he keeps his head back," advised Sefton.

Suddenly Yoshitake came running out onto the field at full speed. "Are you happy now, Yamada?" he screamed as he made straight for the pitcher. From all appearances, he was intending to attack, so Nishimi quickly stepped in to head off the manager's momentum. The catcher wrapped him in a bear hug as Yoshitake continued to rave at Yamada. "This is what you get for inviting this *keto* in," he said, pointing to Sefton. "You forget real easy, don't you, what his kind have done to us."

The players looked away in embarrassment. "Oh, c'mon," said Yamada with disgust. "It's not his fault."

"You guys have no pride," yelled the manager as he struggled against Nishimi's grip on him. "Well, you can play with white men. Not me." He broke free and stormed off the field, not once looking back as he disappeared from view.

The others watched him go. There was an awkward silence. Finally, Sefton spoke. "I guess that's it for today, fellas." He bent down and said to the second baseman, "I'm awful sorry, son." The player gave a small wave to indicate he appreciated the concern.

"You have nothing to be sorry for, Mac," said Yamada. "It wasn't your fault. It's this lousy field."

"That's true," said Kurima. "This field stinks." He kicked the infield dirt. "Pebbles, dust clouds, prairie dog holes. I'm sick and tired of playing on this. We need a better field."

"So what should we do?" Nishimi asked.

"We could go to the administration and ask for help," suggested Matsumoto.

"Are you kidding?" Kurima scoffed.

"They don't care about stuff like this," Yamada said. "If we want a better ballfield, we're gonna have to do it ourselves."

"But where would we start?" asked Matsumoto.

Kurima had a practical suggestion. "We could start by clearing the pebbles out of the infield."

"That'd be a good start," acknowledged Yamada, "but we need an overall plan. We need to think about what kind of field we want."

"Grass outfield," said Matsumoto, and everybody laughed.

"In your dreams," someone said.

"No, that's okay," said Yamada. "Let's talk about everything we'd like, and then we'll see what's actually possible."

Nishimi spoke up first. "We need a real backstop. That damn chicken wire is good for nothing."

"We should build some shaded bleachers so the older folks can be comfortable," added Kurima.

"Is someone writing all this down?" asked Yamada.

"If you'd be so kind as to run over to my car," said Sefton to Nishimi, "you'll find a notebook in the glove compartment." Without hesitation, Nishimi dashed over to the car.

Yamada pointed to the second baseman, who was lying still with his eyes closed. "How's he doing?" Yamada asked.

"I think he's gonna live," said Kagawa. The second baseman waved his hand in the air to indicate he was following the discussion.

Nishimi returned with the notebook and handed it to Sefton, who opened to a blank page. "Okay, let's start again," he said, and the players reeled off the items they had already mentioned. When Sefton had caught up, Yamada asked for more suggestions.

"An outfield fence," said Matsumoto.

"Hey," someone else chimed in, "why not dugouts?" The suggestion elicited more laughter.

"Why not?" said Yamada. His words were echoed by several others. "Anything we haven't thought of?" Everybody thought hard, but nobody had any more suggestions. "Okay, Mac, could you pass me the list, please?"

Sefton tore out the page and handed it to Yamada, who read it over. "Clear pebbles. Grass outfield. Backstop. Bleachers. Outfield fence. Dugouts." He chewed his lip as he thought for minute. Finally, he flicked the paper with his index finger.

"I don't see why we can't do it all," he said. "It'll take some ingenuity, but we've certainly got the time. First things first. Clearing the pebbles. We'll need some screening to sift the top layer of dirt. We'll save those rocks, though, and spread them underneath the bleachers to keep the dust down for the fans. Once we've cleared the area, if we can divert that irrigation ditch up at the garden, we can flood the infield and harden it up. Now, about the grass—I've got a cousin on the landscaping crew. He could probably get us some clumps of that Bermuda grass they have by the administration building. That stuff spreads like crazy. Kurima, you're the plumber. How would we water the grass?"

"Well, I suppose we could tap into the line at the end of Block 28, run a pipe down here, and set up a portable sprinkler. Wouldn't be that hard."

"Can you get the pipe to do that?"

Kurima smiled. "Leave it to me."

"Good man," said Yamada. "What about the backstop? We'll need lumber for a frame."

"I have an idea for that," Nishimi said. He winked at Yamada to indicate that he would let him in on it later. "But what'll we cover the frame with?"

"I know," said Kagawa, who was still kneeling by the second baseman. Kagawa was a gentle giant who didn't talk very much, so everybody paid attention when he did. "You know those long pads they use to keep the cement wet while it's curing? They'd be perfect for the bottom of the backstop."

"That's true," said Nishimi. "And I guess we could just double the chicken wire on the top part."

"We can use those pads to cover the dugouts and bleachers, too," Yamada said. He looked at the list. "What about the outfield fence? That's gonna take a lotta wood."

There was a deflated silence. Suddenly, Matsumoto spoke. "Wait, what if we don't use wood. What if we use something else?"

"Like what?" someone asked.

"Like plants," said a voice. They all turned and looked down at the second baseman. Nishimoto was a nurseryman. He opened his eyes and raised his head; two black eyes were developing. "If we planted castor beans, say, ten feet apart, and dug a little irrigation ditch behind to water them—they grow real fast—that would work pretty good for a fence."

"Good idea," said Yamada. "How's the nose?"

"Pretty sore. At least it stopped bleeding."

"You're gonna have a couple of beautiful shiners."

Nishimoto groaned and laid his head back down on his glove. Yamada checked the list. "What have we forgotten?" he asked.

"Bleachers," said Kurima.

"Yeah. That's gonna be a tough one."

Sefton cleared his throat. The players turned to him. "I know a guy who works in the lumberyard up in Prescott. I could maybe talk to him about givin' me a deal on some wood. Thing is, you need finished lumber for seating—you don't want people pickin' splinters outta their keisters."

"We could never afford lumber like that," Kurima said.

"Well, that'll be my contribution," said Sefton. "It's for a worthy cause. I'll foot the bill for the dugout wood, too."

"Are you sure, Mac?" Yamada asked.

"Have you ever known me not to be sure, Jerry?"

Yamada laughed. "Well, then, thank you, Mac. Okay, we got a plan. Let's meet here tomorrow after work. First thing we'll do is lay out the field so it doesn't interfere with this one. There'll be plenty of pebbles wherever we go, so we can get started by clearing pebbles."

The players gathered up the equipment, broke up into twos and threes, and drifted off. Kagawa helped Nishimoto up and put an arm around his shoulder as they walked. Yamada, Nishimi, and Sefton slowly wandered toward the car. Nishimi carried the equipment bag.

"So what do you have up your sleeve for the backstop?" Yamada asked him.

Nishimi got a gleeful look and pointed to the perimeter fence. "Take out every third four-by-four until we have enough to build a good, solid frame." Sefton laughed out loud at the audacity of the idea.

"That's gonna be kinda tricky," said Yamada.

"We do it at night."

Yamada considered. "Yeah, we might be able to get away with that."

"You guys got guts," said Sefton with admiration. He pointed at the equipment bag on Nishimi's shoulder. "Ya want a ride?"

"Nah. This helps me keep in shape. I'll see you guys later." He took off at a trot.

"Guy's got energy to burn," said Sefton as Nishimi disappeared around the corner of a block.

"He's pretty intense," agreed Yamada. "Listen," he said, changing the subject, "that's a very generous offer you made."

"My pleasure. I mean, I got this dough that's been pilin' up—for what? I got no family. My expenses on the road are covered by the club. So I might as well use some of it to help some friends."

"You're an interesting guy, Mac. Full of surprises."

"That's me." Sefton turned serious. "Hey, what's with that manager of yours? What's his problem?"

"Yoshitake? He's a *kibei*."

"*Kee-bay*? What's that?"

"Kibei were born in this country but were sent back to Japan as kids to go to school there. Most of 'em lived with their grandparents. After they finished school they returned to the States. They tend to see things somewhat differently than those of us who grew up here."

"How so?"

"Well, take Yoshitake. He's very bitter about the roundup and about being sent here. I'm just guessing, but I think his allegiance is probably to Japan. He's even mentioned returning there when the war is over. I try to avoid the subject with him. There's enough tension as it is between the kibei and us."

"So the government was right—there are people loyal to Japan."

"There are probably a handful."

"Then it had to be done."

"What had to be done?" asked Yamada.

"You know, putting y'all in camps."

Yamada shot Sefton a look. "What? Are you saying they had to take every last one of us, American citizens included, trample our civil rights, destroy everything we worked for all these years, split up families and neighborhoods, and send us to this godforsaken place and how many others like it?" Yamada was uncharacteristically overwrought. "Is that what you're saying, Mac? Is that what you're telling me? That's what had to be done? And you call this a free country?"

Sefton realized his mistake and retreated. "No, no, no," he said apologetically. "Of course not. I'm not saying that. Forgive me, I didn't mean to touch a nerve." He looked at Yamada to make sure his friend understood, and the sincerity of his look was enough to make the pitcher soften. "I understand the injustice of it," Sefton assured him. "But if there was a possibility that some people, okay, even just a few, would be working for Japan, the government had to do something, right? What should they have done?"

"I don't know, Mac, I'm not the government," said Yamada softly. "All I know is there had to be a better way than this."

Sefton was forced to admit the truth of that. "You're right, Jerry. There had to be a better way."

27

SEFTON SPENT THE MORNING CATCHING UP ON HIS paperwork—scouting reports, expense accounts, miscellaneous notes to O'Neil—and then mailed off his monthly summary. After lunch at Charlie and Josie's diner, he pointed the Packard toward camp; as he drove, he thought about the amazing turn his life had taken.

For the past month, when he was not out scouting—he had found half a dozen more prospects since Joe Branscomb—he was working on the new ballfield with the Fresno players and the nisei from other teams who had joined in the effort. Sunday evenings, and sometimes even on a weekday evening, he visited the Yamadas. He and Annie had fallen in love despite not having had an opportunity to spend any time alone together since their talk at the ballfield. If anyone asked, Mac Sefton would have to say he was a happy man.

When Yamada had asked his parents' permission to apply to college through the American Friends Service Committee program, he also told them of Sefton's intention to sign him to play ball when the war was over. They were initially skeptical about the latter idea, but when he explained the possibilities it opened, they were more kindly disposed to the plan and began to look upon Sefton as an ally.

For his part, Sefton spent an occasional day working in the garden with the family in an effort to further gain the parents' confidence and, of course, to be around Annie. He found he enjoyed the work and their company. In one of his early visits to their room, he had noticed that they all took off their shoes inside, so he started removing his when he came to tea. He found that it made sitting on the floor rather more comfortable. Little by little, the Yamadas began to relax with him and he with them.

Now, arriving at the camp gate, Sefton was warmly greeted by Rizzolio. They joked for a few minutes and then the corporal opened the gate for his *compa*.

Before heading over to the garden, Sefton took a detour to look at the progress of the ballfield. It had taken a week to clear the infield of pebbles, after which a diversion ditch was dug from the main garden's irrigation system, which was supplied by the canal that ran alongside the camp. The water was used to flood the infield, which caused it to harden up when it dried, leaving a nice, fast surface that could be expected to render a fairly true bounce.

Clumps of Bermuda grass had been removed surreptitiously from the lawns around the administration building and planted in the outfield. As he had promised, Kurima had somehow managed to scrounge enough pipe to set up a portable sprinkler that watered the plantings, and the grass already had begun to spread.

The castor beans that Nishimoto planted on the perimeter of the outfield had sprouted and were taking root. The locations of the dugouts were marked out; two large piles of pebbles lay on the sites of the bleachers.

From the car window Sefton looked out at the burgeoning field with wonder. This, he thought, is true passion for the game. Amazing. Where there's a will there's a way.

He slid the car into gear and drove on, but when he arrived at the garden, Annie and her parents were nowhere to be seen. Strange, he thought. They're always here. Oh, well, try the barracks.

Annie answered his knock and beckoned him in. He nodded hello to Mr. and Mrs. Yamada and saw the expressions of anxious concern on their faces. Sefton turned back to Annie. "Is everything okay?"

"Jerry and Isao are in the stockade."

"Why? What happened?"

"They went out last night to take some more posts out of the fence, and they got caught by the MPs."

"Damn."

"The police came by and woke us up in the middle of the night to tell us."

Mr. Yamada said something in Japanese; he was clearly addressing Sefton. He spoke with more emotion than Sefton usually heard from him. Sefton looked to Annie for the translation.

"My father wants to know if there's anything you can do."

Sefton thought. Maybe he could. "Tell him I'll try my best."

Sefton drove down to the administration building and proceeded to Wayne's office. When he entered the outer room, the grump raised one eyebrow from her perpetual typing. "Afternoon, Miss Desmond," he said politely, not bothering with the charm, as he had already discovered that it had no effect on her. Better to just be businesslike. She gave no indication that she had heard him. "Do you suppose I might be able to see Mr. Wayne for a few moments?" Sefton asked.

"Do you have an appointment?"

"I don't, but this is pretty important."

She turned away from her typing with a sigh of utter exasperation, went to the door of Wayne's office, and knocked. At his "Come in," she entered. Half a minute later she emerged and, without looking at Sefton, gave a wave of her hand to indicate that he had been granted permission to enter the inner sanctum.

"Mr. Sefton, what a nice surprise," said Wayne with exaggerated enthusiasm when the scout walked in.

He knows why I'm here, thought Sefton. He's already figured out how much he's gonna skin me for, and he's counting the bills. Gotta play it out though. Follow the script.

He went to the desk and shook hands with the director. Count your fingers, Sefton told himself. Wayne gestured for Sefton to sit down.

"Now, then, what can I do for you on this beautiful day, Mr. Sefton?"

"Call me Suitcase. We don't have to be so formal anymore, do we?" He knew Wayne would like that.

"Alright, but you'll have to call me Chuck."

"Okay."

"So, Suitcase, what do you have in mind? Don't tell me you've found another prospect here in camp!"

Sefton smiled. "I only wish. No, Chuck, that's not it." Jeez, I hate this cat-and-mouse crap. "I'm actually here to talk about Yamada and Nishimi."

"Yamada and Nishimi?" asked Wayne, stroking his chin as he feigned trying to place the names.

What a lousy actor, Sefton thought. "The two guys that were arrested last night for taking posts out of the fence."

"Oh, those two," said Wayne, snapping his fingers to indicate he remembered. "What about them?"

"Yamada's my prospect, you know."

"Is he, Suitcase? Oh, that's right; I'd forgotten that."

In a pig's eye, you did. "Yeah, he's the one."

"Hunh, how about that?"

"So what are they charged with?"

"Stealing government property."

"Well, let's talk about that, Chuck. You know, they weren't really stealing." This gives him an out, Sefton thought.

"Oh? What else would you call it?" asked the director, picking up Sefton's direction.

"Do you know what they were gonna use those posts for?"

"I don't have the faintest idea. I've said it before and I'll say it again—inscrutable Orientals."

Ignore it, Sefton told himself. "They're building a new baseball field, and they need the posts to frame a backstop."

"You don't say! We were aware of the new ballfield, but I had no idea this was part of it."

"Well, it is. So ya see, it's not really stealin' in this case. They were just movin' the posts from one spot in camp to another. Wouldn't you agree?"

"Hmmm, maybe so. I might be able to see it that way."

"In which case you could dismiss the charges, couldn't ya?"

"I suppose I could," said Wayne. "That would be a *grand* idea, Suitcase. Just *grand*."

You son of a bitch, Sefton thought. Oh, well, I came in here knowing it was gonna cost me. "I'll need a couple of days for that," he said. "I'll have to wire."

"Oh, that's fine," said Wayne generously. "I trust you completely."

"I appreciate that," said Sefton.

"Now, why don't you and I take a walk over to the clink and give those boys the good news. I've been wanting to meet this pitcher of yours."

"Okay."

Wayne reached across his desk and leafed through a pile until he found the arrest papers. He picked up his fountain pen and wrote Dismissed across the page and signed it. Then he got up, went to the door, held it open for Sefton, and followed him out. "Miss Desmond, I'll be gone for about fifteen minutes."

"Yes, Mr. Wayne."

As they walked the block to the jail, Wayne suddenly said, "Say, Suitcase, why don't you join the missus and myself for dinner this evening?"

I'd rather be tied to a stake and whipped, thought Sefton. But I gotta stay on good terms with him, so I better accept. Yeah, this way I can drop by to see the Yamadas afterward. "Sounds great, Chuck."

"Terrific. I'll call Margie and have her put on an extra plate."

As they approached the stockade building, the soldier on duty saluted Wayne. "You have a couple of prisoners in here that were arrested last night for stealing government property, if I'm not mistaken," Wayne said.

"Yessir, we do."

"Well, the charges have been dropped."

"Yessir."

"Why don't you let 'em out now, Sergeant?"

"Yessir."

The soldier took the keys off his belt and unlocked the front door of the jail. He disappeared into the building, and after a couple of minutes, Yamada and Nishimi walked out of the building followed by the soldier, who locked the door behind him.

"Mr. Wayne, I'd like you to meet Jerry Yamada and Isao Nishimi," said Sefton.

"Hello, boys," said Wayne. Yamada and Nishimi nodded hello. "I hear you've got quite an arm there, Jerry."

"Thank you."

"Well, I hope to see you pitch one of these days." Yamada said nothing. "You boys are free to go. Mr. Sefton explained to me what you wanted those posts for, so I'm willing to forget about it this one time. But don't be caught doing anything like that again, boys, or I won't be able to be so lenient. Now run along and behave yourselves."

Yamada and Nishimi started to walk away. "Wait up," called Sefton. They stopped. "I'll be right back," he said to Wayne and caught up with the other two.

"Did you have anything to do with getting us out?" asked Yamada.

"Your father asked me to see what I could do, so I talked to Wayne," said Sefton modestly.

"Thanks, Mac."

"That goes for me too," added Nishimi.

"Don't mention it. Listen," Sefton said to Yamada, "tell the family I'll drop by after dinner."

"Good. I look forward to seeing you. I think I'll ask my father to give us one of his famous talks. I think you'd enjoy it."

"Have you ever heard his old man give a talk?" asked Nishimi.

"No," said Suitcase.

"You're in for a treat."

"Mmmm. Look, I better get back to Wayne."

"Okay, Mac. I'll see you later this evening."

Yamada and Nishimi continued on, and Sefton returned to where Wayne was waiting. "Let's walk back to my office and pick up your car," said the director. "I can call Margie and let her know you're coming. And I think I'll tell Miss Desmond that I'm taking the rest of the day off."

"Sounds good to me."

They started walking. "There's something I've been meaning to ask you about, Suitcase."

Shit, what now? "Go right ahead."

"I heard a rather incredible story about Babe Ruth. . . ."

28

WHEN SEFTON GOT TO THE YAMADAS' IT WAS ALREADY dark. The family was seated around the table, and the father indicated for him to join them. When he was seated, Annie poured tea. "I'm sorry that it's almost cold," she said apologetically.

"I don't mind," said Sefton. "Just being here makes me feel good."

After the tea was poured, Mr. Yamada spoke, and his son translated: "My father is very grateful to you for what you did today."

"I'm very glad I was able to help," Sefton responded.

Jerry spoke to his father, and the older man answered, nodding his head affirmatively. Jerry turned back to Sefton. "I asked my father if he would give us a talk. It's a family tradition. He said that he'd be happy to since you've shown yourself to be a true friend and a man of integrity."

"I'm very touched that your father has such a high opinion of me."

Jerry translated Sefton's words. The older man nodded and became pensive. After a minute of reflection he began speaking, looking from Sefton to Jerry to Annie, stopping now and again for his son to translate.

"This is about how to navigate through life. First of all, you have to know what you want. If you don't know what you want in life, you're like a ship without a rudder. Every little wind blows you in a different direction. So the most important thing is to first decide where you want to go." He raised one hand. "*But*—you have to be careful what you decide you want because whatever it is you set your mind on, that's what you're going to get."

During the translation, Mr. Yamada looked at Sefton, who nodded to indicate that he was following.

"Next thing—once you've decided where you want to go, fix that end firmly in your mind and set out with absolute faith that you'll get there. Of course, many things will come along that look tempting, and if you're not careful you can get knocked off course. You have to always keep in mind where it is you're going and ask yourself, 'If I follow this, will it further my journey or will it take me in a wrong direction?'

"Now, things will inevitably happen that require you to set aside your main plan for a while." Mr. Yamada shrugged. "That's life—it's unavoidable. But you must remember that these are just detours in your journey. They're part of your journey, certainly, but they're sidetracks." His brow furrowed as he seemed to be puzzling something out; suddenly, he found what he was looking for. "Like a flat tire on a car trip—once the flat is fixed, you continue on your way, yes?" Sefton nodded. "So, as soon as this business that took you off course is finished up, as soon as this flat tire is repaired, you get right back on your path."

Mrs. Yamada motioned for Annie to pour more tea. Mr. Yamada waited until the cups were filled before he resumed.

"Sometimes you'll get frustrated, discouraged, because you don't seem to be making progress toward your goal. Or maybe you'll become impatient—you're making progress, but it's taking too long. This is where the faith I spoke of earlier comes in. If it doesn't seem like you're getting where you want to go, it means one or more conditions have not been fulfilled, so the time is not yet ripe for the fruit to fall from the tree. These conditions could be inside you, or they could be in the outside world. The only thing you can do at such a time is keep your goal in mind, keep busy, and have faith that when all conditions are right, what you seek will be there for you."

When that had been translated, Mr. Yamada paused to make sure his listeners were with him. Satisfied that they were, he continued.

"Now, this is very important: you have to keep your eyes open, and your mind as well, because what you seek never comes in exactly the form you expect it. So you have to be alert and be able to recognize it when it appears and grab hold of it because if you don't, you may never see it again. Of course, some people are lucky and get a second chance, but you can never count on that. You have to be ready to act when the opening presents itself.

"Because, you see, there comes a time in later years when you realize that your life is not going to be all you thought it would be when you were younger. Unfortunately, there are things that won't work out as well as you wanted them to. But you want your regrets to be small ones. You don't want to regret having missed your golden opportunity. That one you want to have seized."

When Jerry had finished translating, his father looked at Sefton and, in his heavily accented English, asked, "You understand?"

Sefton's eyes opened wide as he took a deep breath and exhaled slowly through pursed lips. "I need to think it over some, but yes, I think I understand."

"*Hai,*" said Jerry to his father.

It seemed a Jerry end to the visit, so after a minute or two, Sefton, not wanting to overstay his welcome, stretched and said, "Well, I think I should be gettin' goin'." He pointed to himself and then to the door.

They all stood. As Sefton and Jerry moved toward the door, Annie took her mother aside. "Mama-*san,*" she whispered nervously in Japanese, "I would like to take a walk with Sefton-*san.*" Instead of the shocked or disapproving reaction Annie expected from her mother, the older woman smiled and giggled.

"I was waiting for this," she said. "I can see how you two look at each other."

"Would you talk to Papa-*san*? Quick, before he leaves."

Mrs. Yamada went to her husband and conferred with him. Mr. Yamada, of course, exhibited surprise. He looked at his daughter. He looked at Sefton, who was talking to Jerry, unaware of the negotiations that were taking place. He looked back to Annie, closed his eyes, pursed his lips, and nodded.

Annie went right to Sefton. "Mac, why don't you and I take a little walk together? My parents have given us permission."

Sefton's heart took a leap at the thought of being alone with Annie. He looked over to the older couple, who smiled at him. Trying not to seem overanxious, he said, "Sure, that sounds very nice."

"I'll just get my sweater," Annie said. "It's probably a little chilly out."

After another round of good-byes, they were on their way out the door when Mr. Yamada spoke. At first, Sefton thought he had changed his mind about letting his daughter out with a white man. He looked to Jerry for the translation.

"My father would like to know if he could possibly make a request of you."

"Of course. Anything."

Jerry nodded to his father. Mr. Yamada spoke again, and his son laughed.

"My father loves beer, but he hasn't been able to get any since the evacuation. He wants to know if you'd be willing to smuggle in some beer for him."

29

THEY WALKED IN SILENCE FOR A COUPLE OF MINUTES in the direction Annie had chosen. She seemed to know where she wanted to go, and Sefton was happy to be led. After a block, they turned to each other with big smiles, hardly able to believe they were together, alone and falling ever more deeply in love. Their hands reached out and clasped. The first-quarter moon was low in the western sky.

They approached a group of men standing and talking under a streetlight. One said something, and they all turned to stare at the passing couple. Annie gave Sefton's hand a squeeze that said don't bother about them.

After a few blocks Sefton caught on to where they were going. "I think I know where you're takin' me," he said, and she squeezed his hand again. A block later they were at the garden.

"There's a bench over here," Annie said, and led him to it. They sat holding hands and watching the moon, savoring the sweetness of being alone with one another.

Finally Annie said, "I love a garden in the moonlight. Isn't it beautiful?"

"If I never realized it before," Sefton replied, "I can sure see it now." He paused for a few moments. "That was quite a little talk your father gave." Annie laughed. "Does he do that kind of thing often?"

"Not often. But whenever there's a reason. In this case it was to thank you."

"Sure gives you a lot to think about."

"It makes sense, doesn't it?"

"It does, yeah. Ya know, it's really strange, but it reminds me of something a soldier said to me a couple of months ago."

"A soldier here?"

"No, this guy I picked up hitchhiking in Oklahoma back in August after I left here. He talked about his dreams and what he was gonna do after the war. Made me think about what I want out of life and about my own dreams."

They were quiet again, increasingly aware of the deepening feelings between them, but before they could become entirely swept up in it, Annie asked, "So what *do* you want out of life, Mac?"

"I'm tryin' to figure it out, Annie."

"You must have some idea by now."

"Well, I thought I did, but lately I'm not so sure anymore."

"I'd say you need to decide—and soon."

"What do you mean?"

"I mean life's a tricky business. Look at all of us here—one day we were secure in our lives, the next day, the rug was pulled out from under us. And we still don't know what lies ahead. Nothing's for sure, Mac. You never know how much time you have left. We act as if we're going to live forever, but we're not. We're all going to die. So you need to make the most of whatever time you have."

Sefton looked at her. The silver moon was in her black eyes. She seemed to him a gem of incomparable rarity and beauty. He put his arms around her and they fell into their first kiss. Their heads swam and their hearts soared.

Time seemed suspended as they hugged and kissed, until Annie realized that she had been gone for a while. "We'd better get back if we want permission to do this again. We'd better go," she said.

"Yeah, you're right," agreed Sefton.

They stood up and started to the gate. Annie stopped. "How is it you've never been married, Mac?"

He took a deep breath. "Never met anyone I wanted to settle down with."

"You've had girlfriends, haven't you?"

"Sure. But nobody that I wanted to give up my work for. I mean, I have a pretty good job. It's just about all I know how to do. And ya can't very well take a wife on the road. So why would I get married?"

"I know why."

"Oh? Tell me." He looked into her velvet eyes, and the answer was there.

30

"O'NEIL SPEAKING."

"Pat, it's me, Mac."

"Mac? Mac who?"

"Very funny."

"Oh, *that* Mac. I musta forgot what your voice sounded like—it's been so long since I heard it."

"Yeah, yeah. Go on, gimme the needle."

"So what the hell would you be callin' about?"

"Didja get my reports?"

"Ya mean the ones that were three weeks late?"

"Jeez, O'Neil, will ya let up on me already?"

"Let up on you? Are you aware of how lax I am with you? There's not another scout in this organization that could get away with the crap that you do."

"Do I deliver?"

"All my scouts deliver, Sefton. If they don't deliver, they don't work for me anymore. This ain't the fuckin' Washington Senators. This is the New York Yankees. Top to bottom, everybody in this organization delivers or he's on a slow boat to China. If you weren't—" O'Neil stopped short.

Sefton was stung. "If I weren't what? A cripple?"

O'Neil's tone softened; he sounded ashamed of himself. "That's not what I was gonna say. I was gonna say if you weren't one of my oldest friends and someone dear to my heart, with Christ himself as my witness, I'd have to kick yer ass."

Sefton laughed. "You're fulla shit, O'Neil. You couldn't kick my ass if your life depended on it, ya little pipsqueak. So save that Irish blarney for someone that doesn't know you any better."

"Okay, we're even now. Let's get on with business."

"Which is all I had in mind from the beginning."

"So tell me about your kids."

"Well, Branscomb's the genuine article. I've seen him catch three games now. Throws like a big-leaguer. Has a real good way with pitchers. Big, strong body. Runs okay for a catcher. He's quiet, but he's a leader. The other players respect him because he's all business. Very focused on the game. His only weakness is he's not much of a hitter. Slow bat. Might improve with instruction."

"Is he signed yet?"

"I'll sign him this week. His old man's been playin' it cute with me, but I've got him. I'm sure of it."

"What level can he start at?"

"I think we could try him at Double A."

"That's good," said O'Neil, "'cause Dickey's thirty-five, and he's really slowing down. He only caught eighty games this year. Maybe he's got one year left. Rosar ain't the quality we need—in fact, we're talking to Cleveland about a trade. The worst thing is, we got nobody in the system that's gonna be able to take Dickey's place. There's a coupla dago kids in St. Louie we got our eyes on—what the hell are their names? Hold on a second." There was a pause while O'Neil sifted through some papers. "Here it is: Larry Berra and Joe Garagiola—ever hear of 'em?"

"No."

"Problem is one's seventeen and the other's only sixteen."

"Well, I wouldn't rush Branscomb along. I mean, he's only eighteen."

"Okay. I ain't got your report in front of me, so remind me—who else?"

"Well, Pulaski, o' course."

"How's he comin' along?"

"Ain't had a chance to get back up there, but I've got a trip planned this week. I'm gonna go over to see Branscomb's family and then double back to see Pulaski."

"And the rest?"

"New kid named Birdsong, from Safford. Pure hitter, left-handed. Beautiful swing. Unfortunately, he doesn't seem to understand what a glove is for. It's a shame. I dunno if we can teach him to field or not. It's too bad ya can't have a ten-man batting order. Ya know, just add one guy who does nothin' but hit. He'd never hafta take the field. That's where a kid like this Birdsong could make it."

"Forget it. That'll never happen."

"Yeah, I know."

"Anybody else?"

"Nobody that's a can't-miss."

"Well, ya never know. It ain't an exact science."

"You're tellin' me."

"How many all together?"

"Eight."

"Good, good. Because they're drafting our guys left and right. It's a bitch. Henrich's been drafted, Hassett's been drafted, Rizzuto's been drafted—even DiMaggio is talkin' about signing up."

"DiMaggio? He's the last guy I'd think would sign up. Why would DiMaggio sign up?"

"He's been taking a beating in the papers. Ya know, 'Ted Williams joined up, and everybody else is in the service, so why ain't DiMaggio?' That kinda thing."

"What if he gets his ass shot off?"

"We'll make sure he gets assigned to a base that has a ball-club, like Rizzuto. They'll never see combat. That's what they're doing with all the players. Except that crazy fuckin' Williams—he signed up to be a fighter pilot."

"Jeez."

"The thing about the war is, it ain't only hurting the big club. All up and down the system, we're losing kids to the service. All the teams are. I don't know if this is true or not, but I've heard that the Browns have an outfielder on one of their farm clubs who's only got one arm! Can ya fuckin' beat that, Mac? A one-armed outfielder!"

"Jeez, maybe I still got a shot."

O'Neil laughed. "Yeah. Anyway, we need bodies to put on the field, especially in the low minors. I've told the other scouts to sign any busher that shows some promise."

"Really?"

"Really."

"Whatever you say."

There was a pause, then O'Neil asked, "So, how's everything else going?"

"Good, really good."

"I'm glad."

"Listen, Pat," said Sefton tentatively, "I got a coupla favors to ask."

"I shoulda known," said O'Neil.

"I need a plate, a pitching rubber, and a set of bases from the Stadium."

"What the hell for?"

"They're buildin' a new ballpark around here, and I'd like to give 'em a gift. It's kind of a charity thing."

"Who's building a new ballpark?"

"It's a civic project—all volunteer labor."

"Why can'tcha just go to a store and buy the stuff?"

"I could do that, but just think what it would mean to this little community to have bases, a home plate, and a rubber from Yankee Stadium in their new ballpark. And I'm sure I don't hafta tell ya that the publicity won't hurt the organization any."

"Awright, awright, I'll get 'em for ya."

"I appreciate it. It'll mean a lot—a whole lot." Sefton hesitated.

"I'll bring 'em down to the winter meetings and give 'em to ya."

"Uh, that's the other thing, Pat." Sefton took a deep breath. "I want you to ship 'em 'cause I'd like to be excused from the meetings." Sefton closed his eyes, held the receiver away from his ear, and waited for the explosion. It came a moment later.

"What the fuck are you talking about, Sefton? Just who the fuck do you think you are? Ya know, one of these days, you're gonna push me too—"

"Pat, calm down and let me explain."

"Why the fuck should I calm down? You piss me off! You drop a fuckin' bombshell on me, and you want me to fuckin' calm down?"

Sefton raised his own voice. "Listen to me, will ya? Will you get your goddamn Irish temper under control and let me explain?"

There was a silence on the other end. Thirty seconds later, in self-consciously controlled tones, O'Neil said, "Okay, I'll listen, but it better be good."

"It's just common sense, Pat. Think about it. Let's say I go to Atlanta in January. It takes me a week to drive out there, I'm there for a week, then what do I do? Drive all the way back here, just to turn around and head back to Florida for spring training a couple o' weeks later? On the other hand, if I stay back east, I lose more than a month of scoutin'. Remember, they play Legion ball all winter out here; it ain't like back east where everythin' shuts down. So either way you look at it, it doesn't make sense for me to hafta go to the meetings."

Sefton knew he had made his case effectively because O'Neil was silent. After he calmed down, O'Neil was capable of listening to reason. "You're a fuckin' pisser, Sefton."

"Yeah, but what would ya do without me?"

"I'd sleep better, for one."

"But your life wouldn't be as interestin'."

"Awright, I've had enough o' this bullshit. I got work to do."

"I'll call ya after I see Branscomb's family."

"I won't hold my breath."

"'Bye, Pat. Don't forget to ship me that stuff."

"Yeah, yeah. Talk to ya later."

Sefton was about to hang up when he heard O'Neil's voice coming through the earpiece. "Wait a minute, don't hang up! There's something I forgot to ask ya!"

"I'm still here," said Sefton.

O'Neil waited a few seconds. Then, "So, uh, how's that Jap pitcher o' yours doing?"

31

IT WAS LATE FALL, BUT IT WAS STILL HOT ENOUGH THAT Sefton filled the desert water bag he had bought in his early days in Arizona. He slung it over the Packard's hood ornament just in case the car chose to overheat on the uphill climb. "Why the hell does everything have to be so spread out around here?" he grumbled, as he got ready to hit the road for Globe and Prescott, a junket that would keep him away from Annie and the others for at least several days—a prospect he found not at all appealing. The familiar sensation of setting out on a road trip, always a welcome feeling in the past, now produced mixed emotions. He shrugged. Oh, well, who am I to complain? he thought.

Whenever he drove through the desert he marveled that people had managed to settle in such godforsaken terrain. He was amazed not only by the towns like Casa Grande and Coolidge and Florence with their couple or three thousand inhabitants, but even more so by the tiny hamlets like La Palma, Randolph, Florence Junction—blink-and-you-miss-'em communities with such neglible numbers of residents that, despite being shown on the map, were not included in the Cities and Towns listed at the bottom with their populations.

How did these places get here? Sefton wondered. A hundred years ago it must have been nothing but Indians. Where did all these settlers come from and why? Who'd want to live out here?

As he drove through Florence Junction, he saw a family beside a tarpaper shack. Half a dozen barefoot kids ran around in the dust, the parents standing idly by, a vacant look on their faces as they watched the car roll by. Sefton was thunderstruck—he knew the look of these people only too well. "Oh, my God," he blurted out to himself, "they're Oklahomans. Jeez, these must be some of the ones that didn't make it to California."

He felt a terrific sadness as he thought about the lives that had been ruined by the Depression and the Dust Bowl, and he realized that the difference in their current circumstances notwithstanding, he would always have a kinship with these people. Then, now, and forever, he was one of them.

Outside Florence Junction, the Packard began the slow ascent to Globe, and the landscape gradually changed from low, saguaro-and-sage desert to sparser, mountainous desert, to bare, rock mountains.

Sefton's thoughts turned to Annie. He could only ever remember being so deeply in love once before, but he had been too young then to really appreciate it, a senior in high school and still wet behind the ears. Now, he was a grown man with an idea of just how hard life could be, and by some miracle—certainly through no deserving virtue of his own—an angel had been sent to help him make it through.

His musings turned to the other Yamadas, each of whom he had grown rather fond of. He thought too about the friends he had made through his involvement with the Fresno team and the building of the ballfield. The whole business was almost beyond belief. He felt like a man who had been granted a fresh start. His mind and heart were alive with possibilities, and he marveled at the sense of adventure that now filled his life on a daily basis. He was overcome with a feeling of gratitude.

The barren, rocky terrain finally gave way to grassy, scrub-oak dotted hills, and when Globe, with its black slag heaps left behind from the Old Dominion copper mine, loomed up before him, Sefton looked at his watch and realized he could not remember the last half hour of the trip.

He was right on time. He stopped to check the address and hailed a passerby to ask directions, then drove the hilly streets to the Branscomb house. When he pulled up to it, the catcher and his father were throwing a ball around in the adjoining field. Sefton got out, waved, and went to the trunk to get a glove.

He limped over and shook hands with the father. "Hello, Jack."

"Howdy, Suitcase."

Sefton turned and called a greeting to his prospect, "Hi there, Joe."

"Hello, Mr. Sefton."

Sefton took up a position for a three-way catch. Jack Branscomb fired the ball to the scout; Sefton caught it and felt the sting in his palm. Oh, brother, he said to himself, the guy's tryin' to impress me with his arm. Kinda jerk who thinks he could have been a big-leaguer if only he'd gotten the breaks. Sefton threw the ball right back to him and indicated with a gesture that he was reversing the direction of the catch. He wanted to take the prospect's throws, and besides, he did not need to have his hand burned up by some forty-year-old has-been who never was in the first place.

When the ball got to the younger Branscomb, Sefton raised his glove and the catcher put it right in the pocket, not too hard, but with just the right amount of juice—exactly the way a pitcher likes to have the ball returned. The kid's instincts are terrific, Sefton thought. They played catch for another fifteen minutes, and just about every throw Joe made was right to the glove.

Then Mrs. Branscomb appeared in the doorway. "Would you boys be innerested in some lunch?" she called.

"Sure would," answered her husband.

Sefton returned the glove to the trunk of the car, took out his briefcase, and followed the others into the small stucco house. Mrs. Branscomb had the table set, and as soon as the three men had washed up and were seated, she put a casserole on the table and served it—macaroni and cheese with navy beans. As Sefton watched the food being shoveled onto his plate, he was hit by a terrible yearning for Charlie's cooking.

"Thank you, Mrs. Branscomb. Sure smells good."

Through the meal and coffee they made small talk. When Jack Branscomb declined a second cup of coffee, Sefton took that as his cue to begin business. "So, have you thought over my offer, Jack?"

"I have, Suitcase, and I must say I think it's a mite low."

"Five hundred is as high as I'm prepared to go, Jack."

"Well, maybe we'll jes' wait for another club."

"You're free to do that," said Sefton. "But I can tell you right now, nobody else is gonna pay what the New York Yankees pay."

"Dad!" said Joe, with a pleading whine in his voice.

"Jack, why don'tcha jes' go ahead and accept Mr. Sefton's offer?" added Mrs. Branscomb from the kitchen sink, where she was washing the dishes.

"Now, you two jes' let me handle this, ya hear?" said Jack sternly.

"Look, Jack, let's not beat around the bush," said Sefton. "This is not some kind of a poker game. You're wasting your time, and mine, if ya think ya can bluff me. I've made my offer. Now, take it or leave it."

The set of Jack's mouth told Sefton that this was a man who hated losing but had nonetheless endured a lifetime of it and knew he was once again facing defeat. He sneered to save face and said, "Awright, you win. Sara, bring the man his briefcase."

"That's okay," said Sefton getting up out of his chair. "I can get it."

After the papers were signed, Sefton shook hands with Jack and Joe. "Congratulations, Joe. Welcome to the New York Yankees organization."

"Thank you, sir."

With the money in his pocket, Jack seemed to relax some. "Tell me, Suitcase, don't ya think Joe should start off in Triple A?"

"Well, that may be rushin' him a little bit."

Jack was disappointed again. "Hell, no. The boy's a born ballplayer. A year at Triple A and he'll be ready for the major leagues."

"I'm afraid it doesn't work that way, Jack. Why don't ya just let us worry about the best way to bring Joe along?"

Mrs. Branscomb finished the dishes and joined them at the table. "Where are you from originally, Mr. Sefton?" she asked.

"Same as you folks," he answered.

"You don't say?" she said. "I thought I heard Oklahoma in your talk."

"Yes, ma'am. You were right."

"So where do you live now?" she asked.

"Oh, I mostly stay in hotels."

"That must be hard," she said sympathetically.

Sefton smiled. "It can get to a body."

"Where are ya stayin' now?" asked Jack.

"Down in Casa Grande."

"Casa Grande? Ain't Casa Grande right near that Jap camp?"

"Yes," said Sefton, stiffening.

"Jesus, if ya ask me, they oughtta ship ever' one of them slant-eyed bastards right back where they come from."

Sefton winced and his jaw clenched. "Oh, I don't know about that. Most of 'em seem like decent-enough types."

"The hell they do! There ain't a single one o' them goddamn yellow sons o' bitches you can trust." Sefton felt his anger rising. "I'm tellin' ya, buddy, don't ever turn your back on one o' them Nips 'cause they're as like to put a shiv in yer ribs as they are to look at ya."

Sefton couldn't take it. "Excuse me," he interrupted, "but I just happen to know some of these people, and you don't have any idea of what the hell you're talkin' about. They happen to be damn good folks. I'm proud to have 'em for friends." He pointed his finger at Jack, his voice rising and his fury mounting. "You're an ignorant son of a bitch, Branscomb—excuse my language, ma'am—and you're just damn lucky that you signed that contract already because if you hadn't, I'da walked out of here and you'da blown your son's chances with the New York Yankees." He stood up. "Good afternoon. Thank you for lunch, Mrs. Branscomb." He nodded to Joe, who sat stunned. "I'll be seein' you at spring trainin', son."

32

BY THE TIME SEFTON REACHED THE OUTSKIRTS OF GLOBE, his anger had subsided. He forced the Branscombs out of his mind and focused on the drive, which was just as precipitous on the descent as on the climb. He rode the brake for much of the way down until the land began to level off.

In Mesa, Sefton stopped for gas. "Fill 'er up with hi-test," he said as the attendant strolled over, "and check the oil and water, if you don't mind." He handed the man the car keys, singling out the one that opened the gas tank.

"Yessir," said the attendant. He opened the tank, set the pump, and inserted the hose. After the pump had been running for a few seconds, he asked, "So, yer plans all set fer Thanksgivin'?"

In fact, Sefton had been invited to Charlie and Josie's for Thanksgiving dinner the following week, and he was looking forward to it. "Yep," he said.

"Tha's nice. You from aroun' here?"

"Casa Grande."

"Oh? Where ya headed?"

"I'm on my way up to Prescott."

"No kiddin'? I jes' now heard on the radio that they's havin' their first snow up there."

"Snow?" The notion had never entered Sefton's mind.

"Tha's right. I wun' go up that way today if I wuz you. Gonna be purty bad drivin'."

Shit, Sefton said to himself. "I guess I'll have to change my plans."

"I would. Be a whole lot easier tomorrow. An' don' fergit to take a sweater."

"Good idea."

The gas pump clicked off. The attendant went around to the front of the car, removed the water bag from the hood ornament, set it down, and lifted the hood. He withdrew the dipstick, wiped off the excess oil with his rag, put it back, removed it again, and looked at the level. "Awl's okay." He unscrewed the radiator cap and peered in. "Could use a touch o' water, though." He went for the can.

Sefton debated whether to return to Casa Grande or to continue on to Phoenix and stay there for the night. He decided on Phoenix, reasoning that it would shorten the trip to Prescott by an hour and a half. The attendant returned with the watering can and brought the radiator level up. "That'll be three dollars and eighty-seven cents," he said, closing the hood and replacing the water bag.

Sefton gave him four dollars in gas coupons. "Keep the change."

"Much obliged."

"And thanks for the tip on the snowstorm."

"You betcha. Come back now."

Sefton waved good-bye and got back on the road. Approaching Phoenix, he was once again amazed by the fertility of the area. It went against reason that what should be desert was farmland. There were miles and miles of cotton fields, citrus orchards, and row crops of all kinds.

When he had first seen the farms, Sefton had not questioned their success or even cared, but in the past couple of months, his contact with the Yamadas had awakened a long-buried interest in farming, and he began to wonder. One day, passing through the area on a scouting trip, he was in a luncheonette and a farmer sat down next to him at the counter, so Sefton took the opportunity to ask about the crops.

"First of all, there's the climate," explained the farmer. "There ain't no frost around here. Second, ya got irrigation. We don't get enough rain to grow nothin', so we don't depend on it. We got wells and we got that Roosevelt Dam up there, and we know exactly how much water we got to work with 'cause it's portioned out to every farmer by the irrigation district. So drought ain't ever a factor. We plow deeper, we use machines instead of mules, and we use sprays to control weeds and insects. Add it all up, and we ain't never had a crop failure around here."

Rather a far cry from the farming that Sefton had known in Oklahoma, where drought, wind, insects, frost, and hail were constant concerns, and any one of them could devastate a season's crop just like that. Maybe there was hope for farmers, he thought.

On the outskirts of Phoenix, Sefton took a room for the night and got an early start the next morning. On the west side of the city, he noticed a dry goods store and recalled the gas station attendant's caution, so he pulled over and went in to buy a sweater. As he looked over the selection, he found himself wondering which one Annie would like. His own inclination ran toward a plain brown cardigan with buttons, but with her in mind, he chose a blue and green argyle V-neck pullover.

Outside Phoenix the Packard began the long, steady haul up to Prescott. Three-quarters of the way on, the grasslands changed to piñon pine, and Sefton saw the first evidence of the previous day's snowfall. By the time he reached Prescott, the ground was covered by several inches of fine, powdery snow, but it was already beginning to melt in the late morning sun. Though the day's traffic cleared the snow from the road surface, an ugly black slush was already piling up along the sides.

At the lumberyard, Sefton put on his new sweater and went into the office. "What can I do for ya today?" asked the man behind the counter.

"I'm lookin' for Eddie Pulaski," Sefton replied.

"You wouldn't be that baseball scout, by any chance?"

"I am. How did ya know?"

"Heck, everybody around here knows that Eddie signed up for pro ball."

"No kiddin'. Hunh. That surprises me. I didn't take Eddie for the kind o' guy that goes around braggin' about himself."

"Oh, no, Eddie never said a word. But Isaac Martinez told just about everybody in the county."

Sefton smiled. "So how can I find him?"

"When you leave the office, turn left and you'll see where the lumber is stacked up. Walk past there and turn right, and you'll come to where the raw logs are layin'. Keep on goin' and you'll see the sawmill behind that. That's where Eddie works. Just ask the foreman. But I better warn ya, it's kinda noisy back there."

Kinda noisy? thought Sefton when he reached the mill—that's the understatement of the year! The high, rasping whine of the saw blades was not only deafening, but nerve-wracking. This is not a place where I'd like to spend any amount of time, Sefton said to himself.

A man he took to be the foreman approached him, removing his earplugs as he walked. "Can I help you?"

"I'd like to talk to Eddie Pulaski for a minute."

"Oh, yeah, you must be the guy from the Yankees."

"Ya found me out."

"Wait here. I'll get Eddie for ya."

The foreman replaced his earplugs and walked back to the saw area. He waited until Pulaski finished his cut and then tapped him on the shoulder. When Pulaski turned around, the man pointed toward Sefton. Pulaski lifted his goggles, looked, and nodded. He turned off his saw and came toward Sefton, looking at the ground as he walked. When he reached the scout, he took out his earplugs. "Hello, Eddie," said Sefton, holding out his hand.

"Mr. Sefton," he said as they shook.

"How ya been?"

"Pretty good."

"You takin' care o' that right arm o' yours?"

"Yessir."

"Good, good, 'cause it's not too long, ya know, before you'll be leavin' for spring trainin'."

"Yessir." Pulaski looked at the ground. "Mr. Sefton," he began, but trailed off. He seemed to be struggling to say something.

"You sure everythin's okay now?" asked Sefton. "What is it, son? Haven't changed your mind, have ya?"

"No, sir."

"What, then?"

"It's just, well, Isaac read over the contract, and it didn't say nuthin' in there about them payin' my way home if I don't make it."

"Is that what's worryin' ya?" Pulaski nodded. "Well, listen here, Eddie. First of all, I don't want you to be thinkin' you're not gonna make it. Okay? Ya got that? I want you to think positive."

"Yessir."

"But if it'll make ya feel better, I'll add it in by hand that the New York Yankees will pay for your return train fare if you fail to make the organization. Okay? Will that put your mind at ease?"

"Yessir, it surely would."

"Fine, Eddie. I'm happy to do that for ya." He paused a moment. "Now, there's somethin' you can do for me."

"Yessir?"

"Some friends of mine need some good wood. They're buildin' a ballpark, and they need some finished lumber for bleachers. Do ya think I could get any kind of a deal here?"

"You'd have to talk to Mr. Chapman about that, sir."

"Mr. Chapman?"

"The foreman."

"Ya suppose ya could introduce us?"

Pulaski scanned the area for Chapman, and when he found him, he said to Sefton, "I'll be right back." He went and got the foreman and returned. Once again, the foreman took out his earplugs. "Mr. Chapman, I'd like you to meet Mr. Sefton. He's the scout who signed me up."

"Howdy, Mr. Sefton. Nice to meet ya."

"The pleasure's mine, Mr. Chapman."

"What can I do for you?"

Sefton explained what he had in mind. Chapman thought about it briefly and then said, "C'mon over this way," and led Sefton and Pulaski toward the stacked lumber. He pointed to a stack off to the side. "Those two-by-twelves over there are seconds. I can cut you a deal on those. You can use those for the benches." Sefton nodded. "The wood for the structure doesn't have to be finished," Chapman continued. He pointed in another direction. "I got some stuff down there that we can't sell 'cause it doesn't meet specs. We usually grind it up for pressboard, but you can have it. You'll be able to use it for the structure. I'll just throw it in for nothin'."

"That's mighty generous of you."

"Happy to help. How soon do you need it?"

"How soon can you deliver it?"

"Well, I prob'ly won't be able to get around to it for a coupla weeks."

"I guess that'll be okay."

"Where's it going to?"

"Down near Casa Grande."

The foreman whistled. "I'm afraid I'm gonna have to charge you for that."

"I unnerstand."

"Delivery'll run, oh, twenty, twenty-five bucks."

"Sounds fair enough."

"Okay, I'll start makin' up a tag for the lumber and the delivery. If you don't mind waiting, you can take it by the office and give 'em a deposit."

"I don't mind waitin'."

They walked back to the mill area, and the foreman opened a door in the small building near the saws. "C'mon in," he said.

Sefton shook hands with Pulaski again. "Thanks, Eddie. You've done me a big favor here."

"Yessir."

"Now I want you to think positive, okay?"

"Yessir."

"Good boy. And I'll send you a letter in care of the yard, saying that your return fare is covered."

"Thank you, Mr. Sefton." He turned and walked away.

Sefton shook his head as he watched Pulaski put in his earplugs. Scared of his own shadow, Sefton thought. Darn shame. He shrugged and entered Chapman's office. The foreman was writing up the bill. He gestured for Sefton to sit in the other chair.

"Now, exactly where are we shipping this to?" he asked.

"There's a small army installation just outside of Casa Grande," Sefton began.

33

LOOKING OUT OVER THE MOONLIT BALLFIELD WITH YAMADA and Annie, Sefton marveled at how quickly the weeks had flown by. He thought back over the events of the past two months.

Thanksgiving with Charlie and Josie had been as close to a feeling of home as he had known at any Thanksgiving within memory. Christmas dinner with Wayne and his wife was more of a chore, but he had used the occasion to secure a pass that allowed him to remain in camp until 2:00 AM on New Year's Eve—the price being a promise to put in an appearance at Wayne's party, but that had been well worth it.

The New Year's celebration with the Yamada family had been something to remember: the dance at the recreation hall and the heartfelt prayers for peace at midnight, the silent walk with Annie afterward, the magnificent *Oshogatsu* banquet at the mess hall on New Year's Day. "We believe," Annie had explained, "that on the first day of the new year it's very important to eat a big meal of the best food in order to nourish your body, mind, and spirit for the coming year." It was not food he had ever seen before, but it certainly achieved the intended purpose; for days and weeks afterward he carried around a feeling of harmony and well-being.

Despite having nothing more than occasional stolen moments, he and Annie grew ever closer. More and more, he felt incomplete when he was not with her. With no more than hugging, kissing, and hand-holding, their attraction to each other blossomed into deep love.

In early January, Yamada's application to the American Friends Service Committee had been accepted. If everything went smoothly, he would enter college the following fall.

And of course, there was the ongoing work on the ballfield: forming the mound; laying out the foul lines and base paths; installing the pitching rubber, home plate, and bases that O'Neil had sent; fertilizing and cultivating the outfield grass and fence; and building the backstop and bleachers. The camaraderie was of a sort that Sefton had not experienced since his playing days, and encountering it once again made him realize how sorely he had missed it. He could not remember when he had laughed as hard as the time Nishimi, during the field's inaugural practice the previous week, had disturbed a hibernating rattlesnake by lifting the backstop pad to retrieve a foul ball that had lodged under there. The catcher screamed and ran all the way out to deep center field while the rest of the players howled with laughter and the bewildered snake beat a dazed retreat in search of a safer hideout.

In the midst of everything else, Sefton had somehow also managed to scare up three more bush-leaguers for the Yankees' low-minors clubs—kids that would not have had a prayer if it had not been wartime. But what the heck, he told himself in justification, it would give them something to tell their grandkids about.

And now, all of a sudden, it was time to leave for Florida. Sefton looked out at the field. "Heckuva ballfield," he said to Yamada. "First-rate. I've played on minor league fields that weren't this good."

"It's too bad you can't wait one more week and be here for the official opening," said Yamada.

"I would've liked that. Unfortunately, spring training is one of the occupational hazards of my business. Then again, a month in Florida isn't the worst thing that can happen to a guy."

"Still, it's a shame. We were gonna ask you to throw out the first ball."

"Now that I'll be sorry to miss." He went into an exaggerated, comic windup, windmilling his arm around three times, bending over until his nose almost touched the ground, kicking his wooden leg up over his head. Annie giggled and Yamada laughed out loud. Sefton concluded his antics.

"Seriously, tell the guys I said I'm very touched and honored. You're gonna pitch that game, right?" Yamada nodded. "Throw a no-hitter for me, okay?"

Yamada laughed. "I'll do my best." There was an awkward pause. "You expect to get an early start tomorrow?"

"Early as I can," Sefton replied. "I've got one or two last-minute things to take care of in the morning."

Yamada extended his hand. "Then I'll say good-bye now. I know you and Annie have things to talk over."

"Thanks, Jerry," said Sefton, taking the pitcher's hand.

"Drive carefully and have a safe trip."

"I will."

"And try to stay out of trouble."

"Not likely."

Yamada nodded to his sister, then turned and walked away. Annie and Sefton stood looking at the field, waiting for Jerry to pass out of earshot. When he was a comfortable distance away, Sefton asked, "Which is more beautiful by moonlight, Annie, a garden or a baseball diamond?"

"I'd say it's about equal. You guys did an amazing job."

"Your brother led the way."

"He told me about the lumber you bought."

"That wasn't a big deal."

"Yes, it was."

"I was happy to be able to do it."

She looked at him and reached out for his hand. "You have a good heart, Mac."

"Thanks, Annie. And what about you? I could hardly believe my eyes when you showed me Jerry's new uniform. Have you told him yet?"

"No. We're waiting until just before the opening game, then we'll show up at practice, all of us together, and present them to the team."

"I wish I could be there to see their faces."

There was a chill in the air and Annie moved close to Sefton, pressing her back into his chest. He wrapped his arms around her. "Annie, can I ask you something?"

"Yes, of course." He hesitated. "What?"

"Does it bother you that I'm ten years older than you?"

"No, of course not. Why? Does it bother you?"

"No, not at all. I was just wondering how you felt."

She turned around so she was facing him. "This is how I feel," she said, and she kissed him. They passed from the realm of the ordinary into the domain of the enchanted, where everything makes sense and nothing is impossible.

"I wish we could just have a normal life together," Annie said after a moment.

"Maybe someday we will."

"Oh? Does that mean you've figured out what you want in life?"

"Well, it's startin' to become clearer to me. At first, ya know, all I cared about was signin' your brother to a contract. But I've sure learned a lot in the past six months, Annie. For the first time in my life, I'm beginnin' to feel like I might actually be able to settle down."

She kissed him. "Oh, how I love you, Mac."

"And I love you." Again they kissed. When they came up for air, Sefton reached into his pocket. "I have somethin' I wanna give you. Ya won't be able to see it very well in this light, but ya can take a better look when ya get home." He pulled a necklace from his pocket. "This was my mother's locket. She gave it to me just before she died and told me to give it to—" He stopped, unable to quite get the words out. "You know."

Tears welled up in Annie's eyes. "Oh, Mac," was all she could say before they came spilling down her cheeks.

"I don't know how I'm gonna make it through the next six weeks, Annie."

"I know. It's the same for me. I'm gonna miss you like crazy. You're such a part of me already. It's like a dream, isn't it, Mac?"

It's the American dream, thought Sefton.

34

IN THE PAST, SEFTON HAD ALWAYS LOOKED FORWARD TO spring training. As a player, he invariably felt reborn when he put on the flannels again, and since becoming a scout, spring training was a place to renew old acquaintances, trade yarns, check up on prospects, and generally take it easy for a few weeks.

Now, however, the trip to Florida was an unwelcome and jarring disruption of his otherwise harmonious existence. Lacking any real enthusiasm for the venture, the week-long drive became an arduous task. More than once, he regretted not having taken the train.

When he reached St. Petersburg, though, Sefton began to feel better. A stroll around the spring training complex with O'Neil the first day in camp helped get him into the spirit. They passed ballfield after ballfield, with players engaged in all manner of baseball-related activities. On one field, the new recruits were doing calisthenics.

"Pretty sorry-ass crop," said O'Neil, his red hair gleaming in the Florida sun. "Half of 'em are nothin' more than warm bodies —high school varsity material."

Sefton looked out over the group. "Where's Eddie Pulaski? I don't see him."

"That's 'cause he ain't there."

"Huh? Ya mean he didn't show up?"

"Oh, he showed up. Everything was fine until the first time they put him in to throw some batting practice. It was Keller's turn to hit. So Pulaski throws a few warmup pitches, and of course he's having trouble finding the plate. And people are getting a little edgy, you know what I mean, 'cause he's throwing so goddamn hard, but Keller ain't paying any attention. He's busy bullshittin' with Dickey.

So the kid's ready, and Keller gets in the cage, and Pulaski's first pitch is a ninety-five-mile-an-hour fastball, right down the middle of the plate. Keller looks at the kid like, are you outta your fuckin' mind? He yells, 'Get this fuckin' moron outta here before I break his head. Get the fuck off the mound, ya little prick.' You know Keller when he gets mad. So Pulaski walks off the hill."

"Shit."

"Then, a coupla days later, they brought him in to pitch in a rookie game. So he takes his warmups, and the first batter steps into the box. Well, ya can see that Pulaski's nervous as hell. He goes into his windup and uncorks a pitch twenty feet over the backstop."

"Jeez."

"Second pitch is behind the batter's head. Pulaski drops his glove on the mound and walks off the field. The next thing I know, he's in my office telling me that you promised him a return train ticket home. I tried to talk him out of it, but it wasn't no use. He was like a scared rabbit."

"Yeah, I know."

"So I gave him the money for a ticket and wished him luck."

"That's too bad."

"Yeah. Well, it ain't your fault. It was worth a shot, as hard as the kid throws."

The calisthenics session broke up, and a player came trotting over to where Sefton and O'Neil stood. "Joe Branscomb," Sefton whispered to O'Neil.

"Hello, Mr. Sefton."

"Hello, son. Joe, this is Mr. O'Neil. He's the head of scouting."

"Pleased to meetcha, son." They shook. "Mr. Sefton tells me some pretty good things about you."

"Thank you, Mr. O'Neil." Over on the field, one of the instructors called for attention. "I better get back," said Branscomb. He turned and trotted back to the group.

"Good attitude," said O'Neil.

"Gets it from his mother."

Sefton and O'Neil walked on. "How's Keller doin'?" asked the scout.

"He seems okay."

"He's not hittin' the bottle?"

"Not so's I can tell. At least not heavy."

"That's good."

The two old friends ambled about for an hour, until O'Neil finally needed to get on with other business. As they parted company, O'Neil said, "You're a sight for sore eyes, Mac. It's good to see you."

"Thanks, Pat. Same here."

In the next couple of days, Sefton settled into the spring training routine. He was, after all, in his element. He ran into longtime friends and associates, many of whom he had not seen since this same time last year. The bull sessions and laughter in the grand-stand and around the batting cage were music to his ears, as people caught up on the past year's happenings and filled one another in on the latest gossip.

Still, every now and then, something would remind him of Annie, and a profound loneliness would creep in. At those times, he felt distracted, isolated, alienated from his companions, and he found their chatter intrusive and empty.

"Hey, Suitcase, how ya doin'?" someone would call as Sefton approached a group around a batting cage. "I heard you been out in Arizona."

The mention of Arizona would bring on the yearning. "That's right."

"Watch out for them cactuses," some card would chime in.

"That's real clever."

"You like it out there, Sefton?"

"I do."

"I was out there once. Shit, I thought I'd die from the heat."

"It gets hot, all right."

"You plannin' to stay out there?"

"I think so."

"Well, to each his own, I guess."

"I guess that's it."

The discussion would drift in another direction, and Sefton would retreat into his own internal musings.

Like a proud father, Sefton made a point of keeping in touch with the players he had signed, and the third day in camp, he went to dinner with Charlie Keller. He was pleased to see that Keller didn't order any drinks; he hated to think that a player with Keller's talent would jeopardize his career because of booze.

"Are ya stayin' off the sauce, Charlie?" Sefton asked.

"I am, Suitcase."

"That's what I like to hear."

At the end of the meal, Sefton tried to grab the check, but the big-league ethic dictated that the player pick up the tab, and Keller deftly snatched it away from him.

When Sefton had been in St. Pete for about a week, he and O'Neil had dinner. "They're thinking of starting Branscomb in Double A," O'Neil said between bites of steak.

"Sounds right to me."

"Kid's very good behind the plate—and coachable. Birdsong, on the other hand, they don't know what to do with him. It's a shame that a kid who has such talent with the bat is such a fuckup in the field."

"It happens." Sefton looked at O'Neil and smiled. "Just like some guys are geniuses with the glove but are completely lost at the plate."

"Now who would you be thinking about?"

Sefton shrugged. "If the shoe fits."

"Ouch. Thank you for the very unkind remark."

"Don't mention it. Why not put Birdsong in Single A ball and see what happens?"

"Yeah, that's probably what they'll decide to do. No matter how bad he plays he can't do very much damage down there." O'Neil thought a moment. "Problem is, he's gonna eat up Single A pitching, so they'll move him up, and the same thing'll happen in Double A, but when he gets to Triple A, he becomes a liability."

"Who knows? Maybe by that time, he'll learn how to catch the damn ball."

The maître d' approached, gave a slight bow, presented a folded note to O'Neil, and walked away. O'Neil unfolded the note and read it. His eyes narrowed. "Shit."

"What?" asked Sefton.

"DiMaggio enlisted. Goddammit."

The following morning, Sefton rose early and made his way to the compound reserved for the big-leaguers. Keller was just coming out of the barracks. "Suitcase," he said, surprised to see Sefton in this neck of the camp—and especially before breakfast.

"Morning, Charlie."

"What the hell ya doin' over here?"

"I'm lookin' for DiMaggio."

"Yeah, ain't everybody. Ya heard?"

Sefton nodded. "Have ya seen him?"

Keller pointed his thumb over his shoulder. "He's packing."

"Thanks, Charlie. I'll catch up with ya later."

Sefton entered the building. He scanned the room and saw DiMaggio, sitting on his bed, packing a suitcase. He watched the center fielder for a moment, remembering the shy, unassuming kid from San Francisco who had been so easy when he first came up. Now it was a different story. Sefton steeled himself and approached. When he got close, he stopped. DiMaggio gave no indication of being aware of Sefton's presence.

"Excuse me, Joe."

DiMaggio did not look up. "Yeah?"

"Mac Sefton, Joe." DiMaggio looked at Sefton; obviously he did not recognize him. "I'm one of the scouts," said Sefton.

"Oh, yeah. Now I remember ya. Whaddya want?"

Sefton took a deep breath. "I have a favor to ask, Joe."

35

FOR THE BETTER PART OF A WEEK, RIZZOLIO HAD BEEN keeping a hopeful eye out for the two-tone green coupe, anxiously anticipating Sefton's return. He was all but certain that the scout would not be happy with the latest developments at the camp. At the same time, he was eager to hear news of spring training and Sefton's assessment of the Yankees' chances in 1943.

When he finally did spot Sefton's car one evening at dusk, the fading light at first made him doubt his eyes. But no, there it was, and there was the man himself. "Suitcase!" Rizzolio cried, as the Packard glided to a stop. "Welcome back!"

"Good to be back, Corporal."

Sefton opened the door and got out. Rizzolio's expression suddenly changed. "Eh, too bad about DiMaggio, huh?"

"Yeah, that's a shame. But I've got somethin' for you."

"For me?"

"Yeah, it's back here." Sefton limped around and opened the trunk. He rummaged through the mess, pulled out a baseball, and casually handed it to Rizzolio with the autographed side up. The soldier took the ball and looked at the signature.

"Holy cow! Ya got dis for me?"

"For you."

"I can't believe it! Joe DiMaggio!"

"Read the other side."

Rizzolio turned the ball over. "'To my good friend, Cpl. Dominic Rizzolio.' Oh, man, I dunno what to say. Suitcase, I'll never forget dis. *Grazie, amico! Mille grazie, mio fratello!*"

If he only knew what I had to go through to get that, Sefton thought. "Ah, it's nothing, Corporal. My pleasure."

"So whaddya think about our chances dis season?"

"Well, it's gonna be tough, but I think we'll be okay. The line-up's taken a pretty good lickin'. Rizzuto, DiMaggio, Henrich, Hassett, Ruffing—they're all in the service. 'Course, all the other clubs've been hit hard too. One thing ya can be sure of is that McCarthy's a smart manager, and he'll do the best with what he's got. We'll just hafta wait and see how things shape up."

"Yeah, I guess so," agreed Rizzolio.

Sefton closed the trunk and limped back around to the driver's door. He turned to Rizzolio, who had gone back to admiring his ball. "Say, Corporal, could you open the gate for me?"

Rizzolio's face fell. "Oh, jeez. I can't, Suitcase."

"Why not?"

"All passes been canceled."

"Why?"

"I ain't exactly sure. It's got somethin' to do with a loyalty oath."

"What kinda loyalty oath?"

"I don't really know, but it's a pretty big deal. They been busin' people outta here for 'bout two weeks now."

Sefton felt a rush of panic. "Where are they sendin' 'em?"

"I dunno. Someplace in California."

"Listen, Corporal, I've really gotta get into the camp." There was a note of desperation in his voice. "I've *gotta* get in. *Capice? Prego!*"

Rizzolio read the alarm in Sefton's face. He clutched the ball in his hand; he could not let his pal down, especially not now. "I understan'. Oh, man, what a pickle. Lemme think for a minute here." He paced up and down. "Okay, listen, here's what we do. Ya drive ya car up da road and park it over there. Then walk back here, I'll toin my back, and ya slip troo da fence. That way, if ya get pinched, I can say I didn't see nuttin'. You'll be okay—da guy in da tower won't see ya in this light. Comin' out, ya do da same thing. I'll talk to da guy that takes over for me an' let him know ya comin'. He'll look da other way and ya slip troo da fence again. Okay?"

"Yeah. Thanks, Corporal."

Sefton did not move. He wanted to say something that would more emphatically convey his gratitude, but before he could find the words, Rizzolio said, "So what da hell are ya waitin' for? Get goin'." They shook hands. Sefton opened the car door and got in. "Good luck, Suitcase."

Sefton nodded. He drove a few hundred yards, pulled off the road, and then hurried back to the gate. Rizzolio was facing away, and Sefton quickly squeezed between two strands of barbed wire, taking care not to cut himself or tear his clothing.

36

ONCE INSIDE THE CAMP, SEFTON BRIEFLY CONSIDERED going to see Wayne, but immediately dismissed the idea. Instead, he made his way toward the Yamadas' barracks.

There were more soldiers out on patrol than Sefton had seen at any other time. Once or twice, an MP looked inclined to question Sefton's presence, but he gave them no chance to stop him and kept moving as if he belonged. He reached the family's room without a challenge, climbed the short steps, and knocked. After a few seconds, Annie opened the door. The first thing Sefton noticed was his mother's locket around her neck.

"Mac! Come in, quick." He stepped in and closed the door behind him. Annie threw herself into his embrace. "I'm so glad to see you," she whispered in his ear, but then separated herself and stepped back. Sefton accepted this as modesty before the rest of the family, and quickly went to shake hands with Yamada. "Hello, Jerry."

"Mac."

Sefton bowed slightly to the parents, and they returned the gesture. The formalities finished, he noticed the condition of the room. Clothing and other personal belongings were everywhere. The walls were bare, the few photos and other decorations having been removed. A number of open suitcases lay about, packed to various stages of capacity.

"What in the Sam Hill is goin' on here?" Sefton asked. Nobody responded. "What gives?"

"We've been relocated again," said Jerry.

"Where to?"

"They're sending us to a camp called Tule Lake in California, up near the Oregon border."

"But why?"

Jerry shook his head. "It makes about as much sense as anything else that's happened."

"Tell me."

Jerry took a deep breath and exhaled. "About a month ago, the government came up with this questionnaire that we all had to fill out. They said they needed to identify the people who were loyal to Japan. There were two questions that caused a lot of people trouble. I can't remember the exact wording, but the first was, 'Are you willing to serve in the armed forces of the United States?' and the second said something like, 'Will you swear allegiance to the United States and fight to defend the country from attack, and renounce allegiance to the emperor of Japan?' I guess they figured this would weed out all the disloyal ones, but it also caused a whole bunch of problems for many of the rest of us."

"How so?" asked Sefton.

"It wouldn't have been a problem for me or Jerry," said Annie. "But for my parents and the other immigrants, they couldn't say yes to those questions."

"Why not?"

"Because they'd lose their Japanese citizenship."

"So then they could become American citizens."

"No, they couldn't," said Jerry. "That's forbidden by law. It's called the Asian Exclusion Act. They can't even own land—the farm was actually in my name. Not only that, but when we were evacuated, all the immigrants were classified '4C'—Enemy Alien. So if they renounced their Japanese citizenship, they'd have no citizenship at all. What would happen to them then? Anyway, everybody who said no to those two questions—for whatever reason—is being sent to Tule Lake. They're calling us the 'no-no boys.'"

"It's just torn people apart, Mac," said Annie. "Families are being split up—some people staying, some going. It's devastating."

Sefton's mind was reeling. "But what about you two? Why are you going?"

"We had to say no to those questions too," said Jerry.

"Why?"

"In order to keep the family together. That's the craziest part of it all. A lot of people like us are being sent to Tule Lake for reasons that have nothing to do with being loyal or disloyal. It's just a mess. And there's no way you could possibly understand the stigma, for these people, of being labeled disloyal."

Sefton could feel his world crumbling. "But what about our deal?" he protested, raising his voice.

"I'm afraid it's off, Mac."

Sefton's frustration suddenly boiled over, and he was shouting. "But you don't have to go out there to California, for Pete's sake. Just tell 'em you made a mistake and say yes to those questions. Your folks'll be okay. You'll all get back together after the war."

With Sefton's outburst, everything in the room came to a standstill; his unseemly display brought on an embarrassed silence. Then Jerry spoke softly. "Do you have any idea what these two people have been through, Mac? If I told you all the hardships my parents have endured for my sake and for Annie's, I'm sure you wouldn't believe me. Everything we are, we owe to them. My dad is fifty-nine, and my mom is two years younger. They came to this country with nothing, and all these years, they've worked and struggled and sacrificed so Annie and I could have a good life. And just about the time when it looked like that was finally secure, everything was pulled out from under them. And now they're being moved again. And you want us to abandon them?"

Sefton looked at the floor. "No, of course not. Forgive me."

"I made that deal with you so I could save up money for a new farm. It would have been hard enough for them, and for me, and for Annie, but we were willing to do it. But this changes everything."

"I understand."

Nobody spoke. Melancholy hung about the small room like a fog. Finally Annie resumed packing. "When do you leave?" asked Sefton.

"Tomorrow morning," answered Jerry.

Sefton put his head in his hand. In the short space of one hour, his life had fallen apart at the seams, and the inner filling that was the meaning of his existence had come flying out in every direction. Sefton looked up. Annie was busy packing. "Annie, could we talk?"

She stopped what she was doing and spoke to her parents in Japanese. They nodded. "I don't have much time, but we could take a short walk," she said to Sefton.

"Okay."

Sefton shook hands with the other three, then he and Annie left. They walked in silence, holding hands, the reality of their impending separation weighing heavily on their hearts and minds. Without any conscious agreement, they found themselves at the garden. Annie opened the gate and they went to the bench.

They sat close together, fingers entwined, thumbs stroking one another's hands. "I hate to leave this garden," Annie lamented. "Things are just starting to come along after spring planting."

"It's gonna be bleak here without you, Annie."

"Why don't you come to California with us, Mac?"

"I wish I could. But I don't see how. I have a job to do here. I can't keep asking for transfers."

"I see," she said softly. "And is that what you have in mind for the rest of your life, Mac? Being on the road? Living out of a suitcase?" Spoken gently, her words nevertheless stung, but Sefton made no reply. "You know I love you, Mac."

Sefton hung his head. He was torn apart.

Annie waited for a response, but none came. Finally, she said, "I guess I better get back. There's still a lot of packing to do." She reached up and put her hand on his cheek, then leaned over and kissed him lightly on the lips. "I'll never forget you, Mac."

At the garden gate, she turned back to Sefton; he was gazing straight ahead, the most heart-rending look of sadness and loneliness etched on his face. Annie turned and quickly walked away, the pain almost too agonizing to bear.

37

SEFTON WAS AWAKENED BY THE LOW ROAR OF UNMUFFLED engines. For a moment he struggled to determine who he was and where he was, until he recalled the previous day's nightmare.

After Annie had left him, he sat on the garden bench for a long time, dazed, not fully able to believe all that had happened. Finally, realizing it was dark, he remembered his arrangement with Rizzolio and limped back to the main gate. He waved to the soldier on duty and, as arranged, the guard turned his back. Sefton crawled through the fence and walked to his car, then drove it down and parked opposite the gate so he could see the buses leave in the morning.

Now, waking up in the back seat, Sefton struggled to clear the cobwebs as he observed the buses moving through the gate and out onto the road. Suddenly he remembered why he was here. He hurriedly smoothed his hair, put on his jacket and hat, and jumped out of the car. He had to pee something fierce, but that would have to wait.

Sefton stood by the car and watched the buses roll out. As each one turned onto the road and went by him, he caught a glimpse of the people inside. He saw Raymond Kurima, the hot-headed shortstop, who raised his hand in farewell. Sefton returned the gesture. On another bus sat Tom Yoshitake. The former Fresno manager shot Sefton a vicious, malevolent look, but the scout ignored it.

And then he saw Annie. Their eyes locked together. Tears coursed down her face. Sefton's heart was gripped by the most acute and unbearable ache as he stood helplessly and watched her go by. Then she was gone.

Sefton remained rooted to the spot as the rest of the buses streamed past. Well after the last one had departed, he was still there, staring blankly at the ground.

Part II
1945–1946

38

SEFTON LAY IN BED, WATCHING THE EARLY MORNING LIGHT steal in, until his hotel room was saturated with rich, golden sunshine, at which point he could no longer excuse his indolence, and he hauled his body to a sitting position. He reached over to the chair, picked up his wooden leg, strapped it on, stood up, crossed the room to the bureau, and looked at his watch. A quarter after six. Another day to plod through somehow.

The days were little more than that to him now—time to fill with essentially insignificant activity. Outwardly, he had returned to pretty much the same life he lived before meeting Annie, a life that he had found quite congenial then, but that held little meaning for him now. With Annie, everything had been suffused with meaning. Without her, he was just going through the motions.

For months after the Yamadas had left for California, Sefton had been devastated. Lost in his own thoughts and feelings, he spoke when spoken to and carried on seemingly normal conversations, but it all seemed hollow to him, as if he were performing in a dumb show that was all form and no content. As time went on, the pain gradually subsided, and he simply went numb. Since then, he had been stumbling along in an indifferent stupor.

Time and separation had not caused forgetfulness, however. He thought of Annie often, and periodically considered writing to her, but then, what would he say?

It had been more than a year since Sefton last set foot in the camp. At first, he had kept in touch with some of the remaining Fresno players to see if there was any word of the Yamada family, but when he did hear some bit of news, it only made things worse and he missed Annie even more, so his visits became increasingly infrequent. He did occasionally drop by to shoot the breeze with Corporal Rizzolio because he liked the kid, but that was the extent of his contact with the camp.

For Sefton the past two years had been devoid of purpose. Even if he somehow had been able to find fulfillment in his work, the times yielded little in the way of bona fide baseball talent as virtually all the able-bodied men were still being inducted into the armed forces. Of his original group of prospects, the most promising were in uniform: Joe Branscomb was in the army and Tommy Birdsong had joined the navy. Eddie Pulaski had been drafted, but applied for conscientious objector status and was serving as an army medic. Even the mighty Yankees had been affected by the war: after repeating as American League champions in 1943 and avenging the previous year's 4–1 loss to the Cardinals in the World Series, they slipped to third in 1944, their roster further decimated by the draft.

As Sefton dressed now, he could feel the August heat already gathering for its daily assault. The mercury had hit a hundred and nine degrees the day before, and today promised to be equally oppressive. What in the Sam Hill am I still doin' here? Sefton asked himself. The vague thought of what he might do to relieve the tedium of the day floated through his head, but nothing came to mind, and he grudgingly resigned himself once again to the emptiness of his existence. Even Japan's imminent surrender, which was being avidly discussed everywhere, was hardly compelling to him, as it would not essentially change anything in his circumstances.

Sefton limped down the street to the coffee shop for breakfast. At least he still had Charlie and Josie. They had become like family to him. He never told them about Annie, but Josie, in her motherly way, had sensed the profound sadness in Sefton after the Yamadas left and had made a special effort to look after him.

When Sefton opened the door of the coffee shop, he was immediately struck by the lively mood; the place was uncharacteristically abuzz with animated chatter. Normally, there was a subdued drone in the room at mealtimes, particularly at breakfast and dinner, as people took pains not to intrude on the privacy of their neighbors' conversations. Even lunch, which was the most outgoing meal of the day, never produced this type of commotion.

"Hey, Suitcase," called Josie above the din as she spotted Sefton come in. "Heard the news?" She reached over, picked up a newspaper from the counter, and held it up: Japan Surrenders! screamed the banner headline. "It's over!" Josie shouted. She held out the paper to him.

Sefton sat down at the counter and nodded hello to the fellow sitting next to him. "What can I getcha, hon?" asked Josie, pouring him a cup of coffee.

"Bacon and fried eggs'll be fine."

Sefton settled into the paper. He skimmed the lead story and its continuation on page two, and then turned back to the front page to scan the related articles. When his breakfast arrived, he picked at it as he leafed through the rest of the main section. Toward the back, a small headline at the bottom of one page leapt out at him: California Jap Camp to Release "No-No" Boys.

Sefton put down his fork. He quickly folded the paper in quarters and read the short article:

> Sacramento (AP)—The War Relocation Authority announced today that the release of Japanese inmates at Tule Lake Relocation Center would begin within days. The camp, located southeast of Klamath Falls, Oregon, has been used to house the infamous "no-no" boys—internees from the ten relocation camps who refused to declare their loyalty to the United States. A spokesman for the WRA said that with the war now over, the "no-nos" were no longer considered a threat to national security. Beginning in February, approximately two thousand residents of the turbulent camp have been repatriated to Japan, and many thousands more are similarly expected to now return to their homeland.

Sefton continued to stare at the page long after he had finished reading the article and was roused from his trance only when he became aware that Josie was talking to him. He had to make an effort to focus on what she was saying.

"Your breakfast's gettin' cold, hon." She pointed at his plate. Sefton looked down at the food and picked up his fork. Josie took his cup and saucer, dumped the coffee, and poured him a fresh cup. Sefton began to eat.

His mind was racing. Images came flooding in as he ate. He thought of the soldier he had given a ride to in Oklahoma and saw the joyful family all together in the front yard, the dog jumping in excited circles around them. He remembered the young man's words: "If you have dreams, you better go after 'em."

Sefton took a bite of his toast. He saw Annie's face. "So what do you want out of life, Mac?" she asked, her black eyes gleaming in the moonlight.

Sefton sipped his coffee and thought of Mr. Yamada. "You don't want to regret having missed your golden opportunity."

As he mopped up the egg yolks with toast, he heard Annie again: "Is that what you have in mind for the rest of your life, Mac? Being on the road? Living out of a suitcase?"

Suddenly, Sefton felt a fog lift and he was back in the present. He looked around the coffee shop. He had no idea how long he had been sitting there, but the place had all but cleared out. He stood up, aware only of an immediate and wholly unexpected sense of urgency.

"You alright, hon?" asked Josie.

"Yeah, I'm okay," said Sefton. "But listen, somethin's come up, and I got some travelin' to do. I might not be around for a while."

"Oh, that's a shame." Josie turned to the kitchen. "Charlie, c'mon out here for a minute."

The cook appeared, wiping his hands, as usual, on his apron. "What's up?"

"I gotta hit the road, Charlie," said Sefton. "Can't say when I'll be back."

"You transferrin' again, Suitcase?" asked Charlie.

"Could be, Charlie. Remains to be seen."

"Well, I just hate to hear that, but I guess I gotta wish ya luck." He held out his hand. "Sorry to see ya leave, partner."

"We sure are gonna miss ya, hon," said Josie as Sefton and Charlie shook hands.

"And I'm gonna miss you. The two of you have been real good to me. I'm very grateful to ya both."

Sefton reached in his pocket, but Josie held up her hand. "Uh, uh. It's on us." Sefton leaned over the counter and gave her a peck on the cheek.

"Keep in touch, Suitcase," said Charlie.

"I'll do that. And thanks again—for everythin'." He turned to go.

"Wait," said Charlie. Sefton turned back. "Stop in before ya leave town, and I'll have some sandwiches for ya."

"You're just too good, Charlie."

Sefton limped down the street to the hotel, where he quickly packed his things and bid farewell to the room that had been his home for three years. At the front desk, Sefton settled his bill then went out, threw his suitcase in the trunk, and started up the car. He drove the block to the coffee shop and left the motor running while he hobbled in to pick up his sandwiches, then jumped back in the car and drove out of town, making a short detour by the camp to say good-bye to Corporal Rizzolio before heading north.

39

THE ORDER OF RELEASE HAD COME WITH AS LITTLE WARNING as any of the other mandates to relocate. As the rest of the country celebrated the end of the war, for the internees it meant once again being shunted to a new place. From the day Pearl Harbor was bombed, they had been pawns in the government's chess game, being moved at will across the giant board called the United States. First the community leaders had been yanked from their families and sent to unknown places, then the rest of the people were evacuated to the assembly centers, after which they were shipped to the internment camps; from there some were sent to agricultural jobs or college, and others were moved to or from Tule Lake. Now, as a final reminder that their fate was still subject to the whim of the state, they were being turned loose to try to reestablish their disrupted lives, starting from the bottom up.

In the two years at Tule Lake, Jerry had become increasingly concerned about his parents. The move had not been easy on any of the family members, but he was especially aware of the toll it had taken on his parents' spirits. How would they adjust now that the war was over and their lives were once again uprooted?

As the Yamadas packed their things, Annie wondered what lay in store for her and her family. Where would they go, and how would they survive? They still had the three hundred dollars they received from the sale of their possessions when the relocation order came, but that was hardly enough to buy another farm. No doubt, Mr. Yamada and Jerry would have to take work as nurserymen or gardeners or field hands in order to support the family for the foreseeable future. And almost certainly, they could expect a degree of lingering hostility and prejudice from white people.

Annie also wondered what would become of the Japanese-American community. It had been utterly fragmented; there was no possibility of things ever being the same as before. On every level, the future was unsettled and uncertain. Still, Annie was very glad to be leaving Tule Lake.

The segregation camp had been a seething cauldron of tension, and the time there had not been easy for the Yamadas. The camp was in constant turmoil, as the militant, pro-Japan faction controlled the internal politics of the camp and was perpetually fomenting discord. There were any number of strikes and demonstrations, and the belligerence of that group was met by an equally hostile intransigence on the part of the authorities. After food strikes in November 1943, the government handed control of the camp over to the army, and it was not until February of the following year that the War Relocation Authority was able to wrest control of the place back from the military.

The pro-Japan extremists had held near-absolute sway over the camp, employing strong-arm tactics to terrorize any sector of the population that was not in complete agreement with their views. Yoshitake, nursing a grudge over what had happened in Arizona, had singled Yamada out for petty but constant harassment. It was only Yamada's pitching ability—not even Yoshitake would dream of risking the wrath of the issei baseball fans—that saved him from being seriously roughed up by the former manager and his henchmen. Only after Yoshitake was shipped out, along with several hundred other pro-Japan agitators, to the camp in Santa Fe, New Mexico, did Yamada cease to be a target of the bullyboys' attempts at intimidation.

In addition to all the political strife, Annie had her personal sorrow to deal with. Losing Sefton had been wrenching. For months after coming to Tule Lake, she had been certain that he would somehow manage a way to follow, and she fully expected him to show up at the door one day. When he failed to appear, and did not even write, she began to doubt whether he had ever really loved her and then even started wondering if the whole interlude had actually ever happened.

Over time, Annie managed to dissociate herself from her attachment to Sefton. She went on with her life. On the surface, she was the same Annie who always saw the positive side of things, but to those who knew her well, it was apparent that something had been dampened in her.

Now, packing for the following day's departure, Annie laid her clothes out on her bed and put her suitcase beside them. She released the latches, rested the lid back on the bed, and pulled open a side pocket to drop in a pair of socks. A glint of metal in the pocket caught her eye.

Annie removed the object and held it up. It was the locket that Sefton had given her. She remembered the moment on that winter day, six months after arriving at Tule Lake, that she had finally admitted to herself that he would not be coming. She had been sitting by the window, watching the cold, wind-driven rain, and all at once she knew for certain. She slowly reached behind her neck and undid the clasp, then put the necklace in the suitcase and forgot about it.

As she looked at it now, she felt a dull ache, the kind of pain that sometimes momentarily recurs in a wound long since healed over. Not wanting to reopen that wound, she put the necklace back in the pocket and finished her packing.

For the rest of the day, Annie did a fairly good job of keeping Sefton out of her mind, but that night she dreamt of him. When she woke, her heart was still filled with the dream, but after several seconds she remembered the reality of things, and the joy slowly ebbed away.

It was a moonless night. Annie lay in the dark and felt hollow.

40

THE TRIP HAD BEEN HARDER AND MORE TIME-CONSUMING
than Sefton had expected. He was out of shape for this type of mar-
athon driving; with the pool of talent so diluted by the war, his car
trips had been a lot fewer and farther between in the past couple of
years, and after learning his lesson about driving to spring training
in 1943, he took the train to Florida and back the next two years.
Sefton had thus been able to save quite a few of the gas coupons
that the club had furnished him, which stood him in good stead for
his 750-mile trip west.

He had stopped at the Packard dealership in Phoenix to see
about the possibility of trading in the coupe on a newer-model
sedan, figuring that with a hundred and twenty thousand miles,
the old two-tone had done its duty. Besides, if he ever was able
to find Annie and her family, a four-door would be a lot better
car to have.

The dealer had just shaken his head when Sefton told him what
he had in mind. With automobile production all but suspended
during the war, there was a two-year waiting list for new cars,
and he had nothing in a used sedan that was any better than what
Sefton was driving. He suggested a tune-up.

"How long ya figure it'll take?" asked Sefton.

"Could have it ready to go in a couple hours tops," said the
dealer.

"You're on."

While the car was being tuned, Sefton ate his sandwiches and
studied the map. Calculating that it would cut two hundred and
fifty miles off the trip, he decided to drive up through western Nevada rather than over to Los Angeles and up California's

Central Valley. The area around Death Valley worried him, but he figured with the car freshly tuned, he could baby it along through that stretch.

It took him a day and a half to reach Reno. The car had overheated several times going through the desert, and Sefton was forced to travel at night to beat the insufferable heat. As a result, he was bushed the next morning and pulled over to the side of the road, where he slept in the back seat for a few hours.

He hit Reno around sundown and decided he had best get a good night's rest because there was no point arriving at the Tule Lake camp after dark, so he took a room and paid in advance. He set the alarm clock for five and fell asleep easily.

Toward morning Sefton dreamed that he and Annie were being married in center field at Yankee Stadium. Everyone was there: his father, his mother, O'Neil, the Yamadas, his fellow scouts, ex-teammates, the Yankees, the Fresno team, all the players he had ever signed.

When he awoke, he lay in bed for a couple of minutes, savoring the sweetness of the dream but at the same time feeling the sadness of it being nothing but a dream. Then he remembered that he had no time to waste. What if the Yamadas already had been released from the camp by the time he got there? Seized by the fear that he would be too late and would never see Annie again, he jumped up, showered, dressed, had a cup of coffee and a roll, and moved on.

In Newell, he stopped and had a real breakfast and got directions to the Tule Lake camp. When he pulled up to the front gate it was just after 9:30 and buses were already leaving. Sefton stood by his car, searching the windows for Annie. His heart tightened as he remembered the last time he had seen her, on the bus leaving the other camp, tears streaming.

Bus after bus rolled out of the camp, but he could not find Annie or any of the Yamadas on board. A couple of times, he thought he recognized a familiar face, but the buses passed by too quickly for him to make any contact. Hours passed. As much as he wanted Annie to appear, his desire could not make it happen. Hope gave way to doubt, followed by desperation, and finally, dejection.

Sometime in the evening, Sefton realized he had not eaten since breakfast. He hated to leave, but he needed some food, and it seemed futile to just stand there watching the buses go by. Perhaps tomorrow. Despair in his heart, he opened the car door. He would find a meal, get some sleep, and come back first thing in the morning.

41

AS INSTRUCTED, THE YAMADA FAMILY REPORTED TO THE administration building after breakfast. By the luck of the draw, they had been included in the first group to be discharged. They showed their identification to the clerk at the tables that had been set up outside, and they were handed papers authorizing their release.

Hundreds of people milled around and there was a feeling of elation in the air. After three and a half years of detention, they were finally regaining their freedom. At the same time, there was also an undercurrent of trepidation, as nobody knew what lay ahead.

The buses were lined up in a seemingly endless row. At about 9:00 AM, one of the officials announced the people who would board the first bus. There were handshakes, embraces, and tears as people said their good-byes; then the first group boarded a bus and, after some minutes, it drove away.

A quarter of an hour later, the process was repeated, and a second bus rolled out. More people arrived and reported to the clerks. Babies cried and children ran through the jungle of adults' legs and luggage. By noon, more than a dozen buses had left, and the Yamadas still had not been called.

How fitting, thought Annie, that their internment should end with a wait. They had already endured three and a half years of waiting. Go to breakfast—wait. Go to the shower—wait. Go to the laundry—wait. Go to the bathroom—wait. Stand in line, after line, after line. Once, when she had remarked about how much time was taken up with having to wait for something or other, her father had said, "Try to look at it as an opportunity to practice patience." As always, his advice had a beneficial effect on Annie. She recalled his words as she waited this one last time.

Sandwiches arrived. Midday dissolved into late afternoon. Buses continued to leave without the Yamadas being on them.

Finally, with the sun falling low in the west, their names were called. "Let's get on before they change their minds," said Annie. They boarded the bus for Fresno and found four seats near the back. Jerry loaded their bags onto the overhead rack. The parents sat on one side of the aisle, and Jerry offered his sister the window seat on the other side. She slid in and pushed the window open as high as it would go.

After a short delay, the bus started up and drove slowly through the camp. There was a murmur of anticipation as it passed through the gate and pulled out onto the road. Annie gazed out the window at nothing in particular.

She saw the car before she saw him. The sight of the two-tone green Packard brought on a pang of sadness. There's a car just like Mac's, was all she could think. But a second later, she saw Sefton just as he was opening the door to get in. There was a brief moment of disbelief before she was certain.

"*Mac!*" she shouted out the open window. Sefton immediately recognized the voice and turned to see where it was coming from. Annie hung out the window of the bus.

Jerry was shocked and looked out the window. "It's him," said Annie. "Stop!" she cried desperately, leaping out of her seat. "Let me out!" She moved to get into the aisle, and Jerry quickly jumped up to let her by. "Stop the bus!" she cried, hurtling toward the front. She tripped and fell, then picked herself up and continued down the aisle.

On the side of the road, Sefton limped frantically along in a los-ing effort to keep up with the bus. He felt a surge of panic as the vehicle pulled ahead of him.

"Please *stop!*" Annie yelled at the driver. He slammed on the brakes. "Open the door, I have to get out." The urgency and command in her voice left him no choice but to obey. He opened the door. "Wait right here for me," Annie told him as she jumped off.

Sefton was catching up to the back of the bus by the time she hit the ground, and they flew to each other like a pair of magnets. He lifted her off her feet and held her tightly to him, his heart skyrocketing. She kissed his face over and over.

"Oh, Mac, I can hardly believe it. I was so afraid I'd never see you again." Suddenly, the heart that had been sewn up so tightly for two years burst apart at the seams, and she wept for joy as they embraced for all they were worth.

"There wasn't one day that went by that I didn't think of you," said Sefton as he stroked her hair.

"I know, I know. I thought about you too."

The bus horn honked two impatient blasts. Annie looked up at the windows for her parents and brother. All the faces on the bus were looking down at this foolish *nihonjin* girl making a spectacle of herself with some unknown *hakujin*.

Sefton looked up and saw Jerry's head sticking out of the open window. They smiled at one another. "Jerry," said Sefton, putting Annie gently down. He limped over and Jerry reached down for his hand.

"Mac."

The bus horn tooted again. Sefton pointed to his car. "Get your luggage—we'll take my car."

Jerry turned and spoke to his parents, then looked down to Sefton. "We'll be right there." Sefton and Annie went to the door of the bus to help them off.

"C'mon, make it snappy," said the driver as Jerry handed the suitcases down to Sefton. Then he stepped down and turned back to help his parents. When they were all safely off, the doors closed and the bus roared away.

Sefton and Jerry shook hands again. "Good to see you, Mac."

"And you, Jerry."

Sefton bowed slightly to Mr. and Mrs. Yamada, and they returned the gesture. The father extended his hand. "Mac." They shook. Mr. Yamada spoke in Japanese. Sefton looked to Annie and her brother.

"My father says he has never forgotten what you did for us in the other camp," said Jerry.

Sefton looked at the father and bowed again. "Thank you."

It was almost sundown as they loaded the bags into the car. "Are y'all hungry?" asked Sefton.

"Yes," said Annie.

"Me, too. Let's get somethin' to eat." They got into the car, and Sefton drove to Klamath Falls, where they found a steakhouse.

After they had ordered their meals, Sefton said, "Don't tell your father what I'm doin'," and he ordered a bottle of beer for Mr. Yamada. When the waitress returned and put it on the table in front of him, his face broke out into a broad grin, and he rubbed his hands together in anticipation of his first beer in more than two years.

Over dinner, Sefton said, "I think we should stay here tonight and drive to Fresno in the morning. We need to start lookin' for a farm."

Jerry did not translate. Instead, he spoke to Sefton. "We have no money to buy a farm. You know that."

"I have money. I'll buy the farm."

"I don't think we could possibly—"

"Wait." Sefton held up his hand, interrupting before Jerry could go any further. "Listen, I've had plenty of time to think about this. I want to do this for you and for myself. I don't want to live the rest of my life on the road. I want to settle down with Annie." She beamed. "So please, let's not argue about it, okay?"

Mr. Yamada asked a question, and his son explained to his parents what Sefton had proposed. The older man seemed not to be sure he understood and asked his son to repeat it again. Jerry spoke once more. The father, now certain of what was being advanced, took a deep breath and shook his head. No. Sefton's heart sank.

Mrs. Yamada began whispering to her husband. When she finished, Mr. Yamada thought for a minute, then nodded. He spoke, looking directly at Sefton. When he was done, Sefton looked to Jerry for the translation.

"My father says there is no possible way we could accept this from you." Sefton was crestfallen. "However, he says he now understands that you have a very deep commitment to his daughter, and that she returns your feelings." Sefton nodded, hope rising again. "So," continued Jerry, "on that basis what he can allow is for you to provide a down payment, and we'll make payments until we've matched your down payment, and then we'll be partners from there on out."

Sefton's million-dollar smile lit up the restaurant. He raised his hand to get the waitress's attention.

"Another beer for the gentleman, please."

42

THE FIRST HINT OF AUTUMN WAS IN THE CENTRAL VALLEY air. The punishing heat of summer had yielded to the amicable warmth of Indian summer, and the nights had become cool and invigorating. It was possible to work through the middle of the day now without inviting heat stroke.

On this Sunday, however, the work day ended just before noon. Annie, six months along and showing, came down to the orchard to inform the men that lunch was ready. They packed up their tools and followed her to the grove of live oaks near the house, where Mrs. Yamada had a picnic spread.

When they were seated, Sefton put his hand on his wife's burgeoning abdomen. After a few moments, he said, "I think I felt it move," and kissed her on the cheek. She laughed and ruffled his hair, her black eyes dancing with delight.

Lunch was teriyaki beef with rice balls and pickled vegetables. They dug in with gusto. Sefton dropped a piece of beef on his shirt, which caused general hilarity. After more than a year, he was still not a sure bet with chopsticks.

A light breeze barely stirred the air. The sky was sapphire blue. "This is paradise, isn't it?" asked Sefton rhetorically.

It was a perfect day for baseball. "Ever pitch in a championship game before?" the former scout asked Jerry.

"Ever manage in one?" Jerry asked in return. Sefton laughed. "You have some advice for me, Skip?" asked the pitcher.

"I was just thinkin' that it's gonna be a high sky today. Try to keep the ball on the ground as much as possible or it could cause some problems for the outfielders."

"I'll do my best."

"You're going to win," said Annie.

"How do ya know?" asked Sefton.

"I just know," she said.

After lunch they went up to the house, where Sefton and Yamada changed into their uniforms. "Do you have any regrets, Mac?" asked Yamada.

"About what? Oh, ya mean about quittin' the pro game? Nah, not for a minute. Oh, sure, I miss the excitement of the hunt sometimes, but I never regret being here. This is the best I've ever had it. I feel like a new man, Jerry."

"You seem a lot more relaxed, a lot more peaceful."

When they were dressed they went out to the living room where the others were waiting. "I'm very happy you're all coming today," said Sefton. Annie translated. Mr. and Mrs. Yamada smiled.

"Shall we?" said Sefton indicating the door.

They went outside. "We'll meet you at the car," said Yamada, as he and Sefton headed for the shed where they kept the equipment.

"I don't know who's more nervous, you or me," said Sefton.

"I'm not nervous," Yamada told him.

"Yeah, that's the problem with managin'. Ya got nothin' to do but fret."

"I don't know about that. You've done a heckuva job."

"Thanks."

They carried the duffel bags to the car and loaded them into the trunk. Sefton opened the driver's door and held the seat forward for Mr. and Mrs. Yamada. "It'll be nice when we can get ourselves a four-door," said Sefton.

"We need a good truck first," Yamada reminded him.

"That's true," Sefton conceded.

When his parents were seated, Jerry crawled in the other side, and Annie got into the front passenger seat. They drove up the dirt road that led to the highway, their walnut trees spread out to either side of them. Mr. Yamada said something in Japanese.

"My father says we'll have a terrific harvest if the rains hold off a few weeks," Annie said.

Sefton eased the Packard slowly up the dirt road, carefully keeping the speed down in order to minimize the trailing dust clouds that billowed along behind. He started to reach for the radio dial, but checked himself.

"Anybody mind if I turn on the ballgame?"